DEVIL'S SLEW

DEVIL'S SLEW

A Barrett Raines Mystery

DARRYL WIMBERLEY

Minotaur Books
A Thomas Dunne Book
New York

This is a work of fiction. All of the characters, organizations, and events portrayed in this novel are either products of the author's imagination or are used fictitiously.

A THOMAS DUNNE BOOK FOR MINOTAUR BOOKS.
An imprint of St. Martin's Publishing Group.

DEVIL'S SLEW. Copyright © 2011 by Darryl Wimberley. All rights reserved. Printed in the United States of America. For information, address St. Martin's Press, 175 Fifth Avenue, New York, N.Y. 10010.

www.thomasdunnebooks.com
www.minotaurbooks.com

Library of Congress Cataloging-in-Publication Data

Wimberley, Darryl.
    Devil's slew : a Barrett Raines mystery / Darryl Wimberley. — 1st ed.
        p. cm.
    "A Thomas Dunne book."
    ISBN 978-0-312-64949-4 (alk. paper)
    1. African American police—Fiction. 2. Florida—Fiction. I. Title.
    PS3573.I47844D48 2011
    813'.54—dc22

                                                                2010040694

First Edition: March 2011

10 9 8 7 6 5 4 3 2 1

Dedicated to the older generation and the new,
editors Ruth Cavin and Toni Plummer

Acknowledgments

One of my chief pleasures comes at the end of a narrative, when I get to thank a few of the many persons who, inevitably, know more about my subject than I do. Mel the Guide is one of those people, a kayaking enthusiast and professional tour guide who took time from his day at Gulf Coast Kayak to help me with a detailed scene of the novel. Thanks, Mel. Mike Schmahl, similarly, is an experienced captain of commercial fishing vessels who graciously provided details necessary for scenes related to that experience. A good portion of the story involves characters returned from theaters overseas. I was able to draw in part from own experience and the experience of my classmates, particularly Robert Livingston and Randy Hethrington (aka "No Neck" and "Rowdy," respectively), when creating those characters and scenes. Other details were garnered from public sources or in conversation with officers and noncoms, including a troika of chaplains—great and interesting people. Almost every book in this series derives in one way or another from the counsel of two now-retired lawmen, Russell Mobley and former FDLE agent Erik Erikson. Thanks to you, gentlemen. I get a big kick out of thanking New Orleans native Ryan Marks for helping me ferret out details essential to an early and important scene set in the Big Easy. Thanks, Ryan. Thanks to my family. And thanks finally to you readers. Best to you and yours.

DEVIL'S SLEW

Prologue

Northeastern Afghanistan, 2008

THE FLOWER OF ANGELS

She did not know where *she was, at first.* . . . But then she saw the top-heavy vase silhouetted on its familiar sill. A crocus of saffron, the familiar nectar. Like hay drying. And then the voices, murmured and familiar and rising. Concern. And fear.

I am fine, Gulpari wanted to say, but she could not free the words from her mouth, her throat. Inside the blinds of her eyes she could recall what surely must have been the day's beginnings. After all, the routine never changed. The sergeant-driver. The large camouflaged vehicle. The perfume of uniforms and sweat and that other, foreign ambrosia.

How did you say . . . *Colony?* No—*cologne.* That was it. That was the word, what she smelled. A splash of Brut.

The long stares from neighbors, nothing unusual there. Blast barriers and checkpoints. It had been a long ride, though. Longer than usual, away from the city. The countryside—now she remembered. Wide fields furrowed in long brown lines. A wide pavilion, scrolls of bright fabric hanging like abandoned party favors from poles hastily erected against the invading sun.

A ceremony? Yes. She recalled sitting in company beneath the bright, flowing silks. A beaming local with ties to the Taliban saying for the benefit of those present how wonderful it was to see the new processing facility finally completed. That dignitary replaced by one of Karzai's flunkies.

"Pomegranates for poppies!"

That was the idea. Give locals a way to store and process the pomegranate's fruit and they wouldn't cultivate poppies. "Gone are the days when farmers were forced to give up their children in payment of debt to opium dealers!" That unholy trade would go away, along with the warlords. So the logic went.

As if farmers actually decided what they should grow. As if they had that choice.

"Pomegranates for poppies"—the government's toady faithfully translated a text provided by some public-relations officer who clearly did not realize his intended alliteration would not survive its passage to Pashto.

What was the word—*rookie*? A rookie's error. Gulpari had some dim sense of having noted the lapse with irritation. Why did they need *her* if they were going to tolerate such incompetence?

There were more speeches and platitudes and then tea and cakes and, of course, pomegranate to sample. But all that business was concluded before noon, wasn't it? Surely before *dhur.*

Finished. Completed. Paid in full. Yet here it was morning again?

So what had come of the afternoon? Or the night?

"Look at you!"

It took her sister's rebuke to rouse Gulpari to her present situation. She raised her head—a searing pain.

"Ahh!"

Dizzy, as well. And a taste in her mouth of brass or copper.

Her mother guarding the vase on its sill at the window. Motes of dust floating like barbs in a lance of sunlight.

"Can you . . . close the shutter?"

"*What have you done?*" Her mother ignoring that request without reply.

"I need some water."

"Oh God! Oh God!" Her sister wringing her hands.

Would that be the Christian God or Allah the Merciful? Or the Jesus of Three Parts? Was tricky interpreting those warring voices of the Almighty. That plurality of Prophets.

Gulpari rolled over and was surprised to find her elbow meeting the mat at her own front door. In the foyer, an Englishman might say, deposited on a slab of stone just inside the paddock that secured her family's jealously guarded hearth.

"What have you brought to us?" the mother asked without inflection, staring like a vulture from her stony perch. "What have you done?"

Gulpari's protest strangled in her tainted mouth.

What had she done? She had gone to work! She had kept her family from starving! She had become educated—a woman in Nangarhar! And a Christian, too! What more could be done? What more could be expected?

"'Beautiful flower,'" the old woman spat.

Alluding to her name. A flower of Afghanistan, simple and chaste.

"Some blossom, you are. Thank God your husband is away. You should go, too. Before he gets back."

Husband . . . Why should Shamsi resent her? What had

she done to deserve derision and fear from mother and sibling? Gulpari tried to bring her knees to her bosom, and that was when she felt the raw ache between her legs. Saw the stain inside the cotton legs of her *salvar.*

"No, *no* . . ."

Her sister looking on in horror. In disgust.

"How could you?"

"I did NOT! I did NOT!"

"Then what happened, Gulpari! Explain yourself!"

Explain, yes. The interpreter required now to interpret herself.

She felt unhinged, unmoored. Swirling on capricious winds. A speck anxious for any anchor.

". . . I don't remember," she said finally.

Her mother's lip curled upward. "Not a good strategy."

The old woman's hand stretching like a stick from the folds of her burka to the vulnerable urn.

"It's true!" Gulpari dragged herself up by the frame of the door on legs that felt like water.

"Before God, I do not know!"

Leaning on the lintel as though it were a whipping post.

"I DO NOT REMEMBER!"

1

Northwestern Florida, 2010

LITTLE LEAGUE

There is a Florida that has nothing to do with Disney World. Nothing to do with palm trees or Holiday Inns. Tourists are neither courted nor coddled in this part of the Sunshine State and you can go a hundred miles and never see a golden arch. If you are a criminal, however, particularly a violent criminal, there's a good chance you will run into Barrett Raines.

An hour and a half's drive south from Tallahassee gets you to Perry, once a safe haven for Florida's enthusiastic Ku Klux Klan. Nowadays and just south of the Taylor County line, you enter the presently constituted Tallahassee Regional Operations for the Florida Department of Law Enforcement. For Special Agent Barrett Raines, the seven counties comprising that jurisdiction were home turf.

"The Bear" was born and raised on the Gulf Coast not far from Taylor County and knew every road from Perry to Old Town like the back of his pie-size hand. The people of the region were as familiar to Agent Raines as the roads traveled.

There was not a sheriff in Florida's Big Bend unfamiliar to Bear Raines, and no murder, theft, embezzlement, fraud, or malfeasance was outside his purview.

But not this morning. On this morning, Barrett took his restored muscle car up to the Walmart in Perry, picked up a couple of baseballs, a bat, and a glove and was heading out with his twin sons for their late-season Little League game. The boys would be playing in Mayo, a little over twenty miles distant. Was not a complicated route. You take Highway 27 out of Perry and the next town south is Mayo, which is the county seat of Lafayette County and the only town *in* the county. A tourist would not call the drive scenic. During the half hour or less that you're on the road from Perry to Mayo, you're maybe thirty miles from the Gulf of Mexico, but you'd never know it. The influence of the pulpwood industry—impossible to miss in Perry—is not much diminished in the twenty-something miles between the Highway 27 Bar and the Mayo First Baptist Church. Hundreds of thousands of acres of slash pine crowd narrow ditches that shoulder a blacktop slicker than snot on a doorknob. Driving past those trees can be hypnotic, unvarying rows of branchless trees fracturing the sun into flashes of light and shadow. Like seeing a stroboscope through a picket fence at seventy miles an hour.

You drive as if in a maze. No vista. No horizon. Only a Band-Aid of sky overhead. You roll down the windows and gag with a fresh contagion. It's the mill. The spawn of Buckeye's industrial chimneys follows the road like a fever, a thick, pungent odor, something like sulfur, the fruit of pulp breaking down in enormous chemical vats to become a package for Fritos or the papyrus for some earnest scholar's dissertation.

Only the shells of double-wides and abandoned vehicles

break the monotony of this pastoral, those artifacts displayed as tableau on pallets of palmetto. The vestiges of an older and original culture invisible to the accidental tourist are long familiar to Agent Raines. Nearing the county's seat, Bear spots a familiar shotgun shack listing on stumps of loblolly, its cedar shingles torn at random, revealing eaves of pine or cedar. Was Preacher McCallister's old place. There was the old Allis-Chalmer rusting nearby, a hand-turned tractor. A steel crank fit just beneath the radiator to engage a pin. Once the crank pin was engaged, you rotated the crank to turn the engine over. There were a half-dozen ways you could get hurt in that process.

"Always pull 'er up," Preacher reminded Barrett every single time. "Don't push that crank down. She kicks back while yer goin' down, you done broke yer arm. And you want a loose grip—don't trap that thumb." There were other things to remember. Make sure the clutch was not engaged. Make sure the PTO was disengaged. Make sure the damn throttle was pulled back. Was frustrating in hundred-degree heat to crank and crank and crank, only to find out the carburetor was starved for fuel. Those memories sparked with the loose cough of a tractor every time Bear saw that old piece of machinery rusting along Highway 27.

Other memories trailed close behind. The unrelenting heat. The tar and filth. The aching back bent to harvest leaves trapped in white-hot sand. Stinging nettles. Rattlesnakes. No telling how many rows of sand lugs Bear had cropped behind McCallister's recalcitrant tractor, a black boy bent to the ground with white teenagers, equal in the tobacco field, segregated everywhere else. Those days, thank God, had passed, if not all of their effects. Many of the boys with whom Bear shared labor had grown to be fathers. Some of them were friends.

Every artifact drew some sight, sound, or smell from the well of Barrett's memory. It might be a tobacco barn moldering beneath a grove of hickory or water oak. It could be the rusted rollers of a sugarcane mill. But those brief glimpses of a segregated past were fading, rusting, or rotting to oblivion. A modern tourist driving along 27 would be opaque to the associations redolent in Special Agent Raines. Passers-through were more likely to see manufactured homes looking out over an aging Toyota or Ford. Maybe a trampoline on the side. That, and legions of migrant workers, Latinos camped along the blacktop, their children kicking cigarettes and soccer balls.

The changing face of labor reflected huge changes in an economy based in agriculture of one kind or another since the Civil War. Long before Barrett's boyhood, there were cattle drives to rival those in Texas. Barrett used to coax his grandfather for stories of timber barons and turpentine wars, tung-oil groves and hogs herded in endless droves across an unfenced loess that stretched from Cedar Key to Valdosta.

There was, however, a price paid for that earlier prosperity. The tidewater cypress and loblolly pine that fed the saws and planers of massive mills were gone forever. Deep-well irrigation and unchecked tracts of pine combined to kill the table of water, and the link of tobacco with cancer made that crop less attractive. Was rare these days to see the Golden Leaf grown within sight of Highway 27. Farmers who proudly proclaimed themselves both faithful and conservative blamed the government for cutting price supports for tobacco.

The most recent recession only magnified a poverty that was systemic. Abandoned chicken houses sagged within sight on either side of the highway, a hundred yards or more of narrow and cheaply built shelter, fabric and lathe and wire, open at either end and begging to be razed. The fields were mostly gone to scrub, and migrants had replaced the indigenous labor of white kids and African-Americans. It was Latinos from Texas or across the border who now planted, suckered, harvested, and cured whatever small plots of tobacco remained. Or raked pine straw at the modern wage of twenty-five cents a bale. The Florida Department of Law Enforcement was established largely in recognition that sheriffs in rural jurisdictions simply did not have adequate funds, facilities, or personnel to police the growing variety of crimes and criminals in their counties. The FDLE was their intrastate bulwark and partner. Or sometimes competitor.

Dixie County offered a fair snapshot of the jurisdiction. A deputy in Dixie County routinely facing drug runners and domestic violence made less than thirty thousand dollars a year. Of course, living was cheap. You could get three bedrooms and two and a half baths and a garage to go with it for less than $150,000. The problem was that with an income per capita of less than fourteen thousand dollars annually, locals could not afford to take advantage of the deals readily available to retirees from DeLand or Sarasota. Natives joked that the start-up house for newlyweds in Dixie was a deer camp. Barrett was cousin to a newlywed, in fact, who renovated an abandoned tobacco barn for her first home, and Bear himself remained in the first home he ever bought, a modest Jim Walter ranch-style installed a spit from the Gulf.

Agent Raines was, moreover, the only black man in his county with a house of any kind on Deacon Beach.

Locals were used to doing without, but the Crackers and poor whites who had grown up with the Bear were now competing for jobs and groceries with newcomers to the Big Bend. These were the pensioners, professionals, or pirates from Tampa or Orlando or farther afield who came to Florida's northwest with hedge funds, Jet Skis, and a second or third alimony. Lots of toys and condos sprouted up and down the coast from Steinhatchee when times were flush, but that prosperity did not trickle down. The transplants were not much interested in improving their adopted community. They were not concerned that pine trees and prisons provided the mainstay of employment for people in Lafayette and Taylor counties. They were not inclined to vote for bonds dedicated to improve education or health care for a population much more rural and isolated than those in the rest of the Sunshine State.

And yet these retirees and entrepreneurs were surprised to discover that the single mom working at the Piggly Wiggly or the old geezer at the gas station smiled with unabashed schaudenfreude at the spectacle of foreclosed condos and failing 401(k)s. An animosity between the haves and have-nots that only simmered when money was easy now erupted like pus from a festering wound. Especially along the coast. Barrett began to see security fences and cyber-keyed gates on the littorail up and down from Steinhatchee. Kids at school divided along lines of money and class. Churches splintered into self-selected congregations. About the only time you saw locals and transplants in proximity was at a Friday-night football game. That, or Little League.

Little League had become one of the few places where the real estate agent from Daytona and the native-born laborer from Mayo mixed company with relative ease. Barrett was glad to see his own sons side by side with kids from South Florida or South America or even farther. He barely had the car stopped before Ben and Tyndall spilled out, a pair of seventh graders eager to take the field. Had taken a drive of only twenty-five minutes to reach a ballpark that for thirty years was denied to black people. Barrett was glad his sons did not share that memory.

"Don't forget your gear, boys," he called out as he opened the trunk.

Ben and Tyndall dashed back to grab a bat and balls. Bear dropped off the extra bat at the visiting team's dugout, then tapped the concession stand for an ice-cold Coca-Cola before hitting the bleachers. Anyone watching would have seen a black man about as tall as a refrigerator, with rounded shoulders and a head the size of a pail, lounging in jeans and Windbreaker across a pair of aluminum risers. The bleacher actually groaned with his weight. A cap pulled low advertised the boys' team—DEACON BEACH SHARKS.

This was a father-son game and so most of the fathers were on the field. Not Barrett. A forearm shattered by gunfire the previous year was strong enough to pull a trigger or paddle a kayak, but the impact of a ball on a bat was not yet tolerable and might never be. Even so, Bear loved watching his boys mingling with the other kids. Many natives still had a hard time accepting the notion that their Cracker region was now home to folks hailing from Mexico to Morocco. The Sharks and Hornets offered proof of a changing demographic, middle-school black and white kids fielding grounders and catching fly balls side by side. Barrett spotted the one kid from India—his father was retired from Microsoft and a fanatic for cricket. One boy of Vietnamese parents showed promise. Only two Latinos, though. They needed to work on that, getting the migrants involved in Little League.

Damn near all of the fathers were familiar to Barrett from boyhood. Brady Hart was coaching Mayo's team, a short, compact man with thick, thick eyebrows and a crop of hair gone from red to gray. Barrett used to ride a school bus with Brady. They used to get together every hunting season, Barrett with his Remington and Brady with a battered magazine-fed, bolt-action Marlin. Damn thing had a thirty-six-inch barrel and was fully choked. Brady used to joke that he bought the gun for geese or airliners. They'd had some good times in the woods over the years. And then lately on the water. Bear bought his kayak secondhand from Brady Hart's son and got his first lessons from "Coach" on the Gulf of Mexico. It was great rehab for Barrett's arm. Also part of an ongoing project to overcome his fear of open water.

"Jus' keep a cell phone and a GPS," Brady told him one morning as clouds built like anvils on the horizon. "Yer lost, I'll come getchu."

"What if I drown?"

"Well then, there won' be no need."

They had another bond as fathers of twins, though Brady's boys were much older and struck with tragedy, the firstborn killed while still a teenager by some drunk driver on the Old Town bridge. The younger twin was deeply affected and endured some rocky years through high school before finding a niche in military service, coming home after two tours on a dangerous and contested field.

Mike Traiwick was the other coach, probably about the same age as Brady's surviving son, much younger than Brady himself, certainly, and not yet a father. Traiwick was a tall drink of water, eyes set close as a grouper's, pale and bald.

Mike came to Deacon Beach from parts unknown to take over the local and failing newspaper, and he'd jumped into his adopted community whole-hog—church and school and Little League. His latest cause célèbre was to establish a counseling center and job court for returning veterans. He'd already gotten space for the center at the Advent Christian Village in Dowling Park. Barrett's wife would be hosting the premier fund-raiser. Neither Mike nor Brady was one of those frustrated athletes trying to relive an imagined glory on the backs of boys. Thank God. Both men were patient with the kids, but specific with direction and discipline.

Speaking of direction—the game began with an invocation given by a priest. Father Frank Swain was a widowed Episcopal minister reordained as a Catholic. Barrett knew it was possible for some married or formerly married ministers to be extended that dispensation, but Frank was the first he'd ever known personally. Swain was affable, but he maintained a priest's reserve. He affected a kind of anachronistic appearance. Wore suspenders, even in summer. Had hair parted down the middle like Bob McNamara, and bifocal glasses. He had a cross stitched below the crown of his baseball cap and almost never spoke of personal experiences. It was a year before Bear learned from Mike Traiwick that Father Frank had been stationed barely five klicks from Barrett's own artillery unit during Desert Storm. But where Barrett's service overseas ended with that active duty, Chaplain Swain joined the reserves and returned for two more tours, administering once again the rites of Communion and Reconciliation in Iraq, and then in Afghanistan. When Mike Traiwick began casting about for a site to help returning veterans, it was natural for Father Swain to offer his church.

"Let us pray. . . ."

Handy thing about having a priest start your game is that his prayers are bound to be a lot, lot shorter than any evangelic's or Pentecostal's. The boys barely had time to take their caps off before they were back on the field.

Barrett settled back with his Coke. Was wonderful to nurse a soft drink as innocents coached by competent adults competed in an untarnished game. Could be exciting, too. Top of the seventh inning, the Sharks were one run back when Benjamin Raines advanced to third on a walk and his dad felt the tickle of the cell phone in his pocket.

"Bear, it's Smoot."

Smoot Rawlings. Sheriff of Dixie County.

"Yes, Smoot."

"Bear, I hate to ask you, but I'm short and I got a situation out on Devil's Slew."

The Slew—Barrett was already calculating. A huge swamp just across the county line. Took ten minutes just to reach it.

"What's the situation, Sheriff?"

"Got us a GI with a Kalashnikov and a hostage."

Jesus.

"Any ID?"

"It's Quentin Hart."

Quentin Hart . . . Quentin? Brady Hart's son!

Barrett now lumbering off the bleacher and toward the dugout. Mike sees him coming.

"Problem, Bear?"

"Got a call. You see after my boys?"

"No problem."

Bear jogs past the Hornets' dugout on his way to the Malibu. There was Brady coaching his team, sending a sign to his pitcher. A good man. A man Barrett had known since he was a boy.

What do you say to somebody in a situation like this? What do you do?

Barrett cradles his mobile phone.

"Smoot, I'm on my way."

2

Devil's Slew

Barrett hit a hundred and twenty miles an hour before sliding off the blacktop and onto the farm-to-market route that ran smack-dab into the county road that turned to sand and mud on the way to Devil's Slew. The Malibu was running on redline, the Harley four-barrel dumping 89 octane to a '369 with fresh plugs and an aftermarket ignition kit. Had to swap cogs as the asphalt turned to sandy loam. There was only one road into Devil's Slew, a pair of ruts following an old railroad bed.

Smoot could not have given directions to Quentin's mobile home. Place like this, you either knew where to go or you didn't. Even after repeated injunctions from the post office and Homeland Security, there were no road signs to guide you. The Malibu threatened to spin out at every curve, and if she did, there would be no way to recover. Take two steps off these narrow, winding ruts and you'd sink to your waist in a bog that was antediluvian. Many a truck and car had slid off into Devil's Slew, and none of them got pulled out.

The place was actually a slough, of course, or, more accurately, a whole expanse of sloughs, hundreds of acres of bog settling below sea level in a trough miles inland from the Gulf. The Slew was once a boon to fishers and hunters and trappers going after wild hogs and panthers. Barrett had seen lynx and eagles and gators big as goddamn bass boats. Courses of freshwater streams and creeks crisscrossed the marsh in those years, ideal arteries for bream or bass and their wily and ancient predators. Barrett's uncle used to trap otters in Devil's Slew.

Some time in the early fifties, the property was sold to Buckeye, but even though the Slew was put off-limits to hunters and fishers, it was never drained or developed. The Slew's topography did change over the decades. A dense ring of secondary growth exploded with a falling water table to clog the many bogs and hollows and marshes and quicksand that made up Devil's Slew. Vines tangled in profusion around the ubiquitous pine or water cypress or the surviving tung-oil tree or Florida maple, morning glory and milkweed competing with pepper vine and creeping cucumber to hide the iron jaws of traps set by old-timers in their halcyon days. The slough's interior remained a wild and dangerous place. Barrett vividly recalled being trapped in a sounder of feral hogs on land almost as isolated as the Slew. Another memory linked to landscape.

Barrett felt the rear end slide a tad and eased off the accelerator. He wished he was in his cruiser. He felt naked without his radio and shotgun. Not to mention the vest.

"ETA, Bear?"

Smoot's query sounding terse and tinny over Barrett's cell phone.

"Two minutes. Less," Barrett barked to the open speaker. Was fortunate that Quentin's trailer was located on the relatively high ground near the railroad bed. Some Donald Trump wannabe had years earlier talked Buckeye into selling a strip of marsh along that iron highway, with plans to sell four- or five-acre plots to the ignorant, if moneyed, masses pressed by population and skyrocketing expense to look for land in northern Florida. No waterworks in Devil's Slew. No sewage. Snakes and mosquitoes and long, long summers. Those speculatively acquired plots changed hands half a dozen times before being parceled out one at a time to locals or cash-poor pilgrims looking for a dirt-cheap place to float their house trailer or RV. The first and only time Barrett visited Quentin's place was to pick up the kayak that Brady's son had put up for sale.

He could see Quentin's truck up ahead, a GMC hitched to a Coachmen trailer framed by marsh and quicksand on a stamp's worth of dry land. The trailer was a fifth-wheeler, one of those pull-alongs designed for a gooseneck hitch. You could see a push-out extending the bedroom, a hose for gray water. The hell did he do for sewage? There was no trampoline alongside. Nothing but the truck, the trailer, and the Morgan portable out back. Bear expected to see at least a pair of cruisers bracketing the scene, but the only marked vehicle in sight was Sheriff Rawlings'.

Smoot had his Ford Interceptor partially protected behind a water oak thirty, maybe forty yards from the trailer. Nothing behind but a bog and a pair of redbud trees that would not bloom until the return of spring. Barrett scanned instinctively for cover. The only barrier to bullets besides the water oaks and Smoot's vehicle was a portable building on the back side of the trailer. Toolshed? Meth lab? Whatever. It would be poor protection against a marksman with a Kalashnikov.

Bear slapped his Malibu into second and was looking to park when a single round shattered the windshield and a payday on the passenger's side.

"JESUS."

Barrett gunned the Super Sport behind the barricade of Smoot's cruiser, snatched off his seat belt, and came tumbling out of the Malibu, his Glock already chambered.

BAM-BAM. Two more rounds and the Malibu's passenger-side window dissolved into shards of safety glass.

"The hell, Smoot, you could have told him I was the pizza boy."

"Don't think he's interested."

Smoot Rawlings, sheriff of Dixie County. Imagine Coach Bobby Bowden with a badge and holster and a straw hat. Smoot was only average height, rotund, genial as a shopping mall Santa Claus. Had a soft belly, with a zipper running from sternum to pubis, that surgery made necessary in the same engagement that shattered Barrett's forearm.

BAM—another round. This time into the cruiser's wheel well. Barrett winced.

"Please tell me you got backup, Sheriff."

"I got a pair of deputies at Dead Man's Bay on a domestic and two men out with the swine flu."

"That include Roy?"

"Roy's on administrative leave."

A polite way of saying he was drying out.

Barrett shook his head. "I can call a team from the Jasper office, but there's no telling how long it'll take for 'em to get here."

"The fuck you think I called you, Bear?"

Two lawmen on bad ground across from a marksman with military experience and an automatic rifle.

"You've seen the hostage?"

18

Smoot nodded shortly. "Shelley Lawson. Girlfriend."

About that time, a muffled curse burst from the trailer's interior with a woman's scream. Something like glass breaking.

"Not too heavy on 'friend' at the moment," Smoot amended.

"You speak to Quentin?"

"Tried."

"We've got to stall him, Smoot. Buy some time to get a real negotiator in here."

"Feel free."

Rawlings handed over a bullhorn. Bear took it.

"QUENTIN, THIS IS BARRETT RAINES. BARRETT RAINES, FDLE. THE HELL YOU TAKING SHOTS AT ME, QUENTIN? I BOUGHT YOUR KAYAK."

Bear thought he could see a leaf of blind open at a window somewhere around what was probably the kitchen.

". . . Bear? That you?"

A voice swallowed in the miasma. But it was a start.

"BEAR RAINES, THAT'S RIGHT, QUENTIN. YOU KNOW ME. WHY NOT SET THAT WEAPON DOWN AND LET'S TALK?"

". . . I'm talked out."

"NOT WITH ME, QUENTN, I'M FRESH MEAT."

"Are you? Well. I'm not!"

And next thing you knew, he came out charging. There was no warning, no preamble. Just a short, thickly muscled kid with the same bushy brows as his daddy bursting through the flimsy screen door and sprinting across the sammy earth with a banana clip feeding a deadly weapon on full automatic.

"JESUS!" Smoot swore and leveled his shotgun across the hood.

"QUENTIN!" Barrett tried once more over the bullhorn.

But there wasn't time.

Cops have a rule of thumb, the twenty-one-foot rule.

Roughly says that if a man gets to within twenty-one feet of you with a handgun or knife, even an untrained man, then a lawman must consider himself in mortal peril. Twenty-one feet. Sounds arbitrary until you see the demonstration. An officer taking out his weapon, a suspect charging. Most folks never get off a round if the assault starts inside twenty-one feet. Most officers allowing a deadly threat inside that perimeter will die on the spot.

Smoot Rawlings wasn't about to fudge that boundary. Neither was Agent Raines.

Quentin Hart died a good ten yards from Smoot's cruiser. The coroner found equal weights of buckshot and 9 mm slugs. Impossible to say whose round got there first. It didn't make any difference to Quentin. Not to Sheriff Rawlings, either. And certainly not to Barrett Raines.

A clean kill—the required report would exonerate both lawmen. But it didn't feel clean to Bear Raines. Did not feel clean at all.

They found Shelley Lawson cowering and incoherent on the trailer's kitchen floor, a GI-issue flak vest strapped over her Walmart blouse.

"Oh my God. On my GOD!"

"Shelley, you're safe. We got an EMS on the way."

"Oh my God, ohmyGod!"

Doesn't matter whether it's two minutes or thirty: When you have a victim at a crime scene, it seems like it takes an eternity for the paramedics to arrive.

"Shelley ain't gonna be much help," Smoot predicted as the medics finally bundled her away.

"Didn't look like she was beaten," Barrett observed. "No obvious bruises. Not a mark on her face. You know of any other incidents?"

Smoot shrugged. "Nothing specific, just what Brady kinda

let out. Usual stuff. GI back from service. Girl used to having her own way. Little rough settling in."

A little rough. Barrett let that go.

Smoot had swapped his shotgun for a plug of Red Man. "Only thing his girlfriend said on the nine one one was that Quentin was crazy an' had a gun. Then Quentin, why, he took the phone, 'cording to Dispatch, and said if we come out here, he'd kill her."

It would take a half hour for the EMS to arrive and another hour and twenty minutes before the FDLE's Mobile Crime Lab came lumbering into view, and during that time Barrett Raines could not bear to look at the body of Quentin Hart. Bear had seen many violent deaths, of course. He'd even killed his own murderous brother in the line of duty and had to face Corrie Jean afterward. But this was the son of a good man, who Bear had long considered a friend. A man he had known since way before Little League.

What was he going to say to Brady Hart? How do you tell a father that you killed his son?

"Watn't your fault, Bear," Smoot said gruffly. And then: "I'll tell Brady."

Barrett shook his head.

"We'll do it together."

The FDLE Mobile Crime Lab arrived, delaying that awful negotiation. One of Smoot's deputies had been detached to guide the van to the scene. Barrett recognized the senior tech behind the van's wheel; Bob Blanchard had been lifting prints and casting tire tracks for a decade. The junior technician, however, was unfamiliar.

Unfamiliar but hard to miss. Julie Fannon was obviously an athlete, tall and strong. She unloaded a pair of seventy-pound cases off the van as easily as most men would heft a briefcase. A North Florida girl, Barrett guessed, some Cracker's daughter. Looked to be in her late twenties. Wide hips and dishwater-blond hair. Her ponytail was tied off with an ordinary rubber band. No pretensions there. Pale blue eyes. Sunburned.

Bob puffed along behind his junior partner.

"Bear, you ever have a body drop at an actual goddamn address?"

"Sorry to drag you out here, Bob."

The senior man was already unrolling the familiar yellow tape. Within minutes, the two techs had set up their grid and began an inward spiral search. Took the best part of the next hour for them to reach the trailer's interior. Blanchard emerged at one point to display half a dozen evidence bags, each with cartridges inside.

"NATO rounds," Blanchard offered. "Five five six millimeter. Get 'em anywhere."

"How about the weapon?"

"It's a Kalashnikov. You were right. Czech, too. Not a cheapie."

"Pretty hefty weapon to threaten a girlfriend, don't you think?"

Julie Fannon spoke up quietly. "Was the only weapon in the trailer. Though I did find extra rounds in the shed out back."

"Learn anything from the body?"

By which Smoot meant the corpse of Quentin Hart. The body of Brady Hart's son needed separate transport to a medical examiner, so for the present Quentin remained where he fell.

"Taking him to Jacksonville?" Bob asked peremptorily.

"Either there or the Gainesville ME," Barrett replied.

"There's gonna be blowback from the rifle," Smoot predicted. "You'll find powder on his hands. Arms, too, probably. No doubt the boy fired at us."

"Can't get a cleaner shoot than this." Blanchard offered his opinion as freely as usual. "Domestic violence. Perp turns the gun from his girlfriend to the cops. Seen it a million times."

But Barrett noticed that the FDLE's junior technician did not second her senior's assessment.

"Ms. Fannon?"

"Yes, sir."

"That the way you see it? Clean shoot?"

"Oh, yes, sir. Only . . ."

"Yes?"

"Well, Agent Raines, doesn't it seem odd to you that the deceased would put his hostage in a flak vest? I mean, if he was abusing her, if that was his purpose, why when ya'll got here did he put her on the floor inside an armor of Kevlar?"

Smoot Rawlings shrugged. "Just wanted her out of the way is all."

The tall girl nodded. "Out of the way. Yes, sir. That's prob'ly it."

But Barrett once again felt the small itch at the back of his brain that he had learned from hard experience was dangerous to ignore.

"Ms. Fannon."

"Just Julie is fine."

"Julie, then. Why don't you walk me through the scene. Give me your impressions."

"Goddammit, Bear," Blanchard objected. "You don't need to be traispin' all through our evidence."

"I been around crime scenes before, Bob."

"Well. Awright, then."

"Smoot?"

"You see anything interesting, I'm sure you'll tell me."

"Just follow my steps, you don't mind, Agent Raines."

"Yes, ma'am," Bear replied, acknowledging the young woman's authority.

The first place she paused was at the door of the travel trailer.

"Cheap aluminum, you notice," she said. "Kind of door common on RVs and such."

"Yes."

"And you said he came bursting out. I believe Sheriff Rawlings actually said 'Busted out like a bull from a barn.'"

"Just about exactly what he said."

"And yet look, Agent Raines, there's not a dent on the door. There's no warp in the frame. And the lock—it's open."

"You think that's significant?"

"Well, sir, if you were holding a hostage and you had two armed lawmen outside, would you have your front door unlocked?"

Barrett smiled. "I doubt it."

"And if, as the scenario goes, this boy was hyped-up and half-crazy and firing rounds everywhere, would he bother to unsnap a flimsy lock before he came barreling outside with a Kalashnikov on full automatic? And if he came charging like a bull through a cheap tin door—locked or not—wouldn't it be bent or buckled or dented someplace in the frame?"

That's when Barrett found a salve for the itch in his brain.

"You don't think Quentin ever intended to hurt his girlfriend, do you, Ms. Fannon?"

"Well, I called the medics and they told me there's not a mark on her. Not to say you can't emotionally abuse a woman—of course you can. Fact, that's the most common form of abuse. But if I understand ya'll's summary of the nine one one call, the girlfriend didn't call in to say she was being beaten or abused. She called saying that the perp had a gun and was acting crazy."

24

"You think he was crazy?"

"I don't think you think he was, sir."

Barrett smiled. "Call me Bear. And you're right; I don't think the boy was crazy. At least not in the sense that he was out of control of his actions. First off, he waited till the sheriff was out here before saying anything about having a hostage. And then he made no demands. He just starts shooting. You taken a look at the sheriff's cruiser? And my Malibu?"

"Got a bunch of glass."

"My car alone must've taken a half-dozen rounds. But what you can't tell by looking is that the first round went through the windshield on the passenger's side. The *passenger's side*."

"Maybe he just missed," Julie offered.

"Was every round a miss? 'Cause every round taken by my car or Smoot's cruiser was either on the passenger side of the windshield or away from the part of the vehicle where we were taking cover. And I'm betting if you check those redbuds behind the cruiser, you'll see that when Quentin charged us, he was shooting over our heads."

"So he wanted ya'll alive?"

"Must have." Barrett nodded. "In fact, I think Quentin went to some trouble to get the law out here. To dangle a bait we could not refuse."

"What for?"

"To kill him."

Was that sunburned skin suddenly pale?

"So you think . . . You think this was a *suicide*? Suicide by cop? Is that what you're tellin' me, Bear?"

"I read a study recently, claimed that over a third of these kinds of scenarios are invitations for suicide. Don't know if I buy that, but in this case I am sayin' that a military man with a Kalashnikov and combat experience wouldn't miss two targets forty yards away unless he wanted to. And only an insane man or somebody wanting to die would charge across forty yards of damp ground into a shotgun and a Glock."

She nodded. "But then just to go along, I guess the hard question would be—"

"Yes?"

"Well, it's the question never gets answered in a suicide, isn't it? Or almost never. It's the *why*. If you're right, then what made Quentin Hart so desperate or afraid or despondent that he would rather be shot by cops than live?"

"I don't know. But on the chance that this is a proxy suicide, I'm gonna have to ask you and Bob to make another careful sweep over the scene. Especially the trailer. Only this time you're not looking for glass or fiber or fingerprints. This time you're looking for a note, correspondence to family or buddies, computer chatter—anything that might give a picture of what was inside this boy's head."

"Yes, sir," she said, the ponytail bobbing with her head. "Will do."

It was nearly dusk by the time the crime scene was sifted to satisfaction, the evidence logged, and Quentin Hart's body bagged for a trip to the ME in Jacksonville. In that time, somebody must have broken protocol, probably the local 911 operator, because as Quentin was being loaded onto a gurney, another vehicle, a familiar pickup, came rooster-tailing dangerously down the solitary sand road. Sheriff Rawlings spat out his chewing tobacco and stepped briskly into the breach.

"It's Brady Hart. Looks like that priest is with him."

Brady almost ran his pickup into the van transporting his son, screaming fury at the medics: "YOU LEAVE HIM ALONE, GODDAMN IT! LEAVE HIM ALONE!"

Father Frank joined Barrett and Smoot to intercede.

"Let the man have some time with his son," Smoot told the technicians, and then Barrett watched with everyone else as Brady Hart cradled his bloody son in his arms.

"What happened here?" the father croaked finally. "Who did this to you, Quentin?"

"He didn't give us any choice, Brady," Sheriff Rawlings answered stiffly.

"'Us'? The fuck is 'us'?"

It was Barrett's turn.

"He came at us with an assault rifle, Brady. Lawson called nine one one and got the sheriff out. I came and tried to talk to Quentin, but he just wouldn't listen."

"The hell are you saying, Bear?"

"Quentin came out of the trailer shooting, Brady. You can see the cars—he didn't give us any choice."

"You? You black son of a BITCH!"

"Coach, you don't mean that," Father Frank murmured at his side.

Brady Hart shrugged off the priest's arm and took a step toward Bear Raines.

"You killed my son? You son of a bitch, YOU KILLED QUENTIN?"

Smoot put himself squarely between the two men. "We returned Quentin's fire, Brady. That's *we*. Both of us— Quentin didn't give us no choice. Now, that's sorry, I know it is. And I can't imagine what you're thinkin' or feelin', but the fact is, your boy was not interested in talkin'. He came out shootin' and we returned fire, yes, we did."

". . . Jesus! Jesus Christ!"

Brady turned back to his son then, astonished, incredulous.

"Was it . . . was it quick?"

Smoot cleared his throat.

"He didn't feel anything."

Sobbing, Coach Hart collapsed on the gurney bearing his shattered son. A hand that only minutes before had been in a baseball glove now running over the clipped stubble of Quentin's scalp.

Came the inevitable and agonized question. "Why would he do this? Goddammit—WHY?"

Frank Swain kneeling alongside. Praying for an answer?

3

New Orleans

HARRAH'S CASINO

Brenda Mantle could probably have run chips in any casino. Beneath that North Face Windbreaker was a woman with the figure of a Vegas showgirl. Tight ass and flat belly trapped inside a prick-tease blouse and a black skirt. Chestnut hair above a Dutch collar, with breasts threatening to burst buttons off their stitches. With those assets, you could easily imagine Miss Brenda working a table at the Venetian, or a boat in Myrtle Beach or Biloxi. Certainly she fit right in at the New Orleans casino.

Harrah's was convenient, with its own hotel and a pair of others flanking the casino on either side. Nice to have a room close by, especially on a cold and drizzly evening. You could eat at the casino's buffet or walk two blocks to Mother's Restaurant. Best damn country ham anywhere. And unlike the boats up and down the coast, Harrah's in New Orleans offered gambling around the clock, twenty-four hours a day. People flew in and out all the time to try a variety of hands at one of

Harrah's one hundred tables or test the odds on one of the two thousand machines burping, squeaking, and rattling beneath a constant drone of music, Jackson Brown or Elvis or Bono or some other barely popular artist piped in along with the air-conditioning.

Did not look like a casino at all from the outside; there was no phantasmagoric facade, no neon topiary or pyramid. In fact, approaching Harrah's, you could imagine you were entering a courthouse. Thirty-two brass railings lead up a wide terrace of steps framed beneath generic Greek columns to reach a wall of dark glass panels looking over the street like a giant pair of Foster Grants.

On entering, the first thing you see beneath a high ceiling decorated with cotton-candy clouds and rhinestone stars is a podium with a dim light and a nice lady—could easily be Vietnamese or Latino—who asks politely for your driver's license. They swipe your license, but unless you're on a federal watch list or fifteen years old, there'll be no hassle. No record of your name, either. Which can be handy.

There's nothing separating the security desk from the machines, pits, bars, buffet, and restaurant beyond but a waist-high balustrade. Restaurant to the right has a great steak and an interesting painting on the wall. Some blue dog looking over your filet mignon in oil and canvas. Buffet is farther ahead on the right, but, unlike Vegas, you have to play to eat. The candles on the slot machines glow eternally red, yellow, and blue to mesmerize young addicts and grannies propped on stools like mushrooms. The levers are gone on the new machines, but the racket remains, a din of sound dawn to dusk in the front end of the casino.

Table games are situated farther back and segregated into architecturally distinct districts. The Poker Room, where Brenda works, spreads thirty or so tables inside a faux Mardi

Gras. Everything is faked or disguised. The columns supporting the ceiling over the Poker Room double as carnival floats. The perimeter walls defining the Poker Room remain incognito behind a painted facade of French Quarter apartments, brothels, and bars, those establishments rendered in a sloppy simulacrum of wrought-iron balconies in decay, a wallpapered quarter interrupted at intervals with modern boxed-light advertisements of games, specials, and coming tournaments.

A entire wall toward the back side of the Poker Room features prints of players famous for their tournament play. Chris Moneymaker and Doyle Brunson share honors with Johnny Chan and Phil Hellmuth. But there would be no tournament this evening. It would be an ordinary night of Texas Hold 'Em. No limit. Brenda overhears a dealer explaining to some tourist what it means to have a minimum buy-in. Play at the tables is two-five blind, and a handful of regulars were already seated. These were some of the dozen or so players who everyone knew on a first-name basis. Granny was there with her macramé and Agatha Christie. Billy Maunt always came dressed like Johnny Cash, in a black shirt, black trousers, black blazer, and a black wide-brimmed Stetson. Brenda sees "Charlie" Minh stumbling in, a young man staving off his MS with table time. And of course there were always a couple of black kids at the tables, the hoods of their sweatshirts pulled over like a monk's cowl. Like rap stars or gangbangers.

Whatever.

Everybody, local or no, has to sign in at the Poker Room. You have to supply a moniker to handle the cards, but you can use any name you like. Some threesome has already scrawled in as Larry, Moe, and Curly.

Watch out for those guys, Brenda mouths silently.

31

"Your last night with us, ma'am?"

This from her supervisor. Six foot six of bashful Baptist.

"'Fraid so, Harlan."

She shakes the wet off her parka.

"Taking that job in Biloxi, then?"

"Looks like." She lies without flinching.

"Well, we're gonna miss you."

Brenda offers a magnolia smile to the supe before scanning the kidney-shaped tables. She expects a customer will be here this evening, if his pattern holds. A mark of special interest.

Yes. There he is, on the rail.

Brenda threads her way through the tables to the cashier sequestered out of easy sight in a niche behind the tables. Another convenience for a particular kind of gambler, that modest cashier. Shirley would be working the till alone this shift.

"Hey, girl."

"Shirley, wassup?"

"Won't some of your lip gloss, girlfriend. Make me look sexy."

"You don't need anything extra for that, mama."

"Ain't you sweet." Shirley smiles and shoves out racks of chips in ones, fives, twenty-fives, and hundreds.

By the time Brenda returns to the floor, her mark is settled on table number ten. He wouldn't need to color up for a while, which gave Brenda time to tend to her other job. She triggers the mike hidden between her blouse and bosom.

"Lead calling in. I have our man."

"Roger," the reply came five-by to her earphone.

"Lead again. Do I rock and roll or observe only?"

"Your last gig, Lead. Keep it simple."

"Last chance to get him talking."

"Lead, just keep an eye on him. See if you can get him to look into a monitor, maybe."

That wasn't hard. All she had to do was lean over his sunglasses and show some tit. The problem for the camera was that he always wore a long-billed cap and sunglasses.

What did they know? Well, the driver's license was fake; they knew that. And he wore a hairpiece. The photo on his license did not trigger a match anyplace. He was Latino, for what that was worth. Mid-twenties or so. Compact and bearded. The beard appeared genuine. Only clearly distinguishing mark was a tattoo, looked military, a serpent and cross inked across his forearm. He was polite but clearly on guard. Any straight man getting flashed as often as this dude would have been trying to take Brenda back to his hotel. Not this guy. Not interested in sex. And not much interested in cards, either.

They'd been tracking him, Brenda and her team, for about a month. He'd come in, play a couple of racks, cash in his chips, and leave. Drank very little, and whatever conversation she'd been able to draw was reserved for coloring up his chips.

About that time, he nodded and she strolled up, hips swaying. Bright smile.

"Well, look at you again."

He slid a wad onto the table.

"Two racks of green, please, ma'am."

"Sure thing."

Every transaction for chips took place at the cashier's, which meant that chip runners had to be fast on their feet. This wasn't a problem in normal circumstances, as the regulars were usually slow and few in number. But play this evening was brisk, and Brenda worried that she could lose track of her man and the crucial evidence needed.

"Be right back."

She serviced a couple of tables before returning to Shirley,

33

making sure to swap out one of her mark's hundred-dollar bills for a Ben Franklin of her own. It was a good sign that she'd been able to get a large-denomination bill. Usually, he paid in twenties and fifties.

"Here you go, Shirley. . . ."

Brenda slid five thousand dollars under the grille.

"Two green, please."

Shirley recounted the money into trays segregated by denomination and slid out two racks of neatly stacked chips. Same procedure for the next player's request, and the next. You had to work fast. Chip runners who left players waiting didn't get tipped, and in any case, Brenda wanted to keep her mark in sight. She colored up her other players in a quick, tight circuit, completing the round on her mark.

He played three hours straight and tight before he waved her over. She slid her leg along his.

"You have a name, cowboy?"

It was a risk. This mark had made no effort in his seven sojourns at Harrah's to learn anyone's name, much less give his own.

"What's *your* name?" he replied after a pause.

She had her cover ready. "Lacy. Lacy Spoon."

He raked his chips over. "Well, Lacy, right now I'm just an hombre cashing in his chips."

"I gotchu."

"Nothing personal."

She cashiered the remaining chips. Forty-two hundred dollars remained from the five grand that started the evening, and not a single winning hand. She brought back a stack of bills and a complimentary Coke. He took the money without comment, ignored the soda, and dropped a twenty for a tip.

"Don't push it, Lead. Let him go." She heard her team's

direction as the mark left the Poker Room. They could follow him with the cameras, of course.

Eyes in a rhinestone sky.

"Lead here. I got a fresh bill off the target. A hundred."

"Excellent."

"You want me to finish my shift?" Brenda murmured into her mike.

"That's a roger."

Brenda kept an eye out for her other customers as she watched the mark leave. The surveillance would not stop at the casino. Someone would tag the mystery man to the airport, make a note of his flight and destination. He varied his return. Usually it was Orlando, but it could be Jacksonville or Gainesville. Tampa, on one occasion. Three or four times they'd guessed right at home plate, only to lose the target afterward. That in itself was suspicious. Took some conscious effort to shake a tail.

"Missy?" A gambler waved a fistful of currency and Brenda flashed a cheerleader's smile. Compared to her real job, running chips was a snap. She would miss some of the guys and gals she had grown to know in her half year at Harrah's. Somebody was bound to suggest she stay behind for a going-away drink.

"No, cain't," she said, demurring when Shirley made that suggestion. "Got the babysitter to pay."

She checked in her badge and punched the time sheet at the casino desk before picking up her parka. There was always a casual search as you checked out, but nobody was going to look for the hundred in her panties. Not the Baptist supervisor, certainly.

She left the casino, turning left on the sidewalk bordering Poydras to walk against traffic. Pretty quiet for a Saturday night. Probably because of the weather. Late October and cold. A landscaped median split the rain-drenched street into strips of asphalt that caught the reflection of every neon advertisement and passing headlight like mirrors. Cabs coming in all varieties of minivan, sedan, and SUV splashed along either side of the divide. You could see the Riverside Hilton just around the corner. They debriefed in the Hilton. The team was waiting and eager, she knew, to inspect the large-denomination bill she had filched off the target.

There are eyes following Brenda's last walk home, naturally. The apparently homeless man slumped off the curb has a good field of vision, not to mention the two armed agents in the AT&T van across the street. She pulls up the collar of her slicker as a street sweeper lumbers into view just ahead, a monster vehicle hogging the lane. Brenda skips away from the curb as huge brushes churn trash and water into gutters always overtaxed. Her trailing van disappeared momentarily and Brenda instinctively looked to cross the street. Was always better, if possible, to be on the same side of the street as your security detail. She had the radio, of course, and there was the Hilton dead ahead, but even so, it was always smart to keep a line of sight open between yourself and your watchers.

There was an intersection straight ahead, ideal for her purpose. Two cabs were pulled over, a Dodge Caravan and what was almost surely a cop car bought at auction. A man and a young woman in a dark skirt haggling a fare, probably, with a Pakistani driver.

"Scuse me," Brenda offers as she brushed past.

She never sees the Taser.

The driver drills her right behind the ear. A thousand bee stings, a seize of synapse, and searing pain. The man on the sidewalk strips off her Windbreaker. The dark-skirted woman dons Brenda's wrap and crosses the intersection with the

36

light, which leaves the driver and his backup to throw their still-twitching victim into the minivan, where another pair of hands and a needle are waiting. The street sweeper shields all view of that violent transaction, rumbling slowly past gutters silver with rain and filth.

Happens in Mexico City or Bogotá or Baghdad on a weekly basis, kidnappings of high-value targets, often in broad daylight. Brenda Mantle's team reported in a painful postmortem that the only thing out of the ordinary on that Saturday night was the failure of their undercover's radio. Just a burst of static, a technician declared. Then nothing.

"But we could see her crossing the intersection!" an agonized rookie would tell his superiors. "She had the same build, same hair, same clothes. We figured maybe the rain shorted out her wire, but we could see her!"

Taking her usual and predicted route.

"And she looked okay."

In fact, the kidnapper's decoy strolled warm and snug in Agent Mantle's anorak all the way to the Hilton, passing through the hotel lobby in full view of the cameras to reach the loo. By the time Brenda's handlers realized their undercover had been kidnapped, the only things left to inspect were a Windbreaker and a wig. That, and an abandoned street sweeper driven straight off a municipal lot secured by the vigilant employees of the city of New Orleans.

4

Near Devil's Slew

THE CANE MILL

Dawana Jackson learned by text message that Quentin Hart had been shot to death. She was gathering eggs right behind her mama's house at the old sugarcane mill when word came. The phone twittered, she opened the tiny box with the little flag, and there it was:

QTN KIA

Her breathing went suddenly short and shallow. She had to grab the kiln to stand. The panic. That pit in the stomach. And then the impulse to get drunk or get laid or kill some-body. It had happened overseas too often, the sudden noti-fication that a buddy you'd fucked or farted with was suddenly in several pieces. Made you skittish for your own safety. Made you scared and pissed *that* you were scared and pissed.

Quentin dead?

WHN WHR WHO?

She pecked out that query like a chicken worrying a pan of peas.

COPS FUBAR

When the reply came, the "who" was clear enough. The rest was Fucked Up Beyond All goddamned Recognition.

C U LTR

Dawana signed off, cradling her BlackBerry like an egg in her hands. As a girl, she had often sought refuge beneath the corrugated tin roof of her grandfather's sugarcane mill. Was one of the few places she could conjure pleasant memories. The mule plodded in an endless circuit, yoked to the long pole mounted overhead onto the capstan that was the drive-shaft for a pair of counterrotating rollers engaged to squeeze juice from lengths of sugarcane.

Dawana had fed countless stalks of sugarcane into the slender seam between those massive iron drums, watching the juice spill sweet and green into the catching barrel. Bees swarming to those kegs like addicts desperate for a fix. When cane grinding was done, her daddy would hang a play swing from the driveshaft's height, where she would sit perch of an evening, feet dangling, to hear her papa tell stories about Devil's Slew and the Klan and how she should be proud to be part of the only African-American family in the county to own land free and clear and a sugarcane mill.

Their whole community looked forward to cold weather and cane grindings, and every family participated, the men bringing their machetes, the women huddled like witches to fire the kiln. Older folks came, too, enjoying a well-earned leisure. Smoking cigarettes and swapping yarns. The children ran footloose and carefree as a litter of puppies. Dawana used to be one of those innocents, a roly-poly black girl running rings around the boys. Later on she joined her mother at the kettle. Scooping off the boiling foam to make taffy. Pouring the amber syrup crystal clear and thick into whiskey bottles rescued for the purpose. They'd sing at their distaff labor. Dance, too, sometimes. Sometimes Preacher Hewitt would bring his fiddle and you'd see octogenarians too stiff to spit suddenly fluid and mobile, sensual, even, in the ecstatic release of some black spiritual or Appalachian ditty.

And the smell! The nectar of pine resin mixing with the evaporation of raw cane juice?

Good God Almighty!

But only a ruin of that remembered place remained, the old mill long converted to a house for chickens. Milk crates snatched from the local Piggly Wiggly served for the hens' roost. A hasty lining of straw provided insulation and a bed for the eggs. The roof was half gone, strips of corrugated tin peeled back by years of hurricanes, and pine pilings meant to support the eaves and roof were themselves rotting. The kettle that was now a rooster's throne sat askew, its supporting brick oven broken under an unrelenting iron weight.

The mill itself looked out maybe fifty yards to the only home Dawana had ever known outside a barracks, a cedar-shingled sharecropper's shack situated inside a perimeter of cedar posts sagging with strands of barbed wire strung loose as a clothesline. The mounted pole that turned the grinder's gears now looked down to a circle of weeds, and the redolent bouquet of resin and smoke and sweet boiling juice was replaced by the shit of chickens.

It had rained all night. The magnolia tree looking over the

old mill had long ago dropped leaves to the ground, and now they caught the fat drops of early-morning rain in loud particulars.

SPLAT . . . SPLAT . . .

Dawana had gathered close to a dozen eggs under the supervision of a rooster that strutted the edge of the eighty-gallon kettle with that stiff, herky-jerky gait. Ruling his roost like some feathered fucking Napoléon. They poured the steaming syrup into whiskey bottles back in the old days, and every time she gathered eggs, Dawana would find some relic of that labor, a bottle stowed in the years before Parris Island and PCP.

Corporal Dawana Jackson came home lighter and harder than when she left. And yet nearly a year after leaving the Corps, she was back where she'd started, sleeping in the same narrow bed in the same room of the same house she'd known as a child, and with no focused plans to change that situation. Certainly no plans for college or craft.

She was employed, however. Or perhaps *deployed* was the better word.

Or maybe even *redeployed.*

Quentin. Dead. Motherfucker.

"Da . . . Wannnaaaa—?"

Her mama's voice floating through the tears.

"What's takin' you so long, girl?"

"BE RIGHT THERE."

5

The Crusaders

The sun was falling by the time Dawana rendezvoused with the survivors of her outfit, the Bible and .45 secure in the saddlebag of her Harley-Davidson. Over a year back in the world and still they referred to themselves as an "outfit." Still called themselves "the Crusaders," too. A pitiful sobriquet, a plea for identity, for continuity. Like the gun. Like the bike. Dawana got her Bible from her grandpa and her cannon at a gun show in Lake City. Bought the Sportster used off craigslist in a decision based solely on its online advertisement: "A preowned Harley is more than a used bike. It's a battle-tested veteran, a story waiting for a hero."

A story waiting for a hero, now that was righteous. Dawna and her buds wanted desperately to be heroes, though they would never admit it, and they were desperate for any story to fit. They had all been tested, after all. A lake of fire. But their own Special Ops company was disbanded in circumstances that had nothing to do with heroism. And the Crusaders, Quentin included, had a special cross to bear.

Dawana turned off 27 onto a feeder leading to the Fenholloway River bridge. A sour fragrance wafting from the water owed its stench to the effluent of pulp production, courtesy of Buckeye's giant mill. "PME" they called it, with the familiar ring of a military acronym. Nasty shit, apparently. Article in the paper said the discharge was turning female mosquitoes into boys.

What the hell. The flesh is weak.

Dawana gunned her Sportster off the bridge. The Crusaders were redeployed in a mobile home on an acre of land less than half a mile west of the river. Safe from prying eyes behind a shield wall of palmetto and slash pine. Besides Quentin, there were Buddy Hewitt, Raul Carrera, and Sarge. M. Sgt. Terry Godot fashioned himself the glue that held the Crusaders together.

Well, maybe.

Quentin picked a hell of time to get himself killed. They had a drop to make, a big one, and Sarge wanted all hands on board. Dawana kicked down a cog to take the narrow sand road snaking back to the outfit's trailer. Pulling up, she could see some attempt at home improvement. Rope lights ran along the roof of the dilapidated single-wide. A deck thrust catty-corner off the front entry, a jerryrig of cargo pallets piled on top of cinder blocks. Kind of a lawn furniture rigged with duct tape, mosquito net, and PVC.

See how long that lasts, she thought.

Some signs of recreation. A tripod of Kalashnikovs stacked neatly beside a glowing fire. There was a Ka-Bar knife buried near most to the hilt in a dartboard tied to a tree with a length of fish line. Looked like maybe Bud had added a spoiler and a brush guard to his Dodge Ram truck, and Raul had his new Camaro tricked out with spider hubs and halo lights. Must have dropped some coin for that project.

And were those beers stashed inside a commode?

A real boys' club.

She pulled up next to Raul's ride, killed the engine, and kicked down the stand.

"Da-Wan-ah." Bud was already reaching in the shitter to snag her a beer.

"Buddy, Raul. We havin' a wake or what?"

Raul and Bud were already in their cammies and boondockers, playing hearts next to the pine-fed fire on the salvaged hood of a Corolla. Raul Carrera was the only Crusader not from northern Florida. "From Texas," he invariably replied when asked for a place of origin. "The Valley."

The fuck? Was there only one valley in Texas?

Bud and Quentin were Chucks through and through, had attended the same high school in Perry before trooping off to Parris Island. Bud was a lot taller than Quentin, rangy and hairless. Typical Cracker stock. Raul and Dawana first hitched up with Bud and Quentin at SOI-East, honing skills necessary to become a member of a rifle squad. It was another year before they began the more specialized training that got them assigned to the Marine Corps Special Operations Company. That was a story, for sure. And hurting for heroes.

"Shitty news about Quentin." She made sure Bud could see her gun as she took his beer.

"Looks like sister's come to play." Bud lights a cigarette off a pine knot.

"Not gone miss my cut." She frees the bandanna trapping her nappy hair. "That's bullshit, man."

"Nobody staying home tonight, *concita*," Raul assures

her. "Sarge says we go out tonight, Quentin or no Quentin. Which means we a man short. Which means—"

"Which means we need another man. Which would be you," Bud snipes and Dawana slugs him across the jaw.

Takes a while to break that one up, sisters and brothers.

"Fuck you, Buddy!" Dawana kicks a bottle into the fire as Raul drags her off, and it bursts to life like a flare.

"Easy, bitch." Bud's laughing. "You take it too goddamn personal."

"It is damn personal!"

"You two want to kiss and make up?" Raul stands between them. " 'Cause I don' wanta take point worryin' who's naughty or nice."

"Sounds like somethin' Quentin would say," Dawana rejoins and the outfit fell silent.

"Quentin was always the weak link," Bud says finally.

Raul frowns. "Thass cold, man."

"It's true, *compa*. You know it. We all know it."

Bud meets Dawana eye-to-eye.

"You especially goddamn know it."

"All I know is he's dead." Dawana collects her beer. "He's dead, he's gone, and he won't be talkin'. To nobody."

"*Semper* fuckin' *fi*." Raul salutes her.

"We a man short, but we're not a man weak," Dawana declares. " 'And I will strengthen them in the Lord.' "

"Fuckin' A," Bud seconds and then all heads turn as headlights cut a swath through the pines.

Raul reaches for his rifle.

"No, it's all right," Bud says. "It's Sarge."

Gunner Sergeant Terry Godot swung his new Ford Ranger twin into the flickering glare of the outfit's fire pit, checking the suddenly wooden faces now turned in his direction. Measuring them.

45

He dropped from the truck's cab without a cable showing, creased trou and boots spitting, wearing the campaign hat he'd brought back from deployment.

"Is that fucking beer I'm seein', ladies?"

"Goddammit, Sarge. It's for Quentin."

"Bullshit, marine, you don't need Quentin for an excuse."

Dawana and her brother straightened on reflex as their gunny took a place by the fire.

"Give me one a those damn things."

Raul offered a Bud Light and Sarge took it, holding the can carefully away so that the spray would not deface his aging fatigues.

"Mission this evening will be arduous," he pronounced with a long swallow. "At twenty-one hundred we will, as per usual, receive a text message via cell phone, giving precise coordinates for pickup of the product and a brand-new throwaway phone. We take that new phone and product to sea in my boat, where at approximately oh-dark-thirty we will receive a second set of coordinates. That's our buyer's location. He'll be on the Gulf."

Dawana cleared her throat. "And why's the time for those coordinates 'approximate,' Gunny?"

"'Cause we're dealing with fucking Mexicans is why. Greasers. Spics. Assholes. And every swinging dick of 'em working on Tijuana time."

Sarge turned to Raul Carrera.

"Got anything to say, Carrera?"

"No, Gunnery Sergeant."

"Don't know why a Mexican can't keep time—you got clocks in the Valley, don't you, mister?"

"Maybe, Gunny. But I don't think we wind 'em."

The older man barks laughter between chews of Red Man, short staccato grunts of glee. Like a mortar's hoot.

"Fucking Carrera! Only sumbitch in this outfit with a sense of got-dam humor. Now where were we?"

"Your boat, Sergeant."

"Roger. We'll put out as per usual with nets showing. Just like we love shrimping at got-dam midnight. Soon as we're clear of the coast or anything curious, we will wait patiently on our pansy-ass hands for our buyer to text us his location."

"Any idea what our cut's gonna be?" Bud asked hopefully.

"A Roman fortune, if you figure it by the hour. Which I am sure you jarheads are unable to do."

Dawana spoke up. "We appreciate it, Gunny. I appreciate it, 'specially."

Terry Godot frowned. "Got my qualms taking you, Jackson. Gotta be square."

"I won't let you down, Sergeant."

"Here, then."

He tosses her a handheld Magellan. It's a twelve-channel parallel receiver. Wide-area augmentation, too, which would be handy.

"We get the location for the product, yer leadin' us in."

Bud frowned.

"How hard is that, Sergeant? The only road in follows a railroad bed."

"Hewitt, you are truly a dumbass. What the fuck do you think is goin' on in Devil's Slew tonight? Any idea of what or who we would likely encounter were we to ingress on that sorry excuse for a road? Hah? But just in case you hadn't heard, Specialist Hart has managed to call a hell of a lot of attention to that location. Which means the Slew's got more cops on it than maggots on a gut wagon. The sheriff, deputies, a crime van from the FDL of fucking E. Not to mention the biggest nigger in seven counties. No offense intended, Corporal Jackson."

"'Reprove not a scorner,' Sergeant, 'lest he hate thee.' Proverbs nine:Seven."

Sarge swallows a swig of Bud Lite. "Point is, we do not, repeat *do not,* want to paint Agent Raines's radar. Err-go, we cannot be observed anywhere near Quentin's pissant trailer. Which means that if our pickup is in Devil's Slew, as per usual, we'll be coming for it over the bog.

"Don't worry, studs, the moccasins are sluggish this time of year, and if a gator eats your ass, I'll find your shit myself, shovel it in a bag, and bury it by my got-damn petunias. Now, are there any other questions?"

There aren't. At this juncture, there never are.

Sarge nods shortly.

"Awright, then, get your battle-rattle, maggots. And make sure we got reception on our cell phone."

The pickup went off too easily. The Crusaders got their anonymous text message at nine-thirty in the evening, right on the dot, as per usual. Nothing texted but a set of coordinates, latitude and longitude down to the second, accurate within ten or twenty meters even with a civilian GPS. Making matters even easier?

"It's the old turpentine mill." Dawana stabbed the map. "Maybe two klicks out my mama's back door."

"Shit." Bud locked and loaded his weapon as Dawana took up the lead. "I could find the damn thing blindfolded."

"Feel free," Dawana retorted.

They had taken Sarge's truck to a point east of the Slew, pulling the vehicle out of sight in the cover of pines a mile distant from the Slew's uncertain boundary. The turpentine mill lay just inside Devil's Slew, maybe three klicks more.

"My granddaddy usta work turpentine," Dawana commented as she led her platoon into the lowlands.

"Sure he did." Bud chortled. " 'Cause he was a tar baby!"

"Can it, Hewitt," Sarge growled. "We're on patrol."

Marching through swampland is never easy, even humping light. There is no such thing as hiking a straight line and it's impossible to take a heading on a fixed point when you can't see a foot in front of your face. But Dawana found the Dippers over the tree line to fix her march; between those ancient checkpoints and her GPS, the navigation was not difficult. Within minutes, the squad was waist-deep in water and bitching just like they were back in the war.

"Remind you of the fucking marshes or what?" Bud remarked.

"Iraq, maybe," Raul allowed.

"No IEDs at least. We don't have to worry about that."

"Still got traps planted," their sergeant warned. "Old-timers put traps all over this got-damn bog. You get an ankle busted between one of them jaws, you ain't comin' out on my boat."

"Now, there's an incentive," Bud replied. "Truly."

They reached the mill in less than an hour. Not much left to see. Some rotting timbers. The staves of barrels, ghostly in the night as a cage of ribs.

"There's our objective." Dawana flashed her light briefly.

A pair of duffel bags, marine-issue—OD green with a black insignia. Two bags, as usual, set waist-high on a pine stump.

"Sarge—you ever gonna tell us who we're workin' for?"

"Makes you think I know? We waitin' for ladies, let's grab 'em and growl."

Bud and Raul hefted a bag each.

"Hold up. We got to get our new phone."

Sarge grabbed a bag and yanked a brass zipper and Dawana saw what looked like a perfect pile of U.S. currency. Sarge cursed briefly.

"Hand me the other one."

The second bag produced another mobile phone.

Godot snapped it open, checked the battery.

"Five-by. Buddy, hand me your rifle."

Sarge pocketed the new phone and shattered the original with the butt of Buddy's rifle.

"We cannot let these phones fall into the hands of the enemy."

"Yes, Sergeant," the outfit replied in unison.

Sarge tossed the shattered cell phone to Raul Carrera.

"Once we're under way, just toss 'er over the side."

"Yes, Sergeant."

"Awright. And lookee here, lookee here—"

Sarge pulled a package wrapped in tin foil from the duffel bag.

"This is righteous wages, marines. Two thousand large each."

"Minus our tithe," Dawana reminded him.

"Oh Jesus," Buddy groused.

"Ten percent, that's what we said. Ten percent off the top for the war. Ain't that right, Gunnery Sergeant?"

"What we agreed."

"It won't hurt you, Bud," Raul remonstrated.

"Won't help me, neither."

"Help you when you reach them Pearly Gates," Dawana retorted. "Help you when you meet your Maker."

"Sarge, are we in goddamn Sunday school?"

"Ten percent off two grand gives you eighteen hundred dollars, Hewitt. What's that work out to—four hundred dollars an hour? Five hundred? You think you're worth that much?"

"I don't want it wasted is all."

"Before you forget, I am in charge of the tithe," Godot retorted, "and it ain't goin' to waste. It's goin' to kill infidels. What were you plannin', a two-hundred-dollar drunk? Now, grab your gear and get with the program."

Dawana stayed on point to lead the Crusaders out of the Slew, their gunnery sergeant pulling up the rear. In less than an hour, the outfit was back at Terry Godot's Ford truck.

"That was easy." Raul tossed a bag into the pickup's bed.

"'Easy' will get your ass killed."

Gunnery Sergeant Godot now swapping his rifle for the throwaway phone.

"You maggots stow those bags and weapons, *di-di-mau,* 'cause soon as I confirm the pickup, we're goin' shrimpin'."

Local shrimpers dragged their nets during the day, mostly, but Terry and his crew were known to set their nets late at night, dragging for white shrimp until interrupted by their other responsibility, anchoring offshore to cull the shrimp from a bycatch of useless fish and crustaceans.

The bycatch washed overboard or pumped from the bilge generated a slick of oil and juice easily visible to saltwater sportsmen, who took full advantage of that floating line of chum. Sarge welcomed those fishermen, those witnesses to his crew's benevolent occupation.

First chore after netting the shrimp was to cull the catch and get that harvest on ice. Once the shrimp was iced down, they'd put in to Harvey's for a breakfast and beer. The rest of the day was spent in maintenance. The net was always a mess, floats ripped off and riddled with turtle grass and crustaceans. The turtle excluders required constant repair, along with winches and hawsers and generators and pumps, not to mention the electronics. All of that activity providing perfect cover for the boat's other and more profitable application.

Sarge inherited his trawler from an uncle who'd died childless after a long bout with colon cancer. This was a freezer shrimp boat, seventy feet of master boat equipped with a brand-new generator and redundant radar. *The Crusader* came equipped with a Garmin chart plotter and autopilot and enough electronics to keep Bill Gates occupied. Said something about the economy that you could buy a vessel like this for less than a house.

Sarge had his crew aboard *The Crusader* by half-past ten, and by eleven-thirty they were setting a net in the Gulf of Mexico. For their alibi to work, of course, Sarge and his Crusaders actually had to bring back some got-damn shrimp. The outfit only worked four times a week, a light schedule for shrimpers; plus twice a month they had to deliver product, which meant they might not set a net until after eleven at night. The rendezvous coordinates would come in sometime around three in the morning. Took the best part of an hour to secure the nets and shape the ship for the open sea, and Sarge always wanted at least an hour's margin. That was actually the hard part, that last sixty minutes. Nothing to do but wait.

Of course, there was always something exciting about going into deep water. The smell of the wind changing, a deep tang of undiluted brine. Constellations lost in a sky shot with stars, or else darker than the inside of a cow. Some nights, you'd pull under half a moon, or sometimes no moon or ambient light. On this particular evening, the running lights on the shrimper reminded Dawana of a Christmas tree, green and red to starboard and port, white on top. And tonight's work was not a decoy, not an alibi. Tonight, *The Crusader* was about her real business, and Corporal Jackson, finally, was on board for that mission.

Dawana was on the bridge when new coordinates came over Sarge's mobile phone.

"Wanna make yerself useful, Corporal? Write these down."

Dawana recorded the latitude and longitude texted on the phone's small screen.

"Repeat coordinates."

She called out the lats and longs.

"Confirmed."

Sarge snapped the phone shut and turned to Dawana.

"Every pickup we get a new cell phone. We can't get coordinates without it. You clear with that?"

"Yes, Sergeant."

He pockets the hardware.

"Something happens to me, make sure you get the got-damn phone. Now, Specialist Carrera—"

"Yes, Gunny."

"Lay in a course at, say, seven knots."

"Roger, that'll give us . . . two and a half hours 'til contact, Gunnery Sergeant."

Contact at twenty miles. Twenty miles out to sea.

A walkie-talkie squawked. It was Buddy.

"Permission to fly our colors, Sergeant?"

"Permission granted."

They liked to fly their own colors when under way. They had an American flag, of course. That signal flew highest on the mast, then the Marine flag. But the outfit also had colors of its own. Wasn't a flag, really, more like a pennant. And it wasn't elaborate, just a triangle of canvas double-stitched with the outfit's herald, its crescent of arms: a serpent stitched in black over a cross of gold.

"Question, Sergeant?" Dawana was huddled behind her gunnery sergeant in the cabin.

"Certainly."

"How far off are we?"

Sergeant Godot checked his plotter briefly.

"ETA, one hour," he said courteously. And then: "See there? That green patch? That's the mother ship painted on our radar."

"Bud says we always stay on board *The Crusader*?"

53

"That is correct. I take the bags to the receiving vessel by myself. Squad remains behind to secure the ship. And me, of course."

"What if there's a problem, Gunny?"

"Well, that's why we carry weapons, isn't it, Corporal?"

That was their sergeant. Talked like trailer trash till the actual engagement. Then suddenly all professional.

"There's nothing to sweat, Jackson. I watch the bags. You watch me."

What could be easier?

Dawana had never seen the mother ship that was their seaside destination. In fact, the *Mi Casa* was a millionaire's toy, a luxury vehicle nearly twice as long as the outfit's trawler, with a helipad, a pool, and a trampoline for the owner's several children. Lance Corporal Jackson wondered if there would be children aboard this evening. She was actually on the bridge with a pair of binoculars to spot their rendezvous.

"Eleven o'clock, Sergeant!"

"Settle down, Corporal. I see her. Raul—"

"Sergeant."

"At helm. Pull us alongside easy. Stay on your radios, everyone. Jackson, Hewitt—you're our insurance."

Bud was already in the rigging with his rifle. Dawana grabbed her weapon and a pair of magazines on her scramble to reach a position established behind a barricade of sandbags above the bridge. She kept the binoculars, along with the M16 familiar to any rifleman. The *Mi Casa* approached slowly, torching Sarge's boat up and down with a pair of klieg lights.

"Let 'em see us," Godot ordered calmly. "Same drill. Nothing new."

But this time, there was something new. Just there at the stern stood a man in a tuxedo with a bullhorn.

"Ahoy."

"AHOY YERSELF," Sarge called back, and displayed the twin bags in his hands. "THROW ME A LINE."

There was no reply at first, just a shift of players above them. Then a rope net spilled over the side and the voice resumed command over the bullhorn.

"Gunnery Sergeant Godot. Allow me to extend my hospitality to you this evening. . . ."

Dawana heard Bud clear his chamber as a dozen barrels leveled on the shrimper from the yacht's high deck.

Their sergeant did not flinch.

"Not gonna do you much good if I toss these bags into the ocean."

"I will lose some money, señor. You and your crew, on the other hand, will lose your lives."

"Fuck him!" Dawana heard Bud hiss from the nets. "Fuck him. Let's lay down a line of fire and back out of here!"

Sarge came back without hesitation. "Belay that, Jackson."

"Señor? What is it to be?"

Sarge turned to address his own crew. "I don't know what they want, but if it was to kill us, they'd of done that already. So put down your weapons; we're goin' aboard. Hewitt, get the Ribcraft over the side. And let's remember we're marines."

A crossing at sea is never easy, even in calm waters. But if you had to pick a crew to accomplish that task, you couldn't do much better than Special Ops marines. Bud gunned their inflatable outboard over to the yacht, keeping the vessel stable as Dawana followed Raul and Sarge up *Mi Casa*'s uncertain ladder. Bud came last, snaking a towline out for the dinghy.

"For the record, Sarge," Hewitt complained as he climbed, "this sucks."

"Adapt, marine," came the predictable reply.

They got over the railing to find a uniformed crew flanking

a Latino in a tuxedo. He sported a diamond earring, jet black hair spilling loose. A finely boned face ravaged by acne.

"Form up," Sarge ordered his outfit, and the Latino nodded in admiration.

"I would expect no less."

Sarge tossed the two duffel bags onto the deck.

"Delivered as per usual, sir. If you're satisfied with the product, we'd be happy to climb back off your excellent ship."

"Oh, I am confident the product is excellent. And I apologize for the break in our routine. Believe me—I do not like alterations of plan any more than do you, Sergeant Godot. But I have something you need to see, to hear, that jeopardizes all of us."

Sarge remained at attention.

"Got me at a disadvantage, señor. You know my name. May I know yours, sir?"

"Call me Ricky Ricardo," the Latino replied without inflection. "As in *I Love Lucy.*"

He rattled off a command to his entourage in Spanish then. Dawana didn't catch it, but Raul clearly did.

"*Sergeant?*"

"Keep yer powder dry, Specialist."

"'Powder dry,' I like that." Ricky smiled, displaying a peasant's orthodontia in a rich man's mouth. "You will follow me."

Marines were accustomed to bulkheads and hatches and dizzying turns belowdecks, so the trip below was no more disorienting than it should have been.

"Remember," Sarge said quietly. "He wanted to kill us, he'd of done it already."

Dawana told herself that whatever was in store, she wouldn't break. Would not be the first anyway.

Finally, they were herded into— A *gymnasium?* Cost a

pretty penny, too, mirrors and chrome and a floor of bamboo buffed to shine and well equipped with a flat bench and free weights, a treadmill and rowing machine. Even had a soccer net. There was a squat rack set up near the weights, but instead of there being an Olympic bar and plates suspended in that iron frame, what Dawana and her squad saw was—

A man. No, it was a woman. Definitely.

She was hanging naked by her wrists from the top brace of the squat bar; her feet were bound in wire cut well into her ankles to tease a tub of water below. You could see a field generator and a pair of batteries alongside.

Dawana felt a crawl along her spine.

"Our latest catch," Ricardo announced grandly. "From the U.S. Treasury Department, lady and gentlemen. Agent Brenda Mantle."

The woman moaned feebly. A weak arch of her spine. Blood gushed in a fresh foam from her nostrils, and Dawana saw Raul visibly gasp. Abruptly. As if he had suddenly recognized his sister.

Ricky now massaging the diamond in his ear.

"But then one of your crew is already familiar with Agent Mantle."

"Bullshit. " Sarge grated through his teeth. "I never seen this woman or any agent, and neither has anybody on my crew!"

"That is not correct. Is it, Specialist Carrera?"

Raul was pinioned at that point between a pair of Ricky's crew.

"The fuck!" Sarge was boiling. "The fuck are you talkin' about?"

Ricardo extends a hand to one of his flunkies, who hands him a camcorder, a Canon. Ricky displays the modest screen.

"You want proof? I show you. I do not want you to think

that I have no respect for the uniform. I was trained by U.S. military myself. Fort Bragg. I know the meaning of honor, señors, but I also know what it means to betray. I leave you to judge."

His fingers smooth as the silk of his tuxedo as he scrolls through the device's civilized options.

"Ah. Here."

He directs attention to a captured video. It's a small screen, but the image is clear. Some sort of homecoming parade, it looked like. Floats rising in the middle of a spread of tables. A din in the background. A bevy of girls in white blouses and black skirts.

"There? You see?"

Brenda Mantle smiles at Shirley through the cashier's grille.

Godot clears his throat. "Question, señor."

"Of course."

"Where was this taken?"

"Harrah's Casino. New Orleans. We got a woman there looking out for us. She spotted a number of our bills, our counterfeit bills. But we did not know where the bills were coming from, much less that the Treasury Department was interested, until a common thief led us straight to this bitch you see hanging behind you."

"You say a thief?" Sarge challenged hoarsely. "What thief? Who?"

Ricky slides a polished shoe under a duffel bag and kicks it across the polished floor to Raul's feet.

"Open it."

Carrera appealed silently to his sergeant.

"You heard the man."

Raul kneels to open the bag.

"Empty it."

Raul dumps the bag and out comes wad after wad of what

58

appears to be U.S. currency, a pile of crisp, clean one-hundred-dollar bills.

"The best money that money can buy, señors, two and a half million in this shipment alone, and in my business, counterfeit is easier to wash than laundry. In two days' time, these bills will change hands a hundred times. In less than a week, I will have cleaned two and a half million counterfeited dollars for genuine U.S. currency, which I will then use to acquire coke or heroin or whatever drug the gringo can shoot, snort, or smoke for, as they say, pennies on the dollar.

"And the only connection between the fake money and me is at the source. It is only in your hands that I am vulnerable, señors and señorita. Which is why I am extending my hospitality to you this late evening.

"I pay the artist of this product well for his craft. *El artista* pays you wages far more generous than my own employees would receive for such menial responsibilities. And what do we ask of you in return? Hah? Loyalty. That is all. Mistakes can be forgiven. But a man who will betray his benefactor? Never. But back to our small cinema."

He fast-forwards the camcorder and there is Brenda Mantle again, the same woman now spitting blood above her battery-charged tub. But she's unblemished in the video. Cute. Sexy, even. She's framed over a Latino gambler hiding behind a fake beard and sunglasses before a stack of chips.

"*You have a name, cowboy?*"

"*What's* your *name?*"

"*Lacy. Lacy Spoon.*"

"*Well, Lacy, right now I'm just an hombre cashing in his chips.*"

The player reaches out to sweep over his pile of chips; the sleeve of his shirt rides up and there it is, the tattoo, a serpent and a cross. Ricardo strides over to Raul Carrera and snatches back the desert tans covering Raul's arm. But the outfit already knows what's there.

A serpent and a cross inked deeply.

Their emblem, their honor, their flag.

Ricky nods and a punch to Raul's kidneys drops the thief, writhing, to the bamboo floor.

"He's my responsibility," Sarge speaks up hoarsely. "Gotdammit, you want a piece of somebody, take me."

"Admirable. Predictable. Unacceptable."

Raul's legs bicycling weakly his body. Hunched over like a dried pod of beans.

"Your man has taken something like five thousand dollars of the excellent counterfeit for which I have paid in generous, not to mention genuine, currency. But I am not going to kill him. No. And you want to know why? WHY? YOU PIECES OF SHIT! Because this hombre on the floor? He led me by purest chance to this *punta* we got hanging over here."

The tortured woman's bladder lets go then, and Ricky smiles. Then he produces another hundred-dollar bill. Soiled. Bloody.

"We found it in her crotch. While we were interrogating. If this one bill had fallen into the hands of this bitch's superiors, our entire operation might have been compromised, *comprende*? EVERYTHING.

"And she is not the only threat to our operation. Your own boss, the artist of this very denomination, warns me to avoid a local pig of some reputation. His name is Barrett Raines. You know this man?"

Godot cleared his throat. "I know Raines."

"Make sure you stay off his radar, *comprende*?"

"Bear's not even at the Beach anymore. He's with the FDLE."

A goon slams a fist filled with iron into Godot's gut and it's Sarge's turn to kiss the bamboo.

"He lives five miles from your fucking boat!"

Sarge tries to reply. Ricky nods and his goons drag the noncom to his feet.

"The last thing I need is some nigger cop poking into my business." Ricky returned to his camcorder. "You call attention to yourselves in *any* way, you call attention to me. Now, your boss insists my identity is uncompromised and that his marines can be trusted to safely deliver the final shipment. He tells me there will be no more visits to casinos. But I need more than an artist's word to be sure."

Ricardo strolls over to the steel rack beside the batteries. He removes a handkerchief from his tux and wipes her nose.

"Lemme . . . lemmme down. . . . Pl . . . plss lemme . . ."

She slobbers.

"She don't talk so good now, but watch this."

He slaps down a lever to complete the circuit and a scream rips loose. The bulkheads echo with her agony. Uncontrolled, shameless bellows. He kills the circuit and her head falls like a gourd to her chest. The rest twitching. Like a fish on a deck.

"String him up next to her."

"No—NO!" Raul tries to protest, but they are already dragging him to the rack.

Bedlam ensues as Raul screams curses and imprecations. Ricardo's men dragging him to the rack of iron.

"SARGE!" Bud Hewitt blurts out.

"ON BELAY, MARINE."

"But Sarge!"

"He's a thief. He's lucky to live."

Ricky nods appreciation. "You are a man of honor, Gunnery Sergeant, I can tell. And don't worry. The woman—she lasted two days before breaking. We will only chastise your man until morning, at which point he will be returned. I extend this mercy because, thanks to Specialist Carrera, we now have the names of a dozen Secret Service agents, along with operational details relevant to my business."

Ricardo pivots on his polished shoes and Dawana instinctively steps forward to follow.

"Not so quickly, *negro*." He waves her back. "You will stay, all of you, and witness this discipline. And of course I will video your participation."

"You son of a—"

"*Can it,* Hewitt."

Ricardo adjusts the camcorder on a tripod as his goons pin Raul's arms behind his back.

"You owe me one final shipment of product, two and a half million facsimile of U.S. currency, split between fifty- and hundred-dollar denominations. It will be delivered on my schedule and it had better not be short a single dollar or you will all hang on the rack until a death for which you will beg.

"Meantime, you will report to me the habits of a local cop. This nigger Raines. I want to know where he sleeps, where he eats, where he shits. You can text me that information on our secure number.

"But for now, you will witness this discipline. Watch closely, marines, and listen. And remember."

6

The Fund-raiser

Bear Raines tightened the double Windsor at his neck, brushed a speck of lint off his barrel-size blazer, and checked his watch. The opening fund-raiser for the Veterans' Center would begin in minutes, and it appeared everything was on schedule, the tables set, cards placed, the staff assembled. The kitchen was in order, with a veritable feast waiting to be served on the signature teak plates. Credit for that detail and all other logistics went to the owner, who also happened to be Barrett's wife. You could not pick a better hostess for a fund-raiser of any kind than Laura Anne Raines, and a good part of that appeal was completely unrelated to her skill with wait staff or kitchens. Because the first thing you noticed about Laura Anne Raines, if you had a pulse, was that she was drop-dead sexy.

Every marriage has challenges, and in their nearly eighteen years together, Barrett and Laura Anne had faced more than their share of obstacles and prejudice and disappointment, but one thing never changed: The woman could stop a clock.

A smidgeon taller than Barrett, Laura Anne glided between tables on legs a mile long. She had a belly flat as a volleyball player's, but Bear's wife was emphatically not one of those anorexics you see on the cover of *Vogue,* not by a long shot. Her shoulders were wide as a quarterback's. She was wearing a strapless dress for the day's affair that showed off a long, muscled back. She had a very high forehead. Prominent cheekbones. A complexion flawlessly mingled between cream and coffee. And as she aged, Laura Anne abjured cosmetics and supplements and salons. She was all about natural and had lately returned her hair to a 'Fro short as a skullcap. Ever since Barrett had known her, Laura Anne had been a presence, a furnace, unsettling for many men, black or white.

The kind of woman could make a train take a dirt road.

In college, she'd been approached to model, but Laura Anne was neither flattered nor interested. Ms. Raines had a driving passion unconnected to pop culture or to fund-raisers, for that matter, or kitchens. Laura Anne loved music, especially classical compositions. She'd earned a master's degree in music education and had aspirations to teach at Deacon Beach High, but a white man's school board scotched that opportunity. Which led Laura Anne by necessity and tragedy to acquire Ramona's Place.

The eatery was stilled referred to locally as "Ramona's," after Ramona Walker, its original owner. Laura Anne took over the place in the face of locals openly hostile or derisive and had triumphed beyond anyone's expectation. The restaurant itself was a tin-roofed product of renovation and repair, a hopscotch architecture fashioned of cypress, pine, and Hardie board. You went through a door salvaged off a shipwreck to enter a place that had started as a beer joint before emerging in its final iteration as one of the finest places on the coast for steak and seafood. The newest addition added maybe ten tables, for a total of forty or so. A wraparound deck tied onto a pier convenient to diners arriving by boat.

The menu included African-American and Cajun dishes in interesting combination with the bounty of the sea. Okra and oysters, say. Or dirty rice and flounder. You could get yourself a nice rib eye any day, and the catch of the day was always on special, but the specialty of the house from around late September to the first cold snap was mullet and grits. Folks coming to Ramona's, even native southerners, were either intrigued or horrified to learn that you could use the ugly mullet for anything other than bait. More familiar to travelers from Atlanta or Los Angeles or Miami were the oyster stew and soft-shell crab and onion rings. Scallops were scrumptious in their season, and no restaurant on the Gulf could be short of shrimp.

The interior was wide-open, an island bar offering sweet tea or scotch below the slow turn of paddle fans. Naked beams spanned an interior walled on three sides with glass to offer a great view of the canals and grasses beyond. You couldn't see the Gulf, not unless you climbed the widow's watch. In fact, from Deacon Beach to Steinhatchee, there was nothing like a strand, no beach of sand along the littoral. Instead, you saw miles of grass cut with silver lanes marked with buoys, sometimes, or ordinary sticks, those markers relics of an older and less reliable navigation.

And then there was the music.

Smack-dab in the middle of the dining area stood a baby grand piano, a Steinway, and at any interval during the day or evening, Laura Anne might stop from flirtations or filets to take a seat at her favorite instrument where, as jaws

65

dropped all over, the owner of the restaurant entertained her guests with "Claire de Lune" or Liszt's famous rhapsody. Ramona's had become a watering hole for regional musicians, a welcome port in the economic storm. Students or aspiring musicians came from as far away as L.A. and Austin to wait tables in return for the chance to perform. Laura Anne was their Nubian muse.

Barrett Raines smiled to see young folks from far away mingling with locals at his wife's business. Many of the waiters and waitresses gathered for this fund-raiser hailed from Florida State, a brace of musicians with strings and wind instruments eager to play solo or ensemble. Raines watched the young people guide the arriving guests to their assigned seats. Contributors to the Veterans' Center were seated closest to the piano, naturally. Mike Traiwick was there, of course, the keynote speaker for the kickoff. A gaggle of women from the Historical Society pledged five hundred dollars for a seat at Mike's table. Harvey Sykes was a surprise; Bear would not have guessed that the tightfisted owner of Harvey's Marina would put a dime outside his rented slips. And there was Father Franklin Swain.

Father Swain entered the restaurant in black coat and collar. Barrett met the priest's eye as he entered, and Swain walked straight over.

"Father Frank. You seen Brady?"

"Spent most of the morning with him. And Mrs. Hart."

"How's it going for them?"

"Not well. Brady's cursing God and everyone else for Quentin's death. Including you, Barrett. He especially holds you responsible. The way he speaks—!"

The priest shakes his head.

"Put it this way: You'd never know that you and Brady were friends."

Bear was not surprised. Any African-American raised apart in a white community with a history of intolerance knew that all apparent signs of acceptance or respect or even courtesy were in some sense provisional. Contracts voidable only on one side. White folks who would fight if you called them bigoted would without qualm vote to block your sons' entry into a Boy Scout troop or deny your wife a job in the local school.

Barrett could remember Brady Hart's father standing with scores of other angry white men and women to protest the integration of Deacon Beach High School. And yet Brady Hart had not displayed his father's prejudice. He had been decent to Bear, kind even. They played ball together as boys, and as men they had forged memories kayaking, hunting—and then Little League.

But those bonds were fragile, Barrett knew. Brady might be furious with Smoot Rawlings for the role he played in Quentin's death, but for Barrett there would be a hatred that stopped for its justification at his skin.

"I want to attend the funeral," Barrett told the priest. "I want to be there, for Brady as much as for Quentin."

"Wait on him, Barrett. He needs time."

"Could be a long time."

The priest removes his wire-rimmed glasses, reaches for a napkin.

"I s'pose you know he also lost his firstborn son?"

"Traffic accident. I was first on scene after Smoot."

The chaplain shook his head. "Well, clearly Quentin had problems. Had them here, I imagine. Magnified them overseas and brought them home."

Something in that declaration got Barrett's attention. "Frank, did you cross paths with Quentin when he was overseas?"

"Yes. I was assigned through the Navy Chaplain Corps to

67

a marine unit in Nangarhar. There were a core, or maybe cadre, I guess you'd say, of marines and soldiers who attended Mass. Quentin came occasionally, even though he was Protestant. There were one or two other locals in his squad whom I'd see. You might know Ronald Hewitt?"

"You mean Buddy?"

"Bud Hewitt, yes. He and Quentin took a job here locally with another veteran, a shrimper from Steinhatchee—"

"Terry Godot."

"That's Gunnery Sergeant Godot, thank you. Not sure he's a good influence. And then I'm sure you know Dawana Jackson."

"Know her family," Barrett corrected him. "Fact, her mother still lives on the old homestead out near Devil's Slew."

"Really?" Swain smiles. "Well, Dawana was my RP."

"'RP'?"

"'Religious Program Specialist.' A kind of combination acolyte and logistics assistant. Also a bodyguard."

"Bodyguard? For a chaplain?" Bear was surprised.

"Oh, yes." Swain chuckled. "RPs receive combat training specifically for the purpose of defending chaplains."

Barrett was taken aback. "I don't think the army has anything like that."

"Nor does the air force," the priest confirmed cheerfully. "Gives you an idea how highly marines value their clerics."

"Getting back to Quentin for a moment—"

Father Frank adjusts his glasses. "Nothing if not persistent."

"I need to know if there was something eating at Quentin. Anything you can tell me?"

"I can't repeat anything offered in confidence."

"No, course not," Barrett acknowledged. "I was just hoping you had some general observation. See, I am not at all sure that what happened at the Slew was a simple case of domestic violence."

"No?"

"Father, there is some indication, least I think there is, that Quentin was looking to commit suicide by proxy."

"Aah." Swain raised his hand to the part of his hair. "Well, that would explain some things."

Barrett tried to resist asking what "things" might be involved, but Swain was way ahead of him.

"You know, Barrett, one of the reasons these boys get so boxed in is there's really no safe place for them to talk."

Barrett raises his chin to demur. "Isn't the chain of command encouraging troops to get professional counsel?"

The priest's snorts derision. " 'Professional counsel'! Have you ever read the regulations regarding confidential communications between military psychiatrists or psychologists and active-duty personnel? To begin with, a service member, by regulation, cannot get counseling unless he *first* signs a waiver of confidentiality! Now, the chain of command insists the waiver is only intended for extreme circumstances, but a plain reading tells you that any man or woman in uniform can be reported up the chain, and anonymously, for a wide range of broadly defined actions, even those taken under orders in combat.

"So a kid comes in convinced he's shot a civilian. Maybe he has; maybe he hasn't. Maybe the family was killed by shrapnel, but the young marine or soldier doesn't know that, so he comes in and relives the horrible experience with some military counselor. Another GI might have killed a civilian against orders in the wake of an IED. He might have tossed a grenade into a mosque hiding Taliban.

"Beyond the obvious trauma, there is a time bomb ticking in these battered souls, and some of them, not nearly all, come looking for help. They come, they bare their souls to some captain or major, and next thing you know, the rifleman or tank commander or pilot is getting calls from the OSI or NSG for criminal investigation. The men know this, and the women. They're not stupid.

"This is a major reason chaplains are so important in combat units, Barrett. Especially priests. We are the last bastions of confession, the only uniforms in the chain of command who can hear these boys' awful secrets and then keep them *in aeternum*."

Barrett sighed. "Sounds like things haven't changed much since I was in."

"Oh, they've changed. I don't care what politicians drivel; we are in the middle of a religious war that's been playing out for centuries, and in that crusade we are relying on volunteers taken from the most disadvantaged segments of our communities to fight under ambiguous rules of engagement in unpredictable peril for multiple tours. They come home and they need help. They need assistance locally, where they live. The VA simply cannot answer that need, which is why I am backing this center that Mike has proposed with all my conviction."

Barrett smoothed his tie.

"But with respect, Father, that's not the whole problem. Ask most any cop in any military community from Fort Carson to San Antonio and he or she will tell you that returning veterans are committing violent crimes in alarming numbers. Some were felons before they ever put on a uniform. What do we do with those individuals, Father Frank? What do we tell their victims, or their victims' families?"

"We render unto Casear, Agent Raines. You in your way—"

The priest smiles.

"—and I in His."

Less than half an hour by water from Ramona's vibrant fund-raiser, *The Crusader* limped home, its pennant and crew limp and spent. Sergeant Godot put the shrimper on automatic pilot to check in on his squad. Dawana was downing coffee in the galley. Buddy was sucking a beer. Raul shivered under a blanket on a litter. Dawana and Buddy had to carry Raul off the yacht and back to the shrimper. Her BDU was smeared with her buddy's blood.

"But he'll be all right," Buddy kept saying. "He'll be fine."

It was remarkable how torture with cattle prods or car batteries or rope could be accomplished with remarkably little evidence of the ordeal. Raul was stretched, broken, beaten, and electrocuted for nearly three hours, but beyond a few contusions and a broken and bloody nose, he showed very few outward signs of his trauma.

But Raul was broken; there was no doubt. He had the thousand-yard stare, the somnolent response. It was much easier to strip a man's humanity when he was already compromised, of course. A thief does not suffer more on a cross than a man of conscience, but he does not recover as quickly. Much harder to overcome abuse when you know that in some perverted sense you deserved it.

"Bastard could have got us all killed!"

Buddy Hewitt had gone from defending his buddy to cursing him.

"He could've got us killed. All of us!"

"Could have," Sarge agreed.

"I hate what they did to him, but Raul brought it, didn't he? Well, didn't he?"

"He did," Dawana offered her confirmation.

"Put our asses on the line so he could fucking gamble? Play cards? Dumbass fucking wetback!"

"Settle down, Buddy." Dawana left Raul's side for Hewitt's. "It's over now; just settle down. It'll be fine. We're still the good guys. We're the heroes." Dawana mouthing a conviction she no longer felt.

"Hewitt, stay with Carrera," Sarge ordered, and ducked his head to leave the galley. "Jackson, you're with me."

Dawana clambered after her gunny to the bridge. She waited for Sarge to check their course and update the plotter before voicing her own concerns.

"You said we were righteous, Sergeant. You said the money was going to fight the war."

"We are. It is," Godot replied.

"That Mexican's a drug lord! I dit'n sign up to push no kind of drugs, Sergeant!"

"Stow it, Jackson."

"We cain't go servin' two masters, Gunny."

Sarge turned on her furiously. "Kind of got-damn fantasy world do you religious nuts live in? You're gonna pocket one thousand eight hundred dollars for this trip. Eighteen hundred dollars! Which master you think paid them pieces of silver?"

"Wages of sin is death, Sergeant."

"Yer not dead. I'm not. And neither is Raul. Now, got-dammit, I told you when we started on this road that I would do everything in my power to make sure our profits put rounds on ragheads, an' that hasn't changed. I can't control what that asshole Ricardo does with his cut, but I sure as fuck control my own wallet. And so do you, Corporal. And so does our boss—I can guarantee you he's righteous.

"It ain't perfect, I know, but there's no such thing as a clean war, especially against infidels."

Raul's blood was still damp on Dawana's issued shirt.

"What about that Treasury agent? The woman? She's no infidel."

"Collateral damage."

"They crucified her! I don't know if I can get past that, Sergeant. I just don' know!"

His jaws locked.

"Well, you fucking A better figure it out, Corporal Jackson, because we got one more delivery to go. One big one. And we can't afford another weak link on our crew."

Barrett Raines took a backseat once the fund-raiser was under way. Laura Anne seated Frank Swain at a table with Mike Traiwick and the most generous contributors. After the obligatory introductions and feast, Traiwick made a Power-Point presentation of the plans for a new Veterans' Center to be built on the lot behind what used to be Mayo's First Methodist Church. The affair ended with chamber music and a solo on the baby grand, Laura Anne bringing Haydn's Concerto in G Minor to an audience weaned on the Beatles or Willie Nelson.

Everyone agreed it was a swell affair.

Laura Anne had to change clothes for the evening shift, so Bear drove her home, stopping first to pick up the twins from baseball practice. The family was headed back to their Jim Walter home on an unnamed blacktop near Harvey's Marina when Bear spotted a pair of vehicles coming up fast from behind.

A Ford Ranger twin looked to be wide-open, a Harley-Davidson crowding the centerline alongside. Ben and Tyndall turned at the Harley's throaty roar.

"They're coming fast!" Tyndall remarked, and Bear eased

his unmarked vehicle as far toward the shoulder as he could safely manage.

"See if you can get a tag number," Bear told his boys.

"Not today, Bear." Laura Anne laid a gentle hand on her husband's injured arm. "Please? It's just some youngsters blowing off steam. Let it be."

The pickup ripped past Bear's Crown Vic at ninety miles an hour, the motorcycle following so closely that its slip-stream rocked Bear's heavy cruiser. His hands tightened on the wheel.

"Barrett?"

"I hear you."

The headlights from the pickup lit up a line of mailboxes on the sharp curve ahead. Bear saw the truck catch the shoulder, the truck sideswiping the boxes. Tin boxes sailing into the air.

The boys cheered.

"Boys," their mother warned.

Barrett noted the damage and location as he drove by. He would remember the details. White Ford Ranger. Double cab. Driver up front, passengers behind. Male. A black driver hauling ass on a Harley Sportster punked out with running lights and a sissy bar. Pilot had a helmet and battle-dress trousers and blouse. Desert Digital.

"Daddy, look!" Ben shouted, and Barrett watched with his family as the bike's driver shed the BDU.

The shirt catches the slipstream like a parachute and the driver's sex gets immediately established. A young woman now driving topless. Except for her helmet.

The twins howled glee. "She's havin' a good time!" Bear's firstborn crowed.

"Benjamin." Laura Anne offers mock censure as she turns to Barrett. "They're just young."

74

"'Young,'" Barrett echoes mechanically.

"It's not your job to give tickets, Barrett."

"They fled the scene. They damaged property."

She runs her hand inside his thigh. "Nothing that can't be repaired."

"Mailbox is federal property."

"Seems to me I remember a young man I once knew chucked a thirty-pound melon off the back end of a truck riding at a pretty good clip past a row of mailboxes."

"Laura Anne!"

She chuckled. "They're just young. Letting off steam."

"Is that it?"

He frees a hand to find the warm skin at the small of his wife's elegant spine.

"Well, maybe we get home, we can let off some steam ourselves."

7

Supercommuter

Every workday for Agent Raines involved a marathon commute. There were over two hundred miles of coastline in the
Tallahassee-administered region, and seven counties, coastal
and landlocked. The Regional Office for Tallahassee Operations was for years situated in Live Oak, some miles east of
the Suwannee River. A community that had weathered the
recession better than most with an agribusiness augmented
by Walmart and other wholesalers close to Interstate 75,
Live Oak was the most prosperous burg in the region.

The FDLE's Live Oak office was established in what was
originally a redneck's discotheque. The onetime honky-tonk
for two-timers was an unremarkable single-story building, virtually windowless, with a shallow-sloped roof. Its saving grace
was a canopy of magnificent live oak trees and a barbecue pit.
Bear and his fellow investigators salvaged the barbecue pit that
had famously served the disco and regularly put it to use. Come
football season, agents would run an extension cord out to a

rabbit-eared TV and enjoy sweet tea and brisket as the Gators and Seminoles battled for bragging rights.

As the region's counties plunged into economic malaise, tax revenues plummeted and law enforcement suffered. Sheriffs all over the region became increasingly dependent on the Live Oak office for support. Everything from voter fraud to environmental crime passed across some desk or other in Barrett's office. As the FDLE's workload increased, the need for office space naturally increased. No problem. Plans were drawn up and sent through committee to renovate and expand the existing facility. How hard could it be to add space to a building that used to be a dance floor? But as plans, and ambitions, wound their way through the appropriate subcommittees at the legislature, the economy tanked and funds for the expansion were cut, which is to say castrated, and the well-loved Live Oak office was shut down.

Some son of a bitch even took the barbeque pit.

A scramble for temporary space led the FDLE to establish its Regional Office in what agents fervently hoped was a provisional headquarters located in the seat of Madison County. An abandoned high school in Jasper was appropriated for next to nothing and Barrett and his colleagues and their staff moved into a honeycomb of cinder-block classrooms clustered downstairs from the slightly crazed magnolia and two puffed-up assistants charged to administer the school system's payroll.

Just approaching the building was depressing. The flagpole out front was long neglected. The badly landscaped grounds baked in summer and died in winter and the architecture was unvarying and utilitarian. Everything was laid out in rectangles of tile and brick and cinder block. The hallways were still stale with teenage pheromones; lockers rusted on walls layered inches deep in lead-based paint.

It was too expensive to cool the building centrally, so the halls were left to ambient adjustment, leaving the classroom/offices to be cooled or heated by window units that had you either freezing your ass in summer or sweating in winter (as an agent once expressed without apology in Bear's presence) "like a bored chigger in a nigger's navel."

Remarks like these were common when Bear first came to the FDLE. It was clear that many of the older, all-white agents resented the newcomer from Deacon Beach. Lots of bait got thrown Bear's way in those early years, all eyes watching his response. Barrett's response was to use whatever bait he could find to catch bad guys. The Bear became the first African-American to be elevated to special agent in the FDLE and was still the only black agent working in the region of Tallahassee's responsibility. Barrett was by now senior enough to choose his own corner in a cubicle in what used to be the chemistry lab of Jasper High School. A fitting place, Glenda Starling joked, for the explosions sure to come.

Even before Florida ran out of money, the FDLE ran a lean ship. There was hardly a stick of furniture in the office that couldn't have come from Goodwill. In fact, some of the desks were bought at an army-surplus depot. Some equipment you couldn't lowball. Security cameras had to be set up at entry points, naturally—and a metal detector. Separate cameras scanned the parking lot outside.

But Glenda Starling, combination adminstrative assistant and aspiring chanteuse, was a genius at stretching dollars. Every agent's PC was purchased at a fire sale, and not everybody who wanted a laptop got one. When it came to money, Glenda was a hard-ass. Cell phones and radios were parceled out like Christmas gifts, and if the shredder didn't work, you broke out a pair of scissors.

Bear missed the barbecue pit. There was a microwave and

a coffee machine in the old faculty lounge, but agents mostly fed the Coke machine. There was a john in the lounge, too, but the plumbing stopped up so regularly that agents generally opted for the boys' room down the hall. It was embarrassing to line up, as you had in high school, to drop your tool over a urinal that lipped sour and porcelain someplace below your knees.

And of course the move to Jasper meant that Barrett put another forty miles a day onto his commute. Was a little over fifty miles from Bear's ranch-style home to his Live Oak office. Jasper, Florida, was sixty-seven miles from Steinhatchee, which made it over seventy miles from Bear's residence. Once you got to work, it was not uncommon to be called to some distant crime scene, which added even more miles to the daily count on the odometer. Agents displaced from the Live Oak office were assured there was no need to sell homes or relocate; as money got better, agents were promised that a brand-new Regional Office would be built on the Live Oak site.

No one was holding his or her breath.

The routine for agents coming to work was unremarkable. Check e-mails from local sheriffs or Tallahassee. Make sure you'd completed your Race Relations Seminar and qualified with your firearm and contributed to the United Way. Oh, yes, and do apprehend that serial killer or pedophile. Pretty much like any other office. But today would be different. Bear was actually notified as he was driving in that a Treasury agent had been abducted in New Orleans and that the FBI and Treasury were asking all intrastate agencies, along with county sheriffs and the Highway Patrol, to assist in a full-court press. Tallahassee had sent an agent and a federal team to brief the region's investigators.

Barrett was good friends with the agent assigned to liaise

with the feds. "Cricket" Bonet was a pale giant, a sprawling red-haired French-Canadian who for years had been Barrett's partner. Barrett arrived at the Jasper offices, to find Cricket in the faculty lounge, wiping at his trousers with a paper towel.

"The hell you doin', Cricket?"

"Wiping piss of my pants—you use the johns down the hall?"

"Stand back and lean," Bear advised. "Spreads the pattern."

Cricket wadded up his bulk-bought napkin and banked it off the Sears window unit to score in the Walmart garbage can sitting beneath a Mr. Coffee.

"Hell of a place you got here, partner."

Barrett produced a quarter for the coffee fund.

"Java?"

"Thank you, Bear, I could use it. Got an FBI agent and a Treasury dick to herd this morning."

Cricket stood up to adjust his tie and blazer before retrieving his laptop.

"You might want to get one yourself. It's going to be a long day."

You could jive-ass in the hall or in the Lounge, but once you started working a crime, any crime, agents became as serious as undertakers, and when a crime was directed at anyone in law enforcement, the room got quiet as a tomb. Ask almost any American with a badge or a gun his or her worst fear and kidnapping will rank just behind taking an innocent's life or imprisonment.

It was all too common for a policeman or judge to be snatched in Mexico City, or Baghdad, but this sort of crime was extremely rare inside the United States. Law-enforcement personnel who were taken hostage stateside were almost always snatched on impulse or opportunity, usually in connection with a robbery or prison riot. The abduction of Brenda Mantle marked an entirely new level of threat.

The briefing was set up on the stage of the school's auditorium. Somebody plugged in a radiant heater to kill the chill as agents dragged folding chairs in a semicircle before Cricket Bonet and a pair of feds. Barrett recognized the FBI's contribution: He had crossed swords with Larry Finch on another occasion. Water under the bridge, though Finch was as ugly as ever, with a nose like a barnacle growing off the hull of a boat and an Adam's apple the size of a tangerine. Larry must've gotten contacts or LASIK surgery sometime recently, because the glasses were gone.

The FBI's agent was dressed in a style akin to Barrett's, a garden-variety G-man in perma-press slacks, shirt, blazer, and a tie fixed with a Rotary pin. The Sears, Roebuck ensemble— that was the FBI. The Treasury Department's representative, however, was not wearing anything off the rack.

"Agent Pamela Goerne." Cricket introduced the first woman Barrett had ever seen wearing an Armani suit in the flesh.

It was classy, a one-button with besom pockets. Navy with white pinstripes. And Goerne wore it well, the tailored fabric following the contours of a bony frame used to lacrosse or field hockey. She had a windburned complexion, which confirmed time outdoors, and when she spoke, Bear recognized a cultured Massachusetts accent hinting more at Bryn Mawr than Boston. She was red-haired, close to Cricket's color. Green eyes. Average height. The bios distributed by Cricket indicated some smarts: Stanford, Harvard Law, Interpol—then the U.S. Treasury Department.

"Gentlemen—I believe I see gentlemen only in this group, which invites a topic to be deferred—we have a serious situation."

She swiped a finger across a Netbook to activate a slide on a screen salvaged from some classroom.

"Brenda Mantle, Special Agent, Department of Treasury."

The official portrait first. Head-on. Black unisex necktie and jacket. Hair pulled back. She could have been the gal you see at the reception desk before you renegotiate your mortgage: competent, neutral, reserved.

Pam clicked the mouse on its pad.

"Brenda Mantle undercover in Miami."

Somebody started to whistle before censoring himself. Hard to blame any man for that reaction, because here was Brenda Mantle in a two-piece by a swimming pool, and she was hot. Rich chestnut hair. Toned abs and cheerleader legs.

Barrett glanced away from the slide, to see Agent Goerne carefully gauging the reaction of the men around her. A soft *click* brought a new slide.

"Brenda Mantle undercover in New Orleans."

It took Barrett a second to realize that he was looking at a gambling casino. Brenda was smiling at the camera over a rack of chips, a white blouse and dark skirt worn tight to tease, but not to reveal.

One more slide. *Click*.

"Brenda Mantle. Mother of twins."

An audible gasp ran around the half circle of hardened men. Because here was this cute, sexy thing suddenly modest in a sweatshirt and jeans, piling sand on the beach with a young boy and a girl barely out of infancy.

"You see my point, gentlemen?"

They had. Agent Mantle was no longer an abstraction. Nor was she a pinup. She was a comrade and a mother, and she was one of their own.

Goerne killed the slides.

"Here's what we know. Agent Mantle was engaged for

half a year following leads related to the laundering of counterfeited U.S. currency in casinos. As you all know, counterfeiters don't make a profit spending their facsimile; they make money by selling fraudulent denominations to third parties. Whoever acquires that faked currency usually tries to launder it in one way or another to get Uncle Sam originals.

"As do nearly all large casinos, Harrah's uses a mechanical scanner to check large denominations coming through the grille. They'll tell you they run all bills through these machines, but that isn't true. The employees are human. They're pressed. They're rushed, or bored, or sleep-deprived. So we figure that on average, maybe one twenty out of a hundred gets scanned. Probably a third to half of the hundreds get a mechanical scan.

"Thing is, the scans don't usually take place right away. A counterfeiter can come in early in the day or afternoon, basically at the beginning of any shift, and be pretty sure that for the next three or four hours he or she can trade funny money for chips with impunity. That's why we put Agent Mantle on the floor. She trained for two years with our best artists to spot contraband currency and, in fact, had pulled a pair of twenties and one fifty-dollar bill from Harrah's in her first five months. But then something happened, something we didn't expect."

Goerne taps her computer's mouse and a new set of photographs displayed on the wavering screen.

A grainy photo much larger than life filled up the screen. The subject was Latino, though right away Barrett noted that the beard did not seem to match the texture of the hair spilling from beneath the bill of the subject's generic baseball cap. He wore sunglasses. A long-sleeved shirt partly exposed has arms as they extended to rake in a pile of chips.

"Remember the tattoo," Gorene ordered. "I had a sketch made, with copies for you gentlemen."

The photo was too grainy to be precise, but Bear could make out the blurred image of a cross or crucifix. It looked like a dragon or maybe just a snake entwined.

"Meet John Doe," Goerne continued. "We estimate that in his four trips to the casino, this man laundered something close to five thousand dollars of counterfeited currency. Now, I'm sure you know that five thousand in funny money is a piss in the bucket compared to many counterfeiting scams. But what got our interest in this case was that the bills we managed to confiscate had serial numbers in the same sequence as other bills that have been appearing at random up and down the Florida coast for nearly a year.

"Clearly this man, whoever he is, is not a big player. But we continue to believe that he has some association with a large counterfeiting operation situated somewhere in Florida . . . And we also believe this man is connected in some way to the abduction of our agent.

"Here is what we know. One: It was professional. The kidnappers had our own security mapped out and neutralized. Streetside cameras have produced almost no useful information about the perpetrators, though we do know that a street sweeper was used to block the view of a surveillance van posted for Agent Mantle's security, and there were a number of taxis clustered with persons so far unidentified near an intersection that was within sight—"

BAM! Bear jumped in his seat as Pam Goerne slammed her fist into the podium.

"—I repeat, within SIGHT of her hotel!"

She had their attention now. There was a fire trapped inside that designer suit that Agent Goerne wanted to make sure they saw.

Agent Goerne stood aside from the podium.

"The kidnappers employed a decoy, a double who took our eyeballs all the way into the hotel. Somebody probably should have squawked when the target headed for the loo in the lobby, but that's armchair quarterbacking. Bottom line is, by the time we got our people out on the streets, in the wet, in the rain, there was nothing left to find but a wig and a Windbreaker.

"The street sweeper was abandoned. The minivan used to snatch Mantle was using faked decals and credentials from a local cab company. We found that vehicle torched in a junkyard near the airport, which may mean that Agent Mantle was transferred to a private aircraft.

"We are reasonably confident she is alive. We believe that the abductors are foreign; the pattern fits what we have seen in every hellhole from Tegucigalpa to Tehran. The leap we are making in the effort to locate Agent Mantle is that her kidnappers are in some way associated with a large, well-financed counterfeiting operation.

"I'd be the first to admit that this is not a sure bet, but too many things make us believe that this cannot be a grab for cash. Consider first the risk: New Orleans is loose, but it's not Bogotá. Whoever took Agent Mantle was willing to accept a terrible risk of capture, which tells me that her value to her abductors is tied to her extensive knowledge of our own Treasury Department's efforts to defeat counterfeiting operations.

"My huge fear is that whoever took Agent Mantle will kill her simply because they can't know with certainty the point at which she has nothing more to tell."

Agent Goerne paused for a long moment. There was not a sound onstage. Only a kind of tightness. Barrett realized, suddenly, that he was holding his breath.

Bear let go a barrel of air. Chests rose and fell all around.

A couple of self-conscious coughs. A sneeze. Finally, Cricket Bonet rose from his folding chair.

"Okay, you know the drill. You know what's at stake. Let's get her back."

Barrett corralled Agent Goerne before she could leave her high school stage.

"Agent Goerne." He buttonholed her on the rising steps. "I'm guessing you got fingerprints off your gambler. And DNA?"

"We did," she replied, interrupting her descent to answer. "No matches, though. Not on our system."

Well, that was a pretty damn big system. The Bureau's IAFIS already shared over 55 million fingerprints with state agencies, the largest cache of biometric information on the planet. And Bear knew that the feds were working hard to include a DNA sample from every criminal coming through any state's system, but the NDIS was getting resistance from an unholy alliance of liberal activists and libertarians, the same groups siding with the NRA to oppose a federal database recording the ballistics of weapons purchased in the country.

Barrett understood very well the fear that government-held information could be used to punish citizens. More than his white neighbors, Bear was aware that Hoover's FBI had actively targeted everyone from Jane Fonda to Stokely Carmichael. The director apparently took a sexual pleasure in snooping on movie stars and politicians. Even JFK was not immune to that poison. Even so, Raines did not see how any citizen was threatened by having a convicted felon's DNA on file or the lands and grooves of handguns available for forensic comparison.

Thank God there was not a constituency outraged by a database of skin art.

"I'm guessing you did a pattern recognition of the tattoo?" he asked.

Talk about crossover technologies: The algorithms driving programs used by analysts to interpret satellite photography and employed by scholars to authenticate folios attributed to Shakespeare were also used to type and group skin art.

"We ran our suspect's design through the system," Goerne answered him directly. "Problem is that dragons and crucifixes are just too common to be useful. There are literally hundreds of thousands of serpents and dragons and crosses worked into innumerable designs. May be useful for indentifying the individual, but we can't tie it to an organization."

"Well then, how strongly are you wed to the theory that Agent Mantle's kidnappers were likely foreign, or foreign-controlled?"

"That's a tentative position based on the modus operandi, and the sophistication involved."

"Because there are lots of kidnappers in Mexico, Agent Goerne."

"With obvious candidates, yes. The Nuestras and Mexican Mafia have threatened our DEA repeatedly. The Zetas are very active, I'm sure you know, many of them trained by our own military. And every group has its own tag or tattoo."

The identifier most familiar to Bear was the recurring variation on the number 13 used by the Surenos gang. The common tag of "Sur-13" could vary in any number of ways, rendered in dots and dashes, a bar code, or simply a tattoo of the Roman numeral XIII. The number 13 was not meant to represent bad luck; instead, it referred to the thirteenth letter in the alphabet—M, for *Mafia*. The Nuestras and Zetas had their own tags and tattoos.

Agent Goerne extended her hand.

"I don't believe we've been introduced. I'm Pam Goerne."

Bear suddenly felt once again like the boy who didn't know not to spear the biscuits off the plate.

"Pardon me, ma'am. Agent Raines. Barrett Raines."

"So you're the Bear. Cricket says you know this part of the state better than anyone."

"He exaggerates."

"I hope not. Because if we find Brenda Mantle, it's not likely to owe to a computer program or a satellite photo. It's going to be because you or someone like you keeps pounding pavement or quicksand or whatever it is you pound down here."

"If your gambler is holed up in our region, we'll find him, Agent Goerne. We won't quit till we do."

"An obdurate man." She allowed a smile and slipped a card from the pocket of her thousand-dollar suit.

"If you need federal assistance, please call me. Anytime."

The first stop Barrett made after hitting his shins on the pisser and spilling coffee on his shoes was seventy miles of undivided blacktop away. The idea for recruiting local newspapers came as Bear and his team assigned tasks in the wake of Agent Goerne's presentation. The office would issue a BOLO region-wide with the John Doe's description and a sketch of the tattoo—that was standard procedure—but Cricket went on to suggest that local businesses should be contacted directly with the gambler's description and that agents should also leave tips for spotting counterfeited currency.

"We can give the manager at Brake Check or the checkout at Safeway the skinny on how to spot a doctored twenty- or fifty-dollar bill. Of course, the bills our suspect is pushing aren't going to get spotted by amateurs, but that's not the point. The point is to give some tired cashier or bored checkout gal a reason to look at the faces and forearms of their customers. Anybody making six bucks an hour is more likely

88

to be on the lookout for a Latin male with a tattoo if she thinks he's sliding her funny money."

"Could take the same approach with local newspapers, too," Barrett amplified. "We could include a sketch of our John Doe, including a detail of the tattoo, along with an alert to be on the lookout for counterfeit. Every owner of a small business reads his local paper, and nobody wants to be stuck with fake cash."

Cricket nodded his approval and another agent volunteered to prepare a PSA for local radio and television stations. This was the new face of law enforcement, a team effort aimed at recruiting the entire community—cashiers, hairdressers, bus drivers, and white-collar workers—adding those eyeballs to the trained inspection of sheriffs, deputies, and cops. To that end, Agent Raines would be pounding a keyboard along with the pavement to enlist cooperation from Web sites and bloggers and chat rooms.

It would be a mistake, however, to assume that the new technologies diminished the need for face-to-face contact between cops and their fellow citizens. If you wanted a single mom or a hardworking dad or a teenager to take time from work or fun to phone in a tag number or to tip the location for a "person of interest," you had to have earned your community's trust. Barrett had worked for years to establish personal relationships with people from Cedar Keys to Perry, and in that effort no citizen was more important than the man or woman in charge of that most humble and persistent anachronism of American culture—the small-town newspaper.

The *Deacon Beach Herald* had until recently been owned and edited by a woman whom Bear considered a close friend. Pauline Traiwick had been a fixture on the *Herald*, an outspoken, fiery woman who never flinched when it came to presenting uncomfortable truths, even when advertisers threatened to pull the plug. Bear remembered from boyhood the firestorm of local ire following a series of articles Pauline wrote to encourage integration of the then-segregated school system. She lost half her ads overnight. Of course, some of that money came back when those same folks ran ads supporting their runs for the school board.

Eventually, most advertisers returned. You could be mad at your small-town rag, but that didn't mean you wanted to lose it. As the recession set in and papers like the *Boston Globe* and the *Philadelphia Inquirer* faced bankruptcy, papers in small and medium markets remained stubbornly healthy. In some cases, their subscriptions actually grew. In Pauline's opinion, this unexpected durability was rooted equally in the power of vanity and in photographs.

It was vain, after all, though perfectly benign, to want to see your son's pimpled face in the local paper as he was publicly praised for being selected for Boys State, or to see your daughter's profile at her induction into the Beta Club. The 4-H and the Royal Ambassadors and the Rotary Club all got to see their members pictured for one recognition or another.

Not to mention the kids in Little League.

Athletic competition of any kind was guaranteed coverage in local papers, but high school contests gave locals the best raison d'être to keep their subscriptions alive. Where else to pose the homecoming queen with the touchdown king? Where else to capture the agony and ecstasy of small-town victories and defeats? There wasn't a running back or lineman from any class-C school who didn't want to see his picture in the local foldout, along with any girl or boy who sank a free throw or swung a bat.

People living in towns like Greenville or Destin or Mayo or Cross City or Branford packed their Friday-night arenas with the passion of Athenians, those triumphs and disgraces reported the next day to generate Saturday-morning's heroes and villains. The small-town newspaper was for local Crackers their last front porch, their mostly replaced fireplace and hearth. There was no medium simpler to access and certainly none so tactile to reward local achievement or disgrace. Pauline Traiwick had chronicled her community's daily life, and her nephew seemed determined to keep that legacy alive.

Barrett approached the *Herald*'s brick and mortar exterior from the curbless sidewalk on Beach Street. Even from the street, you could see that the building was badly maintained. The mortar looked as though it had been chipped from the wall with grapeshot. Tall panes of beveled glass badly in need of cleaning were set inside lintels showing wood rot, and the double doors' kerf had lost its stripping. You could see gouges on the sidewalk where the door scraped over its sill. Bear grabbed an iron handle the size of a firedog and tugged. Not enough. The November rains had the door swollen in its frame. Bear tried again with his good arm and the door yanked open.

Ding-ding! A brass bell tinkled to cue an older and simpler era, that association dissolving instantly as the owner glanced up from his laptop and BlackBerry.

"Barrett. Come in. I was just laying in pictures from the fund-raiser."

"They turn out good?"

"Everything with Laura Anne. The rest of us are dog-ugly."

The *Deacon Beach Herald*'s owner and editor greeted customers behind a wraparound counter littered with notes related to advertisements and circulation and, of course, local coverage. Bear used to love watching Pauline print the *Herald* off her old KBA, but that machine was now retired out back, along with almost everything else familiar. Of course, the days of hot type were long gone. Mike Traiwick composed and edited his weekly quarto on an Apple computer. And the pictures of local fishermen and hunters and athletes displaying their various trophies were recorded on a Sony digital and then downloaded to be manipulated by software conforming to the *Herald*'s layout. Pixels were cheaper than film, and faster. Mike kept his laptop, also an Apple, on the counter, along with the constantly employed BlackBerry. About the only other equipment in sight were a fax machine and a laser photocopier bought secondhand and rarely used.

A few things remained sacred. Pauline's old oak roll-around still had its place before the magnificent escritoire, whose calfskin pad sloped on a tablet of hardwood leading to a shelf of pigeonholes looking out like so many caves over ballpoint pens and paper clips. And the American flag still hung across the door that exited to the newly raised Butler building out back, the warehouse securing a bank of digital photocopiers, along with paper, ink, and other paraphernalia.

Mike snapped his laptop shut.

"What can I do you for?"

"Business, unfortunately."

"Uh-oh. Whatchu got?"

Barrett produced the sketched rendering of John Doe along with a separate drawing of his tattoo.

"Some of what I'm telling you is good to print. The rest you're gonna have to sit on for me, Mike."

"I know how to respect a source."

"Sounds familiar," Bear replied ruefully, but he went on to summarize for the editor in chief the basic facts related to the feds' suspicion that a large counterfeit operation might be located somewhere in northern Florida.

"We think this man might be involved." Barrett tapped a

xeroxed sketch of the suspect. "We are pretty sure he's Latin, anywhere from late twenties to mid-thirties. We don't know if the beard is genuine or not. Probably not."

"That's not very specific, Bear."

"No, it isn't. But the tattoo's distinctive, and we're hoping that if people are looking for this man as a possible counterfeiter, well, we'll be more likely to get a tip."

"I can get you, say, half a column. Plus the sketches. Anybody paying for this, by the way?"

Bear appealed with a shrug. "Hoping you could run it as a news item."

"Speaking of news."

Mike snapped his laptop open.

"You seen this?"

Barrett felt a knot in his stomach before he even scanned the header.

The item came from CNN. Forty minutes old. Mike read the text aloud.

"'Federal Agent Kidnapped in New Orleans.'" That something I can print, Barrett?"

Bear met his eye.

"Print anything you like from CNN. But I told you up front there'd be some things from me that would be out of bounds."

"That's fair enough." Mike displayed both palms. "But I certainly have the right to ask: Is the man sketched here connected in any way with the agent whose abduction is now being reported on CNN?"

"The truth is, Mike, and this is confidential, we just don't know for sure."

"But you're figuring it is, aren't you? That's why you're here speaking to me. That's why Amy Lawson called me from Jasper to say she'd got an e-mail forwarded from the FDLE warning small businesses to look out for a Latino counterfeiter with a snake and a cross tattooed on his forearm."

"A counterfeiter isn't a kidnapper, Mike, and there are thousands of federal agents involved in all sorts of investigations. Is anybody saying this agent works for the Treasury Department?"

"Was he? Or she?"

"Would you feel some special urgency to run these sketches if I said yes?" Bear asked, unblinking.

"It would give me reason to run them every week for a month," Traiwick replied. "If you think that would help."

"It would definitely help. But I cannot confirm, and I will deny any claim that I confirmed, that the federal agent kidnapped in New Orleans two days ago worked for Treasury or was in any way connected to an investigation of counterfeiters."

Mike now bobbing his head as he scratched notes. "Understood. Of course, as soon as you leave, I'm going to be trolling for public sources."

"That's okay. Like Frank Swain says, we're both doing God's work."

Raines extended his giant paw and Mike's hand disappeared.

"We have an understanding, neighbor?"

"Course, we do, Bear. Always. And tell Laura Anne once more for me, will you, that she gave our Veterans' Center a huge head start. We already have pledges for over a hundred thousand dollars!"

Bear was genuinely pleased to receive word of the fundraiser's success, but the news from CNN was unexpected. Bear left Mike Traiwick's place, heading for Harvey's Marina. That short drive gave him time to raise Cricket Bonet on his mobile.

"Cricket, you checked out CNN the last hour or so?"

"Just now."

"Is it a leak?"

"No, it's just good reporting. Not surprising, the whole hotel was taped off as a crime scene, investigators pouring in from Atlanta and Washington. Newshounds everywhere. Somebody was bound to find out."

"What's Agent Goerne saying?"

"She says it's worth the burn if it gets people looking."

"It's already helped. Mike Traiwick just committed to run our sketches for four weeks straight."

"Outstanding. Where you headed now?"

"Harvey's Marina."

"Dropping off some sketches?"

"I will, sure, but I have a personal motive, as well. You know that veteran who was shot a few days ago? Involved an assault rifle in a hostage situation."

"I heard something about it."

"Well, I was one of the shooters."

"Oh shit, Bear."

"Anyway, there's some indication the kid was looking to commit suicide. His old gunnery sergeant keeps a boat at Harvey's. I just wanta ask a few questions. It's probably just selfishness on my part."

"*C'est la guerre.* And take your time, Bear. We gotcha covered."

"Thanks, partner." Bear signed off with a twinge of nostalgia. Beyond their professional association, Bear and Cricket shared a history influenced by the prejudice of a larger and dominant culture. Raines had no idea that white people could be prejudiced against other whites until he heard his partner tell stories about being ridiculed for speaking French or about feeling inferior when seeing signs on restaurants or restrooms that mandated ENGLISH ONLY.

Bear knew what it was to see a sign on a water fountain. Knew it only too well. Most days, it was only a distant whisper. But sometimes some asshole in the office or on the street would hurl an insult, or Barrett would hear some slur directed at his children or his wife, and a white-hot rage would threaten to explode.

That's when a badge and a gun were most dangerous.

"I'll be at Harvey's, then," Barrett said, and signed off.

Harvey Sykes's marina, dry dock, café, bait shop, and bodega started as a fishing camp of tin-roofed sheds propped on stilts beside a canal dredged through a half-moon of saw grass and cypress. The canal offered easy access to oyster beds and deep water beyond. The marina was close enough to Deacon Beach or Pepperfish Keys to attract the condo crowd, but removed enough for locals to find refuge in the marina's café or bar.

Commercial fishermen brought their trawlers to Harvey's dry dock for refurbish or repair alongside any number of Makos or Sleekcrafs or Cheetahs. The convenience store was a relatively new addition, and there were probably half a dozen new slips rented out to a variety of pleasure craft and houseboats. Dawana Jackson could see Sarge's houseboat from the deck of the trawler, a luxurious Summerset once owned by a woman convicted for murder.

Dawana and the rest of her squad had been swabbing Terry's trawler under a gray winter sky all morning, doing everything they could to remove any trace of their adventure at sea. Raul Carrera had sprayed blood from a broken nose all over the deck, and his shoulder was dislocated, but there was no way the outfit could risk taking him to an ER, and Raul knew better than to complain.

"Should have left your ass hangin'!" Sarge bellowed at

Raul on the way home from his awful ordeal. "You realize what shit you got us in? And don't think this is the end of it, jarhead, 'cause assholes like that got-damn Ricardo do not forget a thief. Not never."

With that rough encouragement, Sarge yanked Raul's shoulder back into its socket; the Crusader screamed and passed out. Two days later, he was still on the boat. Dawana remained aboard as well, pulling grass off turtle excluders and patching the net when she wasn't tending Carrera. A bright orange patch leaving the channel got her attention. She'd never seen a sail on a kayak before. The small craft leapt like a porpoise across the gray water, pulled as if by an invisible tether on a wedge of Dacron.

So pleasant was that view that Dawana almost missed the unmarked cruiser pulling into the marina's parking lot. The door opened and a black man in a flight jacket and dress slacks piled out. He stood head and shoulders above the Crown Vic's roof, but it wasn't until she saw the wink of the badge on his belt and the bulge of the Glock at his hip that Dawana realized she was looking at Barrett Raines.

"Gunnery Sergeant—that who I think it is?"

Terry followed her finger like a gun sight.

"That's the Bear," he confirmed and glanced up to see the outfit's distinctive pennant catching the breeze. "Shit! Buddy, get that damn flag down."

"Why cain't Dawana do it?"

"Get your ass up there *now*. Dawana, git Raul off the boat."

"What'll I do with him?"

"Drown him, for all I care, but get his ass off my boat."

Barrett Raines spotted Terry Godot's pickup immediately on entering Harvey's rustic parking lot. The Ford Ranger was parked nose out beneath a cypress tree partly shading the marina's slips. The truck was raked fender to fender on the passenger side with the kiss of mailboxes.

Barrett heaved himself out of the cruiser and took a couple of moments to survey the scene. He spotted the rigging of Terry's shrimp boat rising above the roofline of Harvey's bait shop. A frayed American flag hung limp above the cabin, and as he stood by his cop car, Bear saw somebody stripping down another flag set just beneath, but a motorcycle fired up to claim his attention. Raines was about to cross the parking lot when a motorcycle fired up to claim his attention.

It was the same motorcycle Barrett had seen the night of his wife's fund-raiser, the Harley Sportster racing Terry's truck when Sarge clipped the mailboxes. There was the same driver, too, a black female in a military-issue fatigue jacket. No helmet. She had a passenger riding piggyback in desert cammies. His boots were unbloused and he was limp as a sack on her back.

Bear pulled a pen from his flight jacket and made a note to run a 10-28/29 on the Harley's tag, and with that reminder he killed the engine of his Interceptor. Then Raines released the safety on his Glock and made sure a round was chambered.

The gravel crunched beneath Bear's Bates DuraShocks as he heaved out of his car. A glance toward the slips confirmed that Sarge still had his houseboat, but Barrett turned away from the slips and dry dock for a detour across the parking lot to reach Harvey's Café and Bar. He found Harvey at the register with his son Roten, cursing over a computer screen.

"Damn thangs are more trouble than they're worth."

Roten looked just like his dad when Harvey was twenty. Both men were lean and leathered; both had eyebrows that marched in an uninterrupted bridge across their foreheads. Roten eased his father away from the keyboard.

"Daddy, you just need to remember to zero out."

"What I need is a pen and paper!"

"Oh, I don't know, Harvey." Bear dropped into a booth. "I seem to remember you had problems with *x*'s and *o*'s."

"You're a hoot, Bear, you know that?"

"I do."

"Remindin' me of my deficiencies. An' in front of my boy. Who, God knows, has little enough respect for me as it is."

Roten chuckled.

"Yeah, you're just a total failure, Dad. Tell you what. Let me fix the spreadsheet and you take care of Mr. Raines. Though I doubt he's here to snack."

"Oh, he's snacking all right," the older man disagreed as he moseyed on over. "Question is, on what?"

"Got a couple of pictures for you first." Barrett showed Harvey the twin sketches of the Latin gambler and his tattoo.

"We think this guy's passing funny money," Barrett told his old classmate. "He's Latino, as you can see. But the tatoo's the big thing. You see a Juan Valdez with a snake on his arm, let me know."

Harvey swept the artwork off the counter but then hesitated.

"Wait a minute. . . ."

Bear straightened. "What? You seen this man?"

"Cain't tell nuthin from this picture, but the tattoo— A snake, like? Wrapped around a cross? Seem like I seen this here someplace."

"On an arm?" Bear suggested hopefully.

"Damn, if I know, Bear. Prolly nuthin."

Harvey warped a sponge's worth of hair over his brow.

"Sometimes I think I'm gettin' the Alltimers."

"That's all right. Maybe you can help me with another matter."

"We'll see."

"Well, I'm sure you know about Quentin Hart."

"Bad business. I'm owna be at the funeral."

"Wish I could be."

"Nobody blames you, Bear."

"Not true, Harvey, but thanks for saying it. Reason I wanted to speak with you is because I understand Quentin was working for Terry Godot? Hauling nets, what I heard."

"Pretending to anyway."

"What do you mean, 'pretending'?"

Harvey became suddenly circumspect.

"I shouldn't say anything."

"Could be important."

Barrett saw Harvey working his wedding ring.

"I just don't see how Terry's netting enough shrimp to account for the money he's got."

"He's retired from the Marine Corps, Harvey. And the boat's free and clear, what I hear. Some uncle willed it to him."

"I know about the boat, but the Marine Corps dudn't pay retirement in wads of hundred-dollar bills."

"What d'you mean?"

"Terry comes to my bar couple weeks back with Quentin, looked like they'd been arguin'. Anyway, they had a couple of beers and Terry opens his wallet and there's nuthin inside but a fold of C-notes."

"Hundreds? You're sure?" Barrett challenged him sharply.

Harvey looked offended. "Course I'm sure: An' you seen Sarge's truck?"

"The Ranger? Not exactly an Escalade."

"No, but he paid cash for it. Twenty-three thousand, brand-new. Salesman from Lake City told me."

Barrett shrugged. "There's people pay cash for shrimp, and one good night can net you a grand, no problem. As for the truck, I remember first thing I did when I got out of the army was pay cash for my Malibu. Saved every dime I could to get that car."

"I prolly should of kept my mouth shut."

Barrett winked. "I bet you can remember a time when a dollar never burned a hole in your pocket. But you said Quentin Hart was arguing with Terry?"

"He was upset about somethin'."

Barrett mulled that over a moment.

"Harvey, is there anybody on that boat who's not a vet?"

"They's nobody's not a marine. They was Quentin. And now you got Buddy Hewitt and some Mexican and that black girl, name just went out of my head. Drives the Harley out front. Her mama's got a place out toward Devil's Slew."

"You don't mean Dawana Jackson?"

"Dawana, that's her, yeah."

So the chaplain's assistant was the hell-raiser with the Harley. Bear jotted a note.

"Got a handle for the Latino gentleman?"

Harvey shook his head.

"Well, sir, this was helpful." Bear pocketed his spiral pad and pen. "Like I say, I mostly came over to see what I could find out about Quentin's situation, but while I'm here I'll look over Terry's boat, but if I see anything looks out of line, I'll follow up on my own. Catch my drift? You won't be involved at all."

"Thanks, Bear. Give Laura Anne my best."

By the time Barrett Raines hit the pier leading to Terry Godot's trawler, the only flag flying from *The Crusader*'s bridge was Old Glory. Bear spotted Terry Godot on the foredeck. Looked like he was engaged in the repair of some kind of pump. A couple of seals and some spare parts piled together with a pack of Red Man and cigarettes in a plastic milk crate, the workingman's tool chest.

Gunnery Sergeant Godot had Bear Raines in his sights from the moment the lawman left Harvey's Café. No telling what kind of bilge Harvey was spilling, but Terry's personal animus was reserved for Barrett Raines. Terry never crossed Barrett during the years the black man worked as a beat cop in Deacon Beach and had rarely seen Bear since his assignment to the FDLE. But Terry hated the son of a bitch. He hated the way white men who used to openly mock Bear and his nigger family now kowtowed to Agent Raines. He hated the system of preferences that privileged coloreds and wetbacks and lesbians over anything white and straight and male. And then there was the initial confrontation between Terry and Bear that transpired while they were still teenagers.

That business in the cafeteria.

Bear was by then a senior and established as the massive black kid with good grades who abjured football to dribble and shoot. Terry was a sophomore, still unreconciled to his loss of status in a school that, however haltingly, put white kids and blacks on even footing. Terry and his group took every chance they could to make life difficult for the African-Americans in their class. Petty annoyances, mostly. The occasional fistfight. White teachers mostly looked the other way and white students offered primarily tacit support. It was a great place for a bully to excel, and there were many targets.

One kid, in particular, a newcomer to the community, was an easy target. Terry and his nascent outfit would shake Lavon down for lunch money. If the colored boy didn't give up, he was meat for reprisals of all sorts: hot soup poured in his crotch; underwear tossed in the toilet at gym. There were probably half a dozen of these provocations accomplished before the event in the cafeteria. Lavon Hanks was in line, the only black kid in line, which was a mistake, waiting his turn for the usual mashed potatoes or french fries and a waxed carton of milk. Lavon was small, nearsighted, and asthmatic. He was not well liked, even by black kids. A loser so stereotyped as to be shunned by everyone.

"Lavon, lemme see yer wallet." Terry shouldered up to the tenth-grader with a couple of his Cracker friends.

"I don' have nothin'."

"Sure you do," Godot contradicted and his posse snickered in support.

"I spin it awl on lunch."

"I'll just take the billfold, then."

"You ain't takin' shit."

A new voice in the conversation, one Terry would never forget. And there was Bear Raines, already larger at eighteen than most men, black or white, in their small community.

Barrett nodded to Lavon. "Go ahead with your tray." Then he returned to Terry.

"Next time you want some lunch money? Or put somebody's Skivvies in the shitter? You might wanna remember this."

And then Bear kneed him in the balls. It was the first time Godot actually took a straight shot in the family jewels and it was an experience of nausea, pain, and humiliation that he never forgot. Never forgot and never forgave.

Fucking nigger cop.

"Permission to come aboard," Bear now hailed from the pier off the dry dock.

"You don't need my permission, Bear."

"Actually, I do." Bear noticed that Godot never paused from his work.

"Suit yerself."

Bear climbed aboard from a cat amidships and made his way forward.

"Afternoon, Terry."

"Not out here to fish, are you, Bear?"

"I get that all the time." Barrett smiled and unzipped his jacket. "But actually, I wanted to ask a few questions about Quentin."

Terry peeled a cracked seal from its flange and laid it carefully on the deck. Wiped his hands on his trousers.

"Quent was a good marine."

"I don't doubt it."

Sarge pulled a Marlboro from a pack lying inside a tool chest.

"You come here to make yerself feel better, you're at the wrong place."

Bear pulled up an ammo can, took a seat.

"I'm a veteran myself, Terry. You don't have a monopoly."

"Never said I did."

"And I'm guessing as his gunny you made it your business to know where Quentin was at on a damn near daily basis."

"Wouldn't go that far."

"Oh, I think you would. I was just wondering if Quentin had something eating at him. Some kind of baggage."

"The only load Quentin was carryin' was the payment on his trailer."

"What I hear, Quentin paid cash."

Barrett saw a line tighten in Terry's jaw. The old noncom took a careful draw of his cigarette, tapped the ash into his tool chest.

"The fuck is on your mind, Bear?"

"I think Quentin might have used Smoot and me to commit suicide. I think if there was something on his mind bad enough to make him suicidal, you ought to know."

"That's bullshit. People off themselves awl the time and even their families don't see it comin'. You talked to his mama? Or Brady? They see anythin'?"

"Nobody's closer to a marine than his gunnery sergeant, Terry, and it looks to me like Quentin was closer to you than he was to his own family. It's like you still got a platoon out here."

"Band of brothers. Course you wouldn't know anything about that."

Sarge flicked his cigarette over the side.

"Fuckin' ninety-day wonder."

Another miscalculation. It was not a mistake to insult Barrett. Was common, in fact, for noncoms to ridicule the source of any officer's commission. The mistake in this context, though, was Terry's attempt to deflect Barrett's question with so transparent a tool. Made Bear decide to push the interview to, as they say, another level.

"There some business with Quentin Hart you're afraid I'll find out, 'Sarge'?"

The retired noncom flicked his cigarette after the path of his chaw.

"He was weak. Weakest pup in the litter."

"Must have seen something pushed him over."

"We all saw things!" Terry turned, snarling. "The fuck would you know? Every goddamn raghead with a gun or a grenade. IEDs on the streets, in the shitters. Fuckin' cunts carryin' suicide bombs. It ain't like artillery, Bear. It's up close, it's personal, and it never got-damn comes when you expect it.

"And then when you finally get a fuckin' Taliban in your

105

sights, some sumbitch lawyer in Tampa says you cain't en-gage because he's got a roomful of fuckin' cousins might get their sorry ass hurt. Happened every day, every week. And we were supposed to be got-damn different. We were handpicked to go after these motherfuckers and take 'em out, and when we did our got-dam job and we went over there, somebody says, 'Oh, no, you boys are too rough. We're gettin' complaints.' And then they send our ass home.

"Sent home like a squad of got-damn squids. Prob'ly wouldn't have bothered you, 'Agent Raines.' Your notion of war is settin' five klicks off target in a motorized howitzer or whatever the fuck it was. Easy enough to be brave behind ten tons of armor. Or behind a fuckin' badge."

"Easy, now," Barrett cautions gently.

"Pardon fuckin' me."

Barrett plants his hand on his thighs as he rises from the ammo box.

"I understand you have a Mexican working for you."

"What if I do?"

"Got a name?"

Sarge drags a Marlboro through the seine of his chewing tobacco.

"Carrera. Raul Carrera. Buddy asked could I give him some work."

"All right." Barrett jots down the name. "And long as I'm here, you might as well show me around your boat."

"You got a subpoena?"

"Not even."

Terry picks up a fresh seal for his bilge pump.

"Then I don't have to show you a got-damn thing."

8

Fenholloway—the Outfit's Retreat

Dawana Jackson is in her element. She has a man in need, a buddy in arms, and a clear mission to fulfill.

"Hold still, dammit."

She's settled Raul on a ratted-out recliner outside the outfit's single-wide trailer. Raul cradles his wrists on his knees as Dawana applies a compress of ice and water. Field expedient. Ziploc bags filled with hammer-crushed ice and a caul of water. The ligatures circling Raul's wrists are as clear a testament to his ordeal as any stigmata. Would be hard to explain those signature burns as a normal injury. Sarge has given strict orders to Buddy and Dawana to keep their squad mate out of sight until the most visible signs of his torture are diminished.

Shouldn't be too much of a chore, Dawana tells herself. About the only thing showing aside from Raul's busted nose and the effects of a dislocated shoulder are the injuries to his wrists.

Dawana had felt shame witnessing Raul scream on his rack. Part of her was horrified; part of her was scared shitless. Part of her got off to it.

Dawana and Buddy cut Raul down from his torture rack, and it looked like he was going into shock. Even after getting the radioman back to his own boat, it was touch-and-go. Raul's condition was bad enough to warrant a trip to the ER, but that option was quickly vetoed by their gunnery sergeant. "We cain't afford those kind of questions."

"Couple of days, he'll be all right," Sarge predicted.

Now Dawana stood before a rising fire on the outfit's rude patio. The sweet smell of resin released with small explosions of sap from the pine knots fueling the blaze, black smoke rising to mingle with needles of hybrid pine. Dawana was inspecting her buddy's wrists.

"We can wrap 'em with gauze," she declared as she inspected the burns. "Just a wrap around these wrists and nobody'll see a thing. Anybody asks, we can say you got burnt on the generator's exhaust, that's what. Easy as can be."

Raul nods dull confirmation. "*Sí.*"

Buddy throws his K-bar knife into the communal dartboard.

"Goddamn thief."

"Not now, Buddy," Dawana admonished.

Raul watches Buddy stroll over to retrieve his knife.

"Is because of you I did it," the Mexican accused.

"Me? The fuck do you figure that?"

"Is true! You brought me into this outfit! You and Sarge. I did not trust this business, but you talk me into it! Just like when we were overseas."

"Now, don't go there," Dawana interjected sternly. "That was different."

"I always looking for somebody tell me what to do." Raul slobbers into his own beer. "But no more! *¡No mas!*"

"What an asshole." Buddy turns away, disgusted. "You ain't the victim here, compadre! You took a gangster's money—"

"It was so little!"

Raul looks at the gauze Dawana is winding about his wrists.

"I am just a bad man."

"More trash," Dawana declares. "You just set on talkin' trash this evenin', ain't you, Raul?"

"I make one mistake after another."

"Where'd you put the laundry anyway?" Buddy demands. "That money you cleaned in the casino?"

Raul nods toward the trailer. "My footlocker. You want it, you take it."

"By God, I just might."

Raul turns to Dawana.

"They broke me. In front of that woman. They said she lasted two days and they broke me before the sun. Like in the Bible, Peter. The cock crows and I am screaming like a baby. I am not a man. I am nothing!"

Dawana feels a crawl along her skin.

"Now, you hush! You are saved in Jesus, Raul. You been crucified! Your sins are paid, my man. Paid in full!"

Bud snorts. "I'm not so goddamn sure about that."

Dawana turns on him.

"Whatcu woan't, Buddy? Hah? String him up again? Wire his balls and pop out his other shoulder? The man fucked up. He admits it. What more you woan't?"

Raul turns to her and his eyes are wet. "But maybe this was God speaking to me. Warning me. Warning *us*! Maybe this"—

He crossed himself and then made that sign over his several wounds.

"Is jus' a downpayment for our greater sin!"

"Leave it alone, Raul," Buddy warns. "That 'greater sin' shit? Dawana's right; what's past is past. We all agreed. Forget that and you'll burn for sure! We'll all burn!"

"Quiet, the both of you." Dawana slaps her meager supplies into their kit. "Ain't nobody burning. We are Crusaders. Heroes in Christ! We fuck up, we pay our dues, but that don' mean we're bad. You hear me, Raul? You been chastised, but thassa blessing. Really! Listen to me—"

She takes his hands into her own.

"Better for thee to enter life maimed, than having two hands to go into hell."

He pulls away.

"Raul? The hell you goin'?"

"A ride." He nods to the motorcycle. "Clear my head."

Buddy's hand tightens on his knife.

"You ain't goin' anywhere, Valley Boy."

"Buddy—" Dawana steps between Hewitt and Carrera. "What say we give the man some space? I'd say he's earned that. But Raul, I don' know about my bike."

"I been on bikes before." Raul pulls a watch cap from his field jacket.

He straddles the saddle painfully, slipping Dawana's helmet off the sissy bar as he goes. A turn of the ignition key. Lights green. Raul makes sure he's not flooding the engine before he plants a boot on the starter and kicks. The Harley turns over with a throaty roar. Carrera snugs the helmet over his wool cap, then reaches out tenderly to test the throttle and clutch.

"JUST A RIDE," he calls out above the Sportster's rumble. "TO CLEAR MY HEAD."

Dawana made sure Buddy was half-soused and that Raul was well on his way to clear his head or heart or whatever it was he needed clearing before sending a text over her cell phone.

NEED TO C U

She was a little surprised to see the response come so quickly:

MEET @ PARK 1 HR

"Buddy, I need to borrow your truck."

"Fill her up, you can," he replied, and lobbed his knife in the general direction of its cork target.

Dawana put on a fresh set of BDUs and grabbed her olive green jacket along with the keys to the Dodge Ram.

Fuel was down to a quarter of the tank's capacity.

"No way you get a fill-up," Dawana declared aloud. She detoured to the nearest Piggly Wiggly, put in ten dollars of regular, switched on the radio, and then aimed the truck's pressed-steel bumper south on Highway 27. She'd sung along to maybe five or six songs before tooling up to Mayo's single traffic light. A left at the light took her east to the banks of the Suwannee River.

Dawana saw the bridge before she saw the river. A magnificent span of cables suspended the Hal W. Adams over the river Stephen Foster made famous. She crossed high above water clear as amber, making sure to slow down while passing the black & tan always parked beside the weigh station just past the bridge. A few more miles east and Dawana turned left again, this time onto the county road leading to Dowling Park and the Advent Christian Village.

Dowling Park started out as a sawmill. The mill was owned

by Thomas Dowling, the same Dowling who in the early 1900s built the Live Oak, Perry and Gulf Railroad. Mr. Thomas Dowling financed the "Loping Gopher" largely to haul his own lumber and quickly diversified his holdings in land and other commodities to become the wealthiest man in the region. Was around the time of World War I that Mr. Dowling's minister persuaded him to donate the large tract of land that became the Advent Christian Village, a place originally conceived as an orphanage and a home for destitute ministers and missionaries.

In the seventy years following, the Advent Christian Village became almost synonymous with Dowling Park itself, a magnificent development incorporating retirees along with orphans and a host of persons receiving extended care in one of the village's many residential facilities. It was one of the few places in Suwannee County where poverty was not evident. There was always some kind of new building going up, some kind of addition or renovation. The property's western boundary ended on a high bluff that offered a splendid view over the river. To the east was the orphanage and a working dairy.

Dawana eased Buddy's heavy truck over a modest cattle gap to reach a serpentine macadam road that wound its way past a variety of privately owned homes and residences, all shaded by magnificent oak and hickory and magnolia trees and hedged with *Photinia serrulata,* those serrated leaves tipped scarlet, like blood on the points of a thousand spears. Closer to the park's interior were facilities for extended care. Every house, residence, and clinic was girthed with shrubbery indigenous to northern Florida, the perennials framed by banks of azaleas and daylilies that, in spring, would mingle their odors with the smell of hyacinth and magnolia. This late in autumn, you got the damp and fecund odors of Spanish moss and decaying acorns to clear your head.

Corporal Jackson rumbled past the village's surprisingly small chapel before finding a spot to park outside a brick-sided ranch-style building tucked under the trees. Took her two tries to nose the pickup into the slot without tangling the truck's heavy brush guard in a crowding stall of ligustrum. White letters dabbed onto a panel of cedar identified the building as the Northside Residence, an innocuous euphemism for a place where people came to face the end of their lives.

She found Father Swain waiting in the modest office provided for his twice-weekly ministry, a cubbyhole set along a hallway punctuated with IV stands and semiprivate rooms. CHAPLAIN AVAILABLE, the sign on the door invited, even though the Adventists in situ were not abundantly thrilled to have a Roman in their midst. A growing population of Catholic residents, particularly Catholics with money, induced the concession of a priest "on campus."

It made for some awkward moments. Dawana was once intercepted on her way to Father Swain's office by a genial Protestant only too happy to administer any rite. Corporal Jackson insisted on seeing the chaplain whose life she had protected with her own. The priest had an office of his own in the small church in Mayo, of course, but the chaplain's assistant preferred to be reconciled at a distant location and in a secluded sanctuary.

Confession, after all, was supposed to be private.

"Dawana, come in. How are you?"

A crucifix hung in a catenary of brass below Father Swain's stiff white collar. His hair split in a Dagwood part right down the middle. A black short-sleeved shirt, black trousers, and black shoes and socks were as severe as any uniform. The priest stepped from behind his desk and pulled over a chair.

"Sit, please. Let me get the door."

Dawana waited for the door to shut before pulling out the gun from her jacket.

"There's a problem, Father. I need absolution."

The chaplain nodded calmly. As if there were nothing between him and his penitent but a rosary.

"Ask and ye shall receive, Corporal Jackson. But first you must have a clear and contrite heart."

9

Night Rider

At one time, Raul Carrera had a Harley of his own. This was before the war. No telling how many two-wheeled miles he'd logged between Brownsville and Padre Island, and it felt good to once more have a motorcycle between his legs. The Harley-Davidson engine, in particular, had a characteristic vibration that varied with speed and acceleration but never completely damped out. Add to that the rush of wind across your face, the shock of the road never entirely subdued. And then the smells of autumn near the Gulf, cold and damp and fecund. A tang of sea breeze tickling your tongue.

Raul skirted the coast southward all the way from Fenholloway to Pepperfish Keys, sticking to county roads and blacktops and the occasional dirt road, racing along at eighty miles an hour. But even that good vibration was not enough to clear his troubled head. It was past midnight before he checked in with his outfit.

"The fuck are you?" Buddy answered the phone.

"The Keys. I'm headed back."

"You could have let us know where you were."

"The hell am I doin' now?"

"Just get your ass back, Raul."

So much for brotherly love. Raul pocketed the cell phone and climbed back onto the bike. The painkillers he'd been popping all day had him more drowsy than was safe. But once he got back to 27, Raul rationalized that it shouldn't be too bad. Was a straight shot north on 27 to the turnoff for the Fenholloway bridge. Raul got to the highway reasonably alert and observing the speed limit. It was past midnight, not much traffic, though a pulpwood truck driving head-on damn near blinded him on brights. Raul shifted toward the ditch. The truck roared past, its long trailer empty. Nothing crazier than a pulpwooder on a Saturday night.

Only a hint of sky was visible above the wall of hybrid pine on either side of the narrow road, their sappy trunks clicking by like pickets on a fence. A soft, soft shoulder. Raul was fifteen minutes away from his turnoff when he saw a set of headlights small as candles in the mirror bolted onto the handlebar. He shook himself awake, shivering in the slipstream. He hadn't minded the cold on the way out. In fact, he would have welcomed any punishment. But now it was late and he was tired; he wished he'd thought to bring gloves along with his fatigue jacket and watch cap.

He checked his rearview again. Headlights dancing larger in the jiggle of his mirror. Any chance it was a cop car back there? Raul sure as hell did not want to give some deputy or patrolman an excuse to pull him over. He checked the speedometer. Flat on sixty. A mile a minute down a ribbon of blacktop in a chute of trees and the vehicle behind was gaining steadily. No bubblegums tumbling, though, which was a good sign. In fact, judging from the height of the lights, it probably wasn't a cruiser. Just some redneck in a pickup.

Coming fast, though. Coming hard.

Raul shifted his weight to pull the bike even farther off the centerline, teasing the shoulder of the blacktop. The headlights behind blinked twice. Good driver, Raul thought with relief, and flashed his own halogens, indicating it was safe to pass.

Here she came, just off his portside and closing. A little close, to be sure. Raul checked his mirror again, and about that time the truck behind put its lights on high beam.

"Fucking Christ!"

By the time he realized what was happening, it was too late.

It was the second time in as many weeks that Barrett Raines had reason to confer with the technicians assigned to the FDLE's Mobile Crime Lab—even though the site of the crash was not initially regarded as a crime scene. The motorcycle was still burning when the county deputy who first spotted the flames reported a single-vehicle accident. Raul was hurled like a bag of popcorn into a solid pine wall at five thousand feet a minute. The helmet looked like a china cup busted in a bathtub, the face and skull like a grapefruit turned inside out.

The wallet provided identification, a VA card and a Florida driver's license establishing one Raul Jesus Carrera with an address in Miami. DOB 14 August '87. The victim would not be a candidate for organ donation, even though the license indicated his consent to that purpose.

"Nothing here that ain't busted," Bob Blanchard declared. "Inside and out."

Once again proving that even a broken clock is right twice a day.

Walking in from the road, Barrett Raines saw signs of Raul's richochet through an unyielding gauntlet, the bark of trees sheared off and stained with blood and tissue. The torso lay in a separate location from the driver's head and limbs, the intestines burst through his anus like an enormous hemorrhoid. The arms and legs were easy to locate, though it took some time for the cops first responding to realize that the distinctively inked scorpion and cross on the victim's forearm matched the tattoo specified in the recently issued BOLO.

Smoot Rawlings used his BlackBerry to send a digitized picture of the tattoo to Tallahassee's Operations Center. Raul's face was not amenable to photography, but his licensed photo was on record, and that information, combined with the tattoo on the GI's forearm, triggered an 85 percent match with the computer-generated specs for the John Doe so urgently sought by the FBI and the Treasury Department.

It was just about sunrise when Barrett Raines had gotten a call from Cricket Bonet, who told him that the counterfeiter fingered by Treasury Agent Brenda Mantle was a former marine found dead in a ditch on Highway 27. Barrett had driven straight to the scene. He recognized the bike right away. "Might check to see if it's stolen," he advised. "The owner, I am just about positive, is Dawana Jackson."

Bear Raines could take credit for an ID of the motorcycle, but it was Julie Fannon who declared within minutes of arriving that the burning wreck was not the product of a simple accident.

"First off, there was more than one vehicle involved," the tall young crime-scene tech insisted.

Sheriff Rawlings spread his arms. "We got one set of tracks, one wrecked Harley, and one victim."

Julie demurred. "It's true there's no sign of anyone at the site of the wreckage other than the victim. But you look at the road here, you see any skid marks? Not a one. He never even hit the brakes."

Sheriff Smoot Rawlings countered with a tap to the brim of his ever-present straw hat.

"Seen it a million times. Late at night and cold. Boy's tired. Maybe a drink or two. He nods off, and first thing you know he's wrapped around a damn tree."

"Yes, Sheriff, but if you'll walk with me just up the road a piece—"

Bear tagged behind Smoot as Julie Fannon led them another fifty yards north.

She stopped to kneel by the soft shoulder north of the wreckage. "See these tracks? They're recent—the grass is barely sprung back up. Big tires. Prob'ly a truck. For sure somebody pulled their vehicle over to this shoulder of the road. Same side of the road as the wreck."

"Missy, this is half a football field from the motorcycle."

"Yes, sir, but it is up the road from the bike, on the same side of the road, and it's fresh. Now, there's no way anybody could pass by and not see the fire, so either the driver of this vehicle saw the accident after it happened or saw it when it happened—or else the driver had some other reason for stopping."

"And what reason would that be?" Rawlings prompted.

"I'm thinking whoever pulled off the road up here maybe caused this accident."

Smoot snorted his dissent. Barrett Raines took a knee beside Julie Fannon.

"I don't see any footprints. No sign of anybody getting out."

"Not onto the shoulder, no, sir. And the vehicle did not

back down the road, which means either the driver pulled over and then stayed in the vehicle before goin' on about his business or else the driver pulled over, stopped the vehicle and got out to walk the hard road back to the wreckage of the motorcycle."

"So say he walked the road back, so what?" Smoot frowned. "What's that signify?"

"Well, Sheriff, does it make sense to you that somebody not involved with the collision would take time to pull over, get out, walk fifty yards or more back to a pretty spectacular crash site, and then make no attempt to assist the victim? Not even a nine one one call?"

"Maybe they just decided not to get involved," Smoot groused.

"Then why stop at all?" Julie posed that question. "Person wants to be a Good Samaritan, they don't just pull over for a look-see. They get out to help. But there are no footprints to be seen where we are now and none at the site of the wreckage back yonder, which tells me that whoever pulled over here, if they did get out, was not intending to help anybody.

"Whoever pulled over here was either a voyeur or caused the wreck.

"Get a closer look at that bike, I wouldn't be surprised if you find it was hit from the side or maybe from behind. Could be somebody passing too close. Playing chicken. Or for that matter could even have been on purpose."

"That's a stretch of spandex, don't you think, Bear?"

Barrett stood and dusted off his slacks.

"If this victim's not the John Doe we've been looking for, I probably would take a pass, but if Raul Carrera is our New Orleans gambler, he's our only link to counterfeit and Brenda Mantle.

"Plus, I can't help but wonder where he got those wounds

on his wrists. Also why he was driving Dawana Jackson's motorcycle."

"Girlfriend, maybe?" Smoot worked his gum back and forth. "Not that it makes any difference. Could still be an accident."

"Could be, but we need to be sure, Sheriff. Stakes are just too high."

"Shit fire and save matches."

Smoot spat carefully.

"Awright, then. Break out the tape."

The site was designated a crime scene. Carrera's body was bagged for transport to the medical examiner in Jacksonville. The motorcycle was winched onto a wrecker and hauled to Tallahassee, where a forensic examination supported Julie Fannon's reconstruction of the scene.

"Somebody definitely clipped that Harley, and hard." Barrett delivered the verdict to Sheriff Rawlings late the next day. "We're looking for a heavy bumper, most likely not painted and not chrome, either, though the fire complicates that finding. We might get lucky. Whatever hit the bike should have picked up some paint off the motorcycle, probably some metal off the rear fender, and maybe some cuts off the chain, as well. We should contact local body shops 'case the perp tries a repair."

"Roger." Smoot scribbled a note onto his spiral pad. "And what did the ME have to say?"

"Just about every bone was broken, which complicates things, but the ME agreed with us that the wounds on his wrists were definitely ligatures. He'd been tied up. And judging from a hematoma and the painkillers in his blood, the doc believes a shoulder was dislocated before the wreck. There were some other signs of abuse, too, but inconclusive."

"So what we got is a marine took his girlfriend's bike after kinky sex and she runs him off the road?"

"I'd be surprised if sex had anything to do with it." Smoot slides his pen into the holder in his shirt pocket. "We better start interviewing people."

"I spoke with Terry Godot day before yesterday."

"I heard. Hell of a coincidence, don't you think? Two boys, both in the same unit overseas, both working for Terry, and both dead within two weeks of each other?"

"Hazardous duty, for sure, but it won't get us a warrant for anything Terry owns. We can search Carrera's vehicle for links to counterfeit. We can get a warrant for his trailer in Fenholloway. Might get lucky there. But to get on Sarge's boat, we're going to need something connecting Terry and Raul other than a part-time job and military association."

"How 'bout Dawana Jackson? You'd think she'd of reported her Harley stolen by now. Unless she loaned it."

"Either way, gives us cause to speak with her." Barrett kneaded his injured arm. "But before that—"

"Yeah?"

"Let's see who shows up at the funerals."

Anyone involved with the investigation of homicides knows that a significant percentage of killers attend their victims' funerals. Killers attend their victims' rites for various reasons, sometimes to relive the rush of the crime, to revel in the grief of family and friends, or sometimes to seek a perverted penance in the graveside rituals.

Sort of like begging forgiveness from the deer you just gutted.

And then there are some criminals forced by association with their victims to attend funerals they'd just as soon avoid.

Pretty hard for a surviving son or husband to fart off a father's funeral or a wife's. Even a murderer willing to endure social opprobrium avoids behavior that might provoke suspicion.

Whether drawn to the grave for the purpose of reliving a homicide or forced by association with the deceased to attend, many killers come to the graves of their victims, and for that reason cops over many generations have attended those services. Barrett Raines had no difficulty finding a place among Raul Carrera's mourners. However, it took Father Franklin Swain's personal intervention to get Brady Hart's permission for Bear and Sheriff Rawlings to attend his son's funeral.

Quentin Hart was laid to his final rest at ten o'clock on a morning still showing frost. There were surprisingly few family members present. Brady and his wife were the only blood kin attending. Quentin's putative fiancée was conspicuously absent. On the other hand, Buddy Hewitt, Terry Godot, and Dawana Jackson were conspicuously present, that troika of comrades attending both Quentin's funeral and, later in the week, Raul Carrera's graveside service. There was only one other person attending both funerals, and he came in vestments and collar.

"We send an honorable warrior to his grave." Father Frank Swain offered that remark at Corporal Hart's graveside, as well as at Specialist Carrera's.

Bear noted that aside from the onetime military chaplain's participation, there were no trappings of a military funeral. There was no honor guard, no officer to present a folded flag to the surviving parent or relative. No salute of rifles. Just a barren grave, surviving comrades, and their priest. Barrett recalled Terry's bitter description of his unit's service overseas— something about being dismissed? Or maybe just dissed.

"Something here's not right, Cricket."

"There's plenty's not right, partner. But I've got a federal agent kidnapped in New Orleans and funny money floating all over the state of Florida and I don't give a shit what Quentin did in Afghanistan that might have made him depressed or suicidal. And Raul Carrera didn't kill himself, did he? As for Terry Godot, the only thing you have against Sarge is a teenage beef and a mouth."

"You know me better than that, Cricket."

"I know you're barking up a tree a long goddamn way off."

"Okay, okay." Barrett relented. "I admit there's nothing at present connecting Quentin's situation to Raul's homicide or to counterfeiting or anything obvious, but dammit, Cricket, just let me make a few calls, all right? I just want to know enough to rule it out."

"What you want is to put your own mind to rest."

"Fine, then. It's for me. Or call it a hunch."

"Hunch, my ass." Cricket scowled, but then he said, "You're not going to be able to get Quentin's records, but you can make a stab at Carrera's. I'll go along with that. Provided it's quick."

Getting a GI's military record is never quickly done, even for the FDLE. Barrett's first step was to phone a liason attached to Navy Personnel in San Diego to see what military records were available for Raul Carrera. A very efficient noncom explained that service records of military members, deceased or living, were not routinely available for any agency's perusal.

"We need authorization to comply," Bear was told.

"And how do I acquire that authorization?" Barrett inquired.

"You know it would just depend on the circumstances," came the completely unhelpful answer.

It was what Bear expected. The only way he'd be able to get a look at any marine's service record would be to establish the sort of probable cause needed to obtain a subpoena in the civilian world. He had to implicate one of Terry's marines in some criminal matter to have any shot at all.

Corporal Carrera's death was now the subject of investigation as a homicide, which gave Bear some reason to explore his history. Of course, that didn't mean the Navy Criminal Investigative Service would see Carrera's military records as relevant to Bear's civilian investigation, and there was the further problem that, even if they did, NCIS would not release records that were classified or deemed crucial for national security.

But there were two other unusual connections to Carrera's possible homicide that Barrett hoped he'd be able to leverage—Raul's connection to the counterfeiting of U.S. currency and his connection, however oblique, to the kidnap of a Treasury agent. But it would take somebody with a pay grade a lot higher than Bear's to make that case.

Raines thanked his San Diego liaison politely, swapping the office phone for his mobile to dial the Arlington number embossed on the business card Scotch-taped to his second-hand computer.

"Pamela Goerne, Special Investigations," came the Ivy League voice through the ether. "Bear, is that you?"

"It is, ma'am," Barrett confirmed. "And I need your help."

Clearly, Pamela Goerne had pull, because by that afternoon, Barrett received faxed copies of Raul Carrera's DD 214, copies of his performance evaluations, including supporting letters and a citation for a general discharge.

A general discharge was obviously not an honorable discharge, but it did not carry the sting of a dishonorable discharge. Homosexuals could be discharged generally. Sometimes members bargained for a general discharge to prevent Article 15 action or trial for activity proscribed under the Uniform Code of Military Justice. Sometimes sloth on the job or consistently shitty performance could lead to a general discharge.

But Raul's case seemed different.

Specialist Carrera received a G rating on his first PES, which in marine jargon was a rave review. An F or a G rating indicated "exceptional, sustained performance" throughout the reporting period. Raul's second evaluation, however, which took place barely three months later, gave the specialist an A rating on four of the thirteen attributes established for evaluation, which was really bad news. An A rating in even a single category meant that a serious deficiency noted by the member's RS would be documented, justified in writing, and forwarded up the chain for official scrutiny. The second evaluation had been signed, Bear noted, just ten days before Carrera was shipped back to his stateside unit. Apart from the heavily redacted text in the PES was a letter attached and signed by a marine captain, offering further justification for the damning evaluation. Most of that letter was censored, as well, but by comparing documents, Barrett learned that Raul Carerra had been assigned to a Special Operations unit with an MOS designator of 2531, which meant that the marine was trained as a field radio operator. That information corroborated Terry Godot's description of Raul's duties on Sarge's shrimper.

Barrett was surprised to see the unit's designation redacted. Usually, the unit to which a GI is assigned is prominent on his performance evaluations, but Barrett found that specific designators for Raul's unit were inked out, the black felt pen of the censor scoring out all of those details. Only a general description of his unit's mission and the radioman's duties were included in the final performance report.

Bear read the redacted description aloud. "'Marine Corps Special Operations Battalion.'" A few other details of Carrera's short career could be gleaned or deduced. It was not easy to get into any Special Ops squad, and reading between the lines, it was apparent that Raul's unit had been set up for very special operations indeed. The signatures on his PES indicated a streamlined chain of command; in fact, Raul's unit had been under the direct command of a two-star general. A search on the Internet produced a report from the CRO, which identified Major General MacIntyre as commander of Special Ops in the Middle East and Central Asia. It looked to Bear like Raul's had been a stand-alone unit conducting missions pipelined separately from the normal chain of command. Certainly all details of the unit's mission had been kept under very heavy wraps.

The dates on his evaluation indicated that Specialist Carrera was returned stateside less than five months after entering Afghanistan, but the reasons for culling the marine from his unit were concealed behind his supervisors' deliberately broad justifications. "Specialist Carrera showed poor judgment in operations conducted in this theater of operation behavior that which behavior reflects poorly on his unit and the United States Marine Corps. Recommend reassignment to a noncombat capacity until further evaluation can be completed."

So Raul's service overseas reflected poorly, but not poorly enough, apparently, to warrant an Article 15 or courts-martial. Just a quick trip stateside and a general discharge. Bear wondered if Quentin Hart had known something about the circumstances surrounding Carrera's ignominious separation from military service. Surely his gunnery sergeant had to know. Barrett scanned the PES once more and found Terry Godot's signature on Raul's first performance evaluation. Rating? An overall G, exemplary service—the highest rating a jarhead could get. So what happened between Raul's first evaluation and his second? What accounted for the radioman's precipitous fall from grace? It was a tantalizing contradiction, but Bear would not get a chance to pursue it.

Cricket Bonet loomed over his desk.

"Heard Pam Goerne pulled some strings for you."

"She did." Bear nodded to the faxed documents on his desk.

"So did you find anything connecting Afghanistan to Brenda Mantle or hundred-dollar bills?"

"No, Cricket, I didn't."

"Bear, you need to take the afternoon off. Get a little space. Come back fresh."

Barrett stifled an impulse to tell his old partner to get fucked. Cricket was right, of course. Bear was supposed to be looking for counterfeiters and kidnappers. His first responsibility was to Agent Mantle, not Quentin Hart. Maybe he was looking for connections that did not exist.

Bear swiveled his duct-taped chair to check out the view through the jalousie windows. No doubt it was a little chilly outdoors, but the sun was bright. Some breeze, but nothing uncomfortable. He could duck out early and catch Laura Anne at the restaurant. Maybe share a glass of good red wine out on the pier. They hadn't done that in a while. Or maybe he should get himself some exercise. Would be a good day to grab the kayak. Get in some strokes out past the bay.

Cricket seemed to be reading his thoughts.

"Outside, definitely. Just take your phone. Anything breaks, I'll call."

On the coastline and far south of Bear Raines's turf, a middle-aged man and his sunscreened wife were completing their daily exercise. It was a beautiful day to kayak on the Gulf. A sun low and ocher in the western sky bathed the ermine wings of a heron gold and crimson on her way to roost in one of the countless tidewater cypress or yellow-heart pines standing antediluvian sentinel along the coast. An osprey plunged to rake a perch or bream from the riffling water, a redfish impaled on those eager talons.

It was shallow beneath the mulberry and mangrove bordering Pine Island. The water was clear as crystal and barely chest-deep. The Stoakes owned a pair of ocean kayaks. They liked the Peekaboo for its Plexiglas window, which allowed a view directly beneath the hull. No telling what you might see swimming beneath your kayak—a turtle or a cormorant. Any variety of fish, of course. On one of their trips farther from shore, Harriet saw a manta ray pass beneath her flimsy craft, an animal as old as dinosaurs sailing beneath the sea on living wings.

But most of the time they worked closer to shore. Was pleasant to pause from a day's pull to witness pelicans and osprey feeding in their wild cafeteria. Or to see the stiff legs of egrets in the grass. Or to hear the champagne pop of scallops, those tiny and ancient crustaceans released from the sandy bed in an unending and ancient cycle, rising like miniature submarines to reach the surface, to breathe briefly, and then to descend.

A gentle breeze helped push the incoming tide and there was no storm forecast for the day's outing. Even so, experienced sportsmen did not venture into the Gulf or even along it without preparation. You carried water, always. You took some trail mix, or maybe an Igloo with ice and apples. Most modern kayakers took cell phones and GPS units and maps on their intrepid expeditions. And of course you had to plan for the tide. Anybody pulling himself along with a paddle in sixty pounds of plastic knows better than to fight the tide coming home, and Harriet and Harvey Stoakes were nothing if not experienced. They had been on the water for twenty years in oarlocked rowboats, way before kayaking became a sport du jour.

You could tell that Harvey and his wife weren't tourists, or at least not tourists with money. Unlike the nouveau riche, Harvey wore the same shorts kayaking as he did to mow his lawn, those skinny legs extending to a pair of cheap sandals. Harriet was very proud of her own legs, toned and tan. These were the legs of a woman who still taught tennis on public courts in Fort Myers and Tallahassee, and Harriet didn't mind cutting off a pair of denim jeans to display those gams.

But unlike her husband, Harriet was more cautious of the sun. You spent any time on the Gulf, you were a target for UV; combine that exposure with years on a tennis court and it was only sensible to take precautions. Harriet's frayed baseball cap had a strip of cotton cut from a T-shirt pinned at the back of her cap, the flap extending to her shoulders and neck. Harvey said it made her look like an extra from *Beau Geste*. And whereas her husband's bunioned feet were strapped naked in his sandals, Harriet always wore socks and always kept a tube of sunblock handy. Right beside her mobile phone, her Garmin navigator, and her .357 revolver.

Anyone boating in the area of Pine Island or Sanibel might see the two old hoots tooling in and out of the narrow canals and tangles of mangrove that enveloped a variety of private homes constructed along the waterline. They might see the old fuddy-duddies fishing in a soda can or Styrofoam cooler off the water, or some other thoughtlessly discarded garbage. Harriet had modified a shaft from a speargun's quiver to drag in heavier articles. It was much like the smooth-tipped spears work crews used to spear candy wrappers or Starbucks cups from roadside parks or parking lots.

Years of advertisement and public education were augmented by hefty fines to greatly diminish the litter of Florida's highways and parks, but habits offshore remained recalcitrant. There were all sorts of flotsam to be skimmed off the water, the careless refuse of weekend warriors mixing with the callous deposits of commercial fishermen. You could find condoms floating on the Gulf, right along with surfboards and skis and tangles of nylon rope and nets.

And, of course, there were tennis balls.

Fishermen were used to seeing tennis balls floating near the shore, especially on the canals, invariably green and bogging absurdly in the wake of somebody's ski or bass boat. And if you were used to seeing Harvey and Harriet gathering litter off the water, you'd naturally expect to see them depositing tennis balls with their weekly catch of Styrofoam, condoms, and other unsavory detritus.

You probably would not expect to see Harvey and Harriet firing tennis balls at the shoreline like aging shortstops. It seemed just so out of character. Why would these aging hippies pull rubbers out of the water and then turn around to throw other junk in! The hell? Is that what it meant to be a steward of the environment?

In fact, Harvey and Harriet had been steady and unrelenting guardians of Florida's fragile marine ecology for decades. But they were not recreational kayakers. Wardens Harvey and Harriet Stoakes were employed by Florida's FWC, the Fish and Wildlife Commission reorganized in 1999 to enforce laws related to everything from deer hunting to environmental protection. They were officers of the court, with the same authority—in some cases, more authority—as sheriffs, municipal cops, or the Highway Patrol. And the reason the wardens were throwing tennis balls toward the shoreline was to provoke an attack of alligators.

More accurately, Harvey and Harriet used tennis balls to determine which gators were capable of being provoked.

Harriet would rip a ball toward what looked like a log in the water, and in the ensuing explosion of water and mud and vines some twelve or fifteen feet of gator would come crashing out of his lair.

That was a good thing. When a gator reacted to the harmless strike of a tennis ball with this behavior, it indicated that the reptile was not accustomed to, or desensitized by, human contact. Harriet never reached for her handgun when her kayak was rocked by the tumultuous exit of a thousand-pound alligator.

But if Harriet or her husband landed a strike on the snout of a gator and it did not react, or, worse, if the gator slowly churned to line up on their kayaks, you knew you had an animal that was dangerous to human beings.

Dangerous, but almost entirely blameless. Attacks on humans by gators along the coast and in canals had risen precipitously with the press of human population, but that threat was fed, quite literally, off the porches and piers of ordinary people living near water. A man cleaning fish off his back porch or his boat dock throws the entrails into the water and the moccasins and turtles come running.

Gators were sure to follow.

A family might grill steak and chicken out back, but instead of bagging the leavings, they'd toss bone, marrow, and meat into the canal behind their house. For an alligator, this is the equivalent of a Grand Slam at Denny's. Except over time, the service gets to be expected.

And the tip gets messy.

The State of Florida passed laws allowing its FWC to levy stiff fines on commercial operators and private residents who through sloth or intent baited alligators. The first clue to identifying who those folks were was to identify the location of gators unafraid of human contact. Inevitably, that animal would be found feeding close to some careless human of-fender. Of course, if the Stoakes had tooled around the shore with their state hats and official regalia, they'd be less likely to see Joe Six-Pack tossing a pound of spent ribs off his dock. So almost weekly, Harriet and Harvey posed as a pair of harm-less retirees out for a day on the water. They had nailed a re-peat offender early that morning, a private home owner, and by midafternoon they'd spooked a fifteen-footer with a shot to the snout, but as dusk threatened, the weary wardens were no longer looking for monsters to tease with tennis balls.

That didn't mean they passed up the chance to haul crap off the water. Harriet and her husband carried a netted bag specifically for that purpose. Anything that didn't breathe or bleed got tossed into the bag, and not all of it was floating on top of the water. It was very common in the clear water to spot litter on the sandy bed beneath their boats—somebody's running shoe, a laptop, a can of paint thinner. It could be anything. In fact, when Harriet first glided over their last catch of the day, she thought it was a plastic milk carton.

"Hon, I just ran past some trash."

"What is it?"

"Some kind of plastic jug, I think."

"It's plenty shallow, if you wanta snag her."

Harriet glanced at the bag of crap already trailing her kayak.

Her husband smiled. "I'll get it if you want me to."

Harriet hesitated. "Tell you what. Just circle back, you don't mind, and help me relocate it."

"Sure thing, Hickok."

That sobriquet was attached to Harvey's wife because she was deadly with a six-shooter.

She had good eyes for other things, too. On her first pass back, Harriet spotted the litter.

"There it is. Off port."

"Let me."

Harvey spiked the junk like a flounder and hauled it in.

"Soccer ball," Harriet said as her husband snapped the trash off its spear.

But then the kayak shifted with the tide and the ball rolled—

And Harvey Stoakes jumped, screaming, into the water.

Barrett Raines spent the afternoon with his boys. Ben and Tyndall were excited about their semifinal matchup with a visiting team of Little Leaguers.

"And the game's under lights!" Ben was especially eager to chase fly balls under the halogens, just like his big-league heroes.

Tyndall, as usual, was just concerned about screwing up. He'd gotten turned around by a well-hit ball in the boys' previous game and it had cost the Sharks a run. Barrett had a single afternoon to build his confidence.

"Always play farther back in the outfield than you think you need to," Barrett advised. "Then just remember to frame the ball with two hands—both your hands. Now, go on out there and I'll hit you some."

Bear ignored the shock of the bat in his still-recovering forearm as he launched ball after ball into right field. It was great being with the twins, outside, in the bright sun. Laura Anne would come home that evening to find the boys fed and on top of their homework. When Bear got home, he even shooed Aunt Thelma, their live-in relative, counselor, and cook, out of the kitchen.

"I'm doin' for you tonight, Thelma. Go watch *Jeopardy!*"

Thelma was back to her Airstream trailer by the time Laura Anne got home from the restaurant.

"What's this?"

Bear greeting her at the door with a glass of wine and a shit-eating grin.

"Cricket chased me out of the office."

Laura Anne slipped a thin jacket off her wide brown shoulders.

"Tell Cricket he needs to do that more often."

They went to bed, and made love. It was just past seven the next morning when Barrett got an urgent call from Cricket Bonet telling him to rendezvous in Perry for a drive north to an urgent meeting at FDLE headquarters in Tallahassee.

It was ninety-seven miles from Bear's front door to the hub of Florida law enforcement. Barrett got to Perry early, prying Cricket away from Joyce's Café around 7:30 for the drive to Tallahassee.

"Any idea what this is about?"

"Gotta have something to do with counterfeiting." Cricket was tight-lipped. "Pam Goerne's flying in from Washington, and Henry Altmiller's going to be there."

Bear worried the knot in his tie. He checked instinctively for cables on his blazer, checked the crease of his slacks, and put a quick buff on his size-thirteen shoes. Capt. Henry Altmiller noticed those sorts of things. Altmiller was the head of FDLE's Criminal Investigation Division. He was not a cheerleader. Henry didn't pull agents from the field for pep rallies. Whenever you got a call from the captain, you could bet it was serious.

Driving north Cricket scanned the radio for local news. Barrett rested his arm on his unmarked's console and revisited the familiar scenery. The road from Perry to the state's capital ran four mostly straight lanes past miles of rolling landscape. Kudzu weighed down power lines and fences lining fallow fields on either side. There was one pasture in particular that Barrett always looked forward to seeing, forty acres of land graced in its very center with a tiara of dogwood trees. Some hardscrabble farmer averting the blade of his plough year after year to preserve beauty in the midst of profit.

Would be nice come spring to see those trees in bloom.

"Mind if I play a CD?" Cricket asked.

"No, go ahead," Bear replied.

Ninety miles of Gordon Lightfoot later, Bear was grateful to turn off U.S. 19 for the almost-rural boulevard leading to his agency's headquarters. Tall oak trees shaded the curbless street leading to the FDLE. You could still see lots of land that had never seen the foundation of a house. The FDLE's complex lay just ahead, a stone's throw from a facility built to treat patients afflicted with psychosis or schizophrenia. People joked that every employee at the FDLE spent some time in Sunnyland.

The FDLE's architecture was spartan, three quads of brick and glass, three stories high. Agents and other employees typically entered the building from an underground parking lot in the rear. A tall wall of glass protected the only elevator allowing entry. Cricket keyed his card through a magnetic reader. Bear followed him through.

A short ride upstairs took Barrett and Bonet into a narrow corridor. A turn to the right took them past the Putrid Room and the public-relations office to a large conference room. There were already a dozen or more agents present. Captain Altmiller had a seat beside a podium directly across from Treasury Agent Pamela Goerne. Goerne's fingers flicked over a laptop to project a static image on the room's large viewing screen. Just a static image of a television. Looked like a soccer game.

Agent Goerne leaning on the podium, blond as straw and tight as Dick's hatband in another one of those thousand-dollar suits.

Barrett greeted his boss first. "Sir."

"Barrett. Good to see you again. How's Laura Anne?"

"She's fine, sir."

"You know Ms. Goerne?"

"Yes, sir."

Barrett stepped past his captain to offer Pamela his hand. "Thanks for that help with the records."

"Anytime."

But she seemed distracted. Something was definitely out of the ordinary.

"You ready for us, Agent Goerne?" Altmiller's question sounded more like a suggestion.

"I am," she replied.

Captain Altmiller stood from his chair.

"Gentlemen, ladies. Seats, please. I believe most of you know Agent Pamela Goerne, Department of Treasury. Agent Goerne has been involved in an investigation primarily involving our Third District. She has new information today that greatly broadens the scope of our involvement.

"Agent Goerne?"

"Thank you, Captain Altmiller. I will begin by showing you a clip of video making its way around the Internet. Lights, please."

Pam Goerne facing her audience from the podium.

"Just yesterday, the FBI was hand-delivered a DVD containing the material you're about to see. It relates to our investigation of counterfeiting activity, which we believe to be located in your Third District. Be warned that the footage you're about to see is explicit and disturbing."

A click of a mouse and YouTube glowed on the screen.

It *was* a soccer game, much as Barrett had speculated early on.

Except this game played out on a television propped on a TV tray, the small screen flickering with a game in progress. The video's image was secondhand and grainy, framing the TV like a screen within a screen, tiny players in shorts kicking a soccer ball up and down a truncated field.

But then the camera panned away from the television and zoomed out to reveal Agent Brenda Mantle. The mother of two was thrown facedown over a bench in what looked to be some sort of workout facility, her hair falling forward, breasts hanging like udders in a bloodstained top. Her arms were twisted behind her back and tied. A hooded man had his knee in the small of her back, his grappling arms inked with a Z like Zorro's. Two other men, faces concealed behind bandannas, trapped her legs.

"Agent Brenda Mantle." Goerne's voice was tight over the speaker.

A fourth actor in the grisly scene appeared stage right, a Latino man with a potbelly, wearing sweatpants and a Nike body shirt. He turned to the camera with some silent declaration, displaying a knife in his hand—a bolo knife.

Brenda Mantle's head jerking up to recognize that threat, her face framed briefly, terribly.

"*Merde.*" Cricket turned away.

They cut off her head.

The beheading was more horrific for being soundless. You could see Brenda fighting for her life, but you could not hear her screams. You could see the men delight in her death, but you could not hear their taunts.

138

It took all four of the bastards to hold her down, a woman half their size and already spent from torture and abuse. One of the men grabbed her hair like a halter and yanked back to expose her neck for the knife. That, at least, was merciful. The plunge of the heavy blade, the arterial spray. The woman fighting still, blood spilling in a pool to the well-polished floor.

It took minutes, it seemed, to accomplish the rest.

A collective groan rolled over the room, profanity mixed with the sounds of someone crying. Someone else puking.

"Did you—" Goerne began.

"We got it all," Cricket Bonet replied before she could finish.

"I'm sorry, gentlemen, but this is the enemy we face. And it gets worse. I debated whether to show you this, I really did. However, Captain Altmiller agreed with me that it's much better for you to see this here, in this room, than to risk you finding it for the first time on the Internet."

Goerne slips on a pair of latex gloves to retrieve what looks like a hatbox.

"Yesterday afternoon, two FWC personnel working near Fort Myers found this."

She pries off the lid, reaches in, and places a soccer ball on the table.

There isn't a lot of reaction until Goerne rotates the ball, and even then it takes Barrett a second to realize he's looking at a human face. It's a person's face, a real face stitched onto the ball and staring sightless over the conference table. Nothing but holes where the eyes should be. Like a theater mask, gazing out.

It's grotesque. It's distorted.

It's Brenda Mantle.

10

Los Zetas

Altmiller ordered a twenty-minute break. People were rushing to toilets or standing in corners. No one returned to the meeting room early. Agent Goerne began her extended brief by expressing hope that the killers' video of Agent Mantle's decapitation could be traced to its source. She spoke of IPs and multiple routers, but all Barrett could think about was the unnatural extension of a human face over a soccer ball.

"This isn't just about Agent Mantle," Goerne emphasized. "This is an attack on all law enforcement inside the United States. These criminals want us to know that they will kill without impunity and want their competitors to see how powerless we are to retaliate."

"Do we have any idea who's responsible for kidnapping her in the first place?" an agent asked.

"Finally, we do, yes. In fact, they don't even seem to care if we know. Somebody here want to make a guess?"

Barrett spoke up. "Somebody associated with Los Zetas

took her. And I don't think that's a guess. You go back to the video, you'll see a *Z* tattooed on the killer's arm. The *Z* points to the Zetas. Their old radio code."

"Oh shit," somebody said, but a rookie agent seemed perplexed.

"Who are Los Zetas?" he asked.

"Initially, they were our guys," Captain Altmiller answered, and then supplied the background familiar to most in the room. "Years ago, we got the idea of recruiting men from the Mexican army to help us interdict drugs along the border. Their army sent handpicked cadres to our army bases for training.

"I was actually one of that original group of trainers. The DEA also contributed. We gave the Mexicans military hardware and taught them how to use it, taught them how to surveil, how to track and catch drug runners. Looked promising; the Mexicans developed into a crack outfit. What we didn't anticipate was that they'd defect to work as enforcers for drug lords."

Pamela Goerne picked up the narrative.

"There was a group of around thirty turncoats, initially, and it didn't take them long to figure out they could run their own cartel. They called themselves Los Zetas, after their old radio designation, and went on to kill or butcher anyone who got in their way.

"The organization grew like cancer and now runs cocaine, marijuana, and heroin from Nuevo Laredo through Chiapis and into Guatamala. They still pride themselves on being a military organization, and in some sense that's accurate, at least with regard to their hardware and discipline."

Cricket Bonet shook his head. "We arrested Osiel Cardenas in '03 and it didn't make a dent. 'The Lion Who Controls the Handler' is how Mexicans describe the Zetas; and by that, they mean that *we* are the handlers. Los Zetas has killed and tortured DEA agents, not to mention their own police, judges, military commanders, and ordinary citizens. They're turning Mexico into a narco state, but what the hell would they want with Agent Mantle? Did they think she was a narc?"

"If the Zetas thought Mantle was compromising that type of operation, they would most likely have killed her in New Orleans," said Pam Goerne, rejoining the conversation. "This video cements our belief that the counterfeiter Agent Mantle spotted at Harrah's Casino is the same Raul Carrera whose probable homicide is currently being investigated. And we now believe Carerra was gambling with counterfeit money that belonged to the Zetas cartel."

An FDLE agent leaned over a microphone to ask a question.

"Agent Goerne, do ya'll think the Zetas are printing the counterfeit themselves?"

"We don't know," Goerne replied directly. "Right now we are operating on the assumption that Los Zetas has access to U.S. counterfeit in large quantities and varied denominations. If they aren't counterfeiting currency themselves, they are buying it, probably from a Florida supplier. That's where Raul Carrera reenters the picture.

"We are quite sure that shortly before he was killed, Carrera was tortured, a fairly light punishment if, in fact, he was gambling with fold that wasn't his own. A couple of weeks later, he was found dead in what could easily have been mistaken as a hit-and-run accident, which raises the possibility that someone in the Zetas organization decided to silence Corporal Carrera permanently.

"Carrera was not laundering cash for the cartel; the Zetas have a much more efficient mechanism available for that purpose. In fact, they have countless thousands of willing mechanisms. What we now believe is that Los Zetas is acquiring counterfeited U.S. currency and cleaning it through drug transactions in Mexico, which gives them genuine U.S. dollars to buy cocaine or heroin at virtually zero cost to themselves.

"I'm sure you can see the advantages to be gained by using drug money to launder counterfeit. There's the economic advantage, obviously, but more important, cash laundered hand-to-hand is almost impossible to trace. The cartel doesn't have to set up sham businesses or bank accounts to launder their funny money. There are no receipts to juggle or taxes to pay. Money moved in this manner, whether juiced or genuine, never goes into an account that can be frozen or even reviewed. It's brilliantly simple. And it's got to be stopped. Don't forget that this was Brenda Mantle's mission. This was her job."

By the time Agent Goerne completed her brief and signed off, a pall had settled over FDLE headquarters.

"There's not a goddamn thing we can do to help that woman now," a Jasper agent muttered, but Bear contradicted him gently.

"Sure there is. We work our case with Carrera. We find his connection with the counterfeiters. We do that job, we've done something to help."

"Whoever woulda thought a bunch of Mexicans could do this to us? And on our own soil?"

"Been coming across the border for years," Cricket replied sternly. "Ask anybody at ICE or the Border Patrol."

"Or just read the headlines," Barrett added. "Wasn't long ago that the gangs killed an American consulate and his wife. Left a pair of kids wounded in the backseat, for God's sake."

It took the death of a consulate to make news outside the southwest, but Barrett was reading accounts of cartel violence while still an undergraduate in Austin. He'd added a criminal justice major to his English lit studies and learned quickly that a cancer fueled by drugs and drug lords was growing along the banks of the Rio Grande.

The spillover of turf wars was not confined to any particular town. Students in Brownsville were known to duck bullets fired from across the river. Farther west, Laredo's once-vibrant community was decimated by random killings and graft issuing from cartel activity. In one case, a local police chief was murdered within hours of being sworn in. Beheadings were common, almost a signature, the severed heads of informants or opponents tossed into a Dumpster as casually as crusts of pizza.

But the real violence inflicted by the Mexican cartels extended much past gunfire or graft or incessant kidnappings. The rule of law was threatened—on both sides of the border. The cartels had long challenged the integrity of Mexico's institutions, but in recent years they had successfully paid off members of the U.S. Border Patrol, along with constables and sheriffs and city councilmen, to cover the transport of contraband and narcotics.

Of course, anyone involved in law enforcement knew that the chaos raging in Mexico and spilling across the border was fueled by an American appetite for cocaine and other drugs. It was that appetite and addiction that financed crimes against judges, lawmen, and innocent civilians on both sides of the Rio Grande. And now the Zetas had beheaded a Treasury agent kidnapped on U.S. soil.

We can get you—the intimidation long internalized by cops and judges and husbands and wives in Mexico was now visited on the United States. This was the threat advertised by Agent Mantle's slaughter, and all her captors had to do was download a video on the World Wide Web for every cartel, terrorist, or criminal organization to see how vulnerable American lawmen had become.

The message was plain. We can get you anywhere.

Anyplace.

Anytime.

11

Afghanistan, 2008 . . . the Day After

Maj. Steve Saitta was milking the *Stars and Stripes* for news and nursing a glass of prune juice for IBS as he consulted over a one-way radio with a company commander from Nangarhar hell-bent on criminalizing conduct that in any sane war would be commended.

"So you caught this two-striper brewing beer in the chow hall? And you're recommending court-martial? Why not an Article Fifteen? Come back."

Saitta was a JAG in Nangarhar, one of too many judge advocates in uniform who spent too much time either negotiating courses of action for offenses that should never rise to a JAG's attention or, at the other extreme, resisting pressure to ignore truly horrific conduct under the UCMJ that was deemed too politically explosive to prosecute. You heard the word "discretion" a lot when you were a JAG in northeastern Afghanistan. That one and "Pick the hill you want to die on."

Major Saitta finally talked the irate army captain into

agreeing to an Article 15 track for the unauthorized *Brau-
meister*. He was just off the radio, had penned notes onto the
familiar legal pad, and was finally set to supplement his Sur-
fac with prune juice when a tap at the door, too light to have
originated from any GI's fist, offered fresh distraction.

"What is it?"

She was Afghan. Local and devout, judging from the burka
and *habib*. He was about to challenge her presence on instinct, when she pulled a laminated badge from its slight
chain about her delicate neck. He had seen this particular
badge often enough to know what it signified:

Indigenous Interpreter.

He was not surprised to see her hiding the badge. The
Taliban ruthlessly targeted local translators and their families. Everyone in the chain of command was reminded that
these indigs were, in the approved vernacular, "critical re-
sources."

"Yes, please, this is the office of judge advocate?"

"It is." He tossed his juice like a shot of bourbon.

"Please, yes, my name is Gulpari Bhotri."

"Major Saitta, U.S. Air Force," he replied peremptorily,
but he did not invite her in to sit.

"I have come for legal assistance."

"Most do."

She hung in the door half-smiling, as if making great effort to understand the simple sarcasm.

Oh fuck, he'd offended her.

"What can I do for you Miss. . . . Mrs. . . .?"

"I am married. Most definitely."

"Fine, then. Mrs. Bhotri, how may I assist you?"

"I am an interpreter." She displayed her ID like a crucifix.

"I can see that."

"I must report a . . . a rapier?"

"A rapier is a type of sword."

He thrust a ballpoint pen in a feigned riposte and she blushed.

Then it hit him. Then he knew.

"You mean a rape," he said, correcting her. "You mean you need to report a rape? A sexual assault?"

"Yes, yes, that is correct. Forgive me, I am still learning your most excellent language."

He fished over his yellow pad.

"Malleable for sure. Don't know about excellent. So what're the circumstances of the alleged assault?"

"Most egregious," she said, proud of that vocabulary.

"All rape is egregious." He pushed aside his daily laxative. "What I meant was, who, what, when, and where? Start with the who; who is the alleged victim of the rape you are reporting?"

"Was I," she replied correctly in the nominative case.

He sat up.

"You? Were raped? By whom?"

She shook her head, and for the first time he saw the tears pooled in her deep, deep eyes.

"It is as I tell my sister, my mother. I do not know!"

Clutching her badge now like a scourge.

"But I believe there can be only one."

12

Under the Lights

Barrett's day ended with the long drive to Deacon Beach only partially leavened by contemplation of the Little League game he'd be attending. The twins went to bed excited about their semifinal contest "under the lights." Bear hoped Brady Hart would be at the game. Coach Hart had worked hard to make the fall-season league a success. Would be a shame for him to miss his boys' play-off. Bear called Mike Traiwick on the way over to the field, asking if Coach Hart would be on board.

"I don't know, Bear. He hasn't said."

"Mike, if it's a problem, I can have someone bring Ben and Tyndall and I'll just sit out the rest of the season. I don't have to be at the ballpark, if that'll help."

"I don't think that's the right thing to do, Bear. I don't even think Coach Hart would want you to do that. He just needs more time."

Barrett was glad to give himself over to the excited chatter of his seventh-grade sons and their anticipation of the game to come. It was important for any cop to find moments like these, to compartmentalize the day's violence from other duties, other pleasures. He had not forgotten the face stitched onto the soccer ball, but he could put it aside, for a time, in the company of family and friends.

Barrett was grateful his Little Leaguers had a home field on which to play. At the start of the season, they didn't even have a backstop, but Mike Traiwick offered to pay for a ballpark if labor was donated. That's all it took. The fathers all pitched in to cultivate the infield and build the fence. Hank Land donated the Porta-Potties rent-free, and Barrett teamed up with Brady Hart to build the crude backdrop shielding the shitters from view of the stands and field.

It took weeks of friendly labor to build, install, or erect the night lights, dugouts, and bleachers. It took two days just to put up the field fence marking the park's perimeter. Good fences make good neighbors, the poet declared.

But Barrett knew that some fences were better than others.

Bear spotted the lights on their telephone poles, the most expensive equipment at the Shark's home field. You could see proof of the community's new demography in the mix of vehicles converging beneath those mounted lamps, Humvees and Hyundais jockeying for parking spaces with rusted-out Fords and Chevies and Chryslers.

The stands were already half-filled, most of the Deacon Sharks already on the infield and warming up. Barrett saw Mike Traiwick hitting grounders. And there was Father Swain, talking to the Vietnamese kid who'd be pitching.

But Brady Hart?

"Where's Coach?" Tyndall gathered his glove.

"Mr. Traiwick will be coaching," Bear answered his elder son.

"But why?"

"Tyndall!" Ben admonished his twin brother.

"What? What'd I say?"

"You didn't say anything, Tyndall. Ben, be nice to your brother. Now, Tyndall, you know Mr. Hart lost his son and it's been hard for him to get back in the swing of things. Perfectly natural, too. But Coach would want you boys to go out there and do your best, awright? So grab it and growl."

The twins raced to join their other teammates, and Bear made his way over to his usual spot in the bleachers. An early-setting sun left an ocher corona on the teeth of the pines silhouetted on the back side of the field. The weather had everybody digging out winter gear, the locals shivering in Levi's or canvas jackets, the transplants cocooned in parkas from North Face or Eddie Bauer.

There were knots of people in both fashions climbing into the terraced seats, many of whom, maybe most of whom, did not have boys playing. It was just an excuse to socialize. Within minutes, Bear was responding to the friendly queries of neighbors and locals long familiar, and in that time was transported to a galaxy of memories and history far, far away from Mexican cartels and kidnapped agents.

"Bear, can I get you a Coke?"

This from Ed Starling, Glenda's husband.

"Why, thank you, Ed. Lemme get some quarters."

"No way. Enjoy the game. What Glenda tells me you could use the distraction."

Well, that was the damned truth.

The pleasant pop of a hardball off an aluminum bat brought Barrett's attention back to the field of play. He saw Tyndall streak past his twin brother to make an overhand catch beneath the lights.

"He's got a natural talent," remarked someone behind him and Barrett turned, to find Chaplain Swain in the stands.

"Father Swain. Glad you're here."

"Likewise, Barrett. I don't see Coach Hart on the field."

Bear shook his head. "No."

The priest laid a hand gently on Bear's broad shoulder. "Barrett, you don't have to be Catholic to speak with a priest."

That got a rueful smile.

"I get started, I might not want to stop."

Swain handed him a Coke. "You wouldn't be the first."

Bear accepted the soft drink, grateful for company. He settled down with the former chaplain and gave himself up to the game. Barrett's sons were twins, but fraternal, and it was clear that Tyndall was the jock in the family. He was a bulky, broad-shouldered child. Quick, aggressive. Ben was built like his mother, tall and svelt. Benjamin was the scholar in the family, and gifted, but he was also the kind of kid who left his glove at home or forgot to take a piss before the start of the game.

Bear saw his son crossing his legs in the outfield.

"Benjamin!" he said, exasperated, and Frank Swain laughed.

"They are about as different as different can be."

Fortunately for Bear's younger son, the inning ended quickly. Ben tucked his glove on a trot by the dugout, heading straight to the Porta-Potties on the back side of the field.

Barrett watched those skinny legs trot from view as Tyndall came to bat. The older twin now had his attention. A lot of poise for a seventh grader. The count worked to three and two before Tyndall found the pitch he wanted and fired a line drive between second and third.

Bear was cheering his elder son when he realized that Benjamin had been gone too long from the dugout.

"Barrett?" Chaplain Swain was startled as Bear leaped from the stands. "Barrett, what is it?"

He wouldn't have known how to answer. There was no particular indicator, much less evidence, but some deep instinct was shouting to Barrett Raines that his son was in jeopardy.

And when a father gets that vibe, he goes limbic.

A kind of automatic pilot takes over, and that pilot was running the show inside Bear Raines's massive skull. He bolted from the bleachers, running flat out past the stands, around the dugout. It was much darker on the back side of the ball field, the Porta-Potties swathed in shadow and shielded from view. A pasture stretched into the darkness beyond. There was no formal perimeter to fence in the back side of the park, nothing but open ground leading past the trees to the county road beyond.

Barrett skidded on soft earth to find the Porta-Potties and his son. There's Benjamin, thank Jesus! Just out of the loo!

Zipping up his shorts.

But then Bear saw two men emerge from a Suburban parked in the open field behind the park. Two Latinos. Jeans and leather jackets. Hair cut short.

They were armed. Barrett saw this immediately and knew without any doubt what they'd been sent to do.

"BENJAMIN!" Barrett bellowed, and reached for the holster at his hip. There was nothing there. A cardinal rule for any lawman carrying a weapon: Always have it. Always have it loaded. For maybe the first time in his life, Bear had left his Glock in the cruiser.

The killers had not forgotten the rules. Their handguns were military-issue, automatics.

"BENJAMIN, RUN! RUN!"

Had it been Tyndall, such a command would have prompted an instant animal retreat. But Ben was not Tyndall. The younger twin was startled by his father's command and froze like a deer in headlights. An easy target for men trained to slaughter.

"BENNNNNN!"

But then a door burst open on one of the shitters and Bear saw the long barrel of a shotgun.

BOOOOM!

Like a rope, the blast jerked the nearest gunman off his feet.

That's when time stops. Bear running toward his son. The surviving hit man swiveling off the boy to direct fire at the new threat emerging from the outhouse.

Who the fuck—

Brady Hart kicks the shitter's door aside as he bolts a fresh shell into his ancient twelve-gauge Marlin. Full choke. Double ought.

BOOOOM!

The second wad goes wild.

CRAAACK-CRAACK!

The assassin returning fire, pieces of fiberglass spraying Brady Hart like shrapnel. But the coach just keeps coming. Bear watches, amazed, as the old man walks two more rounds into his target.

BOOOOM! BOOOOM!

Two bulbs of buckshot lift the Mexican three feet closer to heaven, and by the time the hit man fells to the ground, he's damn near cut in two.

That's when Benjamin's mind and legs connected. The boy racing to his father's outstretched arms.

"DADDY!"

"It's okay, buddy, it's okay."

Barrett wrapping his son in a grizzly's hug.

"You're fine, Ben. You're all right."

Barrett looks up then, to see the barrel of a twelve-gauge next to his head.

"I meant it for you," Brady Hart declares, tears streaming below his Brooke Shields eyebrows.

"DADDY?"

"Shhh, Ben, it's okay. Coach is okay. . . . Brady? Brady . . ."

The barrel lowers. Brady Hart pulls back the Marlin's bolt and a spent shell ejects with the smell of firecrackers.

"Nobody's losing his children today."

The fallout of the attempted kidnapping of Barrett's son, and the threat to Barrett himself, was, to put it mildly, complicated. First off, the shots behind the park created panic among the spectators and players, the blasts of shotgun and automatics bringing parents from the stands, some streaming onto the field to gather their boys, others jerking shotguns and pistols and baseball bats from their trucks and cars. Barrett's duty as cop was trumped by his responsibility toward his seventh-grade son, who had just witnessed bloodshed and death on what was supposed to be a friendly field.

"IT'S ALL RIGHT!" Barrett displayed his ID on instinct to locals swarming to the Porta-Potties with guns and bats. "SETTLE YOUR WEAPONS. NO WEAPONS, PLEASE."

Weapons dropped one by one, but the crowd would not disperse. Who could blame them? There were two dead hit men spilling blood and guts in the sand behind their Little League park, a seventh grader shaking like a leaf in the wind, his father torn between the twin roles of parent and cop. And by the way, why wasn't Coach Hart with his team?

Barrett kept his son in his arms as he speed-dialed Sheriff Rawlings, called the FDLE to request a Mobile Crime Lab team, and then called his wife. Laura Anne beat everyone else to the ballpark.

Bear was even more worried about his wife's reaction to the violent attempt against her son than he was about the boy's trauma. It had taken Laura Anne nearly a year to get past the depression caused by her own abduction, the first threat to Barrett's family stemming from his role as cop. It had taken years for Laura Anne to reach a place where she didn't blame her husband for precipitating her own terrifying encounter.

And now look what he'd brought on their son.

"Don't talk to me."

Laura Anne brushed past her husband to wrap her son in her arms.

"Laura Anne, it's important that we don't panic."

"That's you, Barrett! You're a man! He's just a boy!"

Franklin Swain tried to intervene.

"Barrett saved Ben's life, Laura Anne. He and Brady Hart."

"I appreciate what you're trying to do, Father Swain, but right now all I want is to get my boy out of here."

"We'll have to interview him," Bear objected weakly. "I have to make some kind of report."

"Yes, well, you know what you can do with your damn report," Laura Anne retorted, and then turned to her son. "Come on, baby."

Benjamin turned woeful eyes to his father, caught in between.

"It's okay, Ben. We can talk at home."

Barrett leaned over to his wife. "But I'm calling Social Services. I want a professional at the house."

She nodded curtly. "Fine."

Sheriff Rawlings arrived about the time Bear's wife was piling her sons into the Malibu.

Rawlings wove through the crowd, working a stick of Big Red furiously.

"Damnation, Bear. This sure as hell ain't Little League."

It was a stroke of some good fortune that Bob Blanchard and Julie Fannon were wrapping up a crime scene near Steinhatchee when they were relayed Barrett's call. The Mobile Crime Lab was on the scene inside twenty minutes. The bad luck was that the technicians got damn near nothing from the crime scene that turned out to be usable.

Julie Fannon warned Barrett within minutes of arriving that efforts to conceal forensic information were evident.

"Look here." She displayed the fingers of one hit man. "He's had surgery on his fingertips. Acid, maybe. Skin graft. Not gonna get anything off this one."

"How about the other?"

"I can lift prints, but I'd bet a dime to a doughnut you're not gonna match 'em."

A glance at a crime scene like the one at the ball field would lead you to expect a trove of information, and in the narrowest sense, that was correct. Both men, for instance, carried a driver's license, but a week's assiduous investigation revealed that both licenses were fakes, their identifiers lifted from the death certificates of Cubans who had once lived in Miami's Little Haitii.

The vehicle had been stolen from a used-car lot in Valdosta, Georgia, where the trail went cold. There were no airplane tickets to follow from the Georgia connection, no credit cards to check. The cash in the Suburban's glove compartment consisted of mixed denominations and was genuine. And as Julie Fannon predicted, the usable fingerprints gotten off the younger assassin did not match those on any database. The killers' Mark 23s were similarly untraceable, and casings collected from the scene revealed their ammo was hand-loaded.

Pamela Goerne flew down from D.C. within the week to get a briefing on the incident. Sheriffs from every county in the district convened for that meeting, along with every FDLE agent in northern Florida. Federal authorities made the decision to share information which to that point had been highly restricted. No longer. Following the attempt on Raines's family, every scrap of information available to federal authorities, including the video related to Agent Mantle's murder, was shared with local law enforcement. The violence directed at Barrett's boy made things personal. There was not a sheriff or deputy in seven counties who did not know Barrett Raines.

"This is the kind of shit's been going on in Mexico and the border for years," Cricket Bonet declared, summing up the situation. "It's not going to work here."

Goerne concluded the briefing, making a point to greet each sheriff and constable personally. She waited until the county's men were back in their cruisers before meeting privately with Cricket Bonet, Sheriff Rawlings, and Agent Raines. She turned to Bear first.

"How's your son?"

"Pretty good, considering. We had a woman from Social come over, and I know a shrink in Tallahassee."

Barrett was referring to the same psychiatrist who had treated Laura Anne.

"I'm more worried about my wife," Barrett went on, with a glance to Smoot Rawlings. "It's like . . . Well, it's a lot like PTSD; she saw Benjamin and it just triggered everything all over again."

He did not elaborate what it had been like to go home

that evening to his modest Jim Walter ranch-style house with the trailer out back. He wanted to be with his son, but as an agent on-scene, there were questions to answer and reports to file. His report had to include his failure to carry a weapon. It also had to include Brady Hart's timely intervention. But even though the question begged to be answered, Barrett's report did not explain why Brady Hart happened to have a shotgun on his person in a Porta-Potty.

"You tryin' to tell me it was just a damn coincidence?" Smoot had been incredulous.

"That's all it was."

"Damned fortunate," the sheriff had said, pressing the point.

"Lots of folks at that game had shotguns and rifles and every other kind of weapon."

"Right. In their trucks, in their cars. And after the firefight started, they came runnin'. But Brady was waitin'."

"Let it go, Sheriff."

"You sure 'bout that, Bear?"

"Anybody asks, just remind 'em it's deer season."

He couldn't wait to get home to see his son. But by the time Bear made the drive back to Deacon Beach that night, it was pitch-dark and late. He lowered the windows in his cruiser, gasping for air like a man drowning. That helped. Pulling up to his modest house, Bear could taste a gentle Gulf breeze, which was soothing. That and the sound of the wind in the pines.

Maybe it would be all right.

Smoot had a pair of deputies watching the place; Bear saw their cruisers out front. A few neighbors from church were congregated, as well; Bear recognized Preacher Theo's minivan and Peggy Magrue's old Corolla. Barrett flashed the dims of his cruiser on approaching the deputies, stopping to thank the men for their vigil before pulling into the carport, where he and Laura Anne made love on summer evenings as the boys slumbered inside.

A few yards behind the carport, an Airstream trailer glowed like a spaceship. This was Aunt Thelma's home. Laura Anne's aunt had come to her meager family simply to live out her years, but she'd quickly become indispensable to her niece and the rest of the family. She was a grandmother to the boys, a stalwart for Laura Anne, an ancient and irreducible rock of ages.

Thank God for Thelma.

Every light in the place was turned on. The carport and winter garden alongside were cast in garish shadows. From the carport, a door led to the kitchen. There was a security light flooding that entry. Even so, Bear tapped the horn of his car to announce his arrival. This was his coming-home habit, his salutation. He beeped the horn and waited for Laura Anne to open the door.

But tonight the door didn't open. Barrett hauled himself out of his cop car and climbed up the short steps beneath the flooding light.

"Baby, I'm home."

Even then Laura Anne hesitated.

"Honey, come on, you know it's me."

"How do I know somebody's not got a gun aimed at your back?!"

Bear remembered that voice, the edge of hysteria, the panic. It had taken Laura Anne a long time to shed that demon. And now it was back.

He tried humor.

"Want me to have a deputy vouch for me? I can wake him up."

"Keep that up, you can sleep in the carport!"

"Laura Anne, please. I was there, too. Don't you think I'm

scared? Don't you think I feel like shit? Please, baby, let me in. Don't do this again!"

A long and uncertain deliberation played out, the murmur of voices rising inside. Finally, Bear heard the snick of a dead bolt, and there was his wife's hand, long and chocolate, lifting the flimsy hook securing the outer screen door.

Laura Anne looked terrible. Her hair was disheveled. She stood there in a bathrobe, her feet bare. Coffee cups littered the sink and crates of bottled water were stacked under the kitchen table with rolls of toilet paper and enough batteries to keep the flashlights on for a year. It did not matter that two cruisers with well-armed officers were posted outside the house to provide protection. That was not enough.

"Jesus Christ, baby, I'm sorry."

She wasn't having any of it.

"How many times is this going to happen, Barrett?"

"Honey, please."

"Is it worth it, husband? Look at me? Is it worth this cost to me, to your family, your flesh and blood?"

He felt the temperature rising.

"Now, that isn't fair, Laura Anne."

"'Fair'? Why don't you go talk to Benjamin about 'fair'! Look him in the eye and tell him!"

He opened his arms.

"Not now, Barrett." She turned away. "Just get inside. With your family. And lock the door."

". . . Agent Raines? Barrett?"

Pamela Goerne's voice brought him back to the meeting. He could feel a fresh flush of heat in his face.

"Sorry, I was just . . . thinking."

The Treasury agent glanced at Cricket Bonet briefly.

"Barrett, if you want off this case, it's done, and with no strings attached. I mean that."

"No." Bear shook his head. "No, if I do that, the sons of bitches have won. I don't want that. I don't want my sons to see that."

She nodded. "I think we may actually have gained the advantage here. The Zetas have clearly overplayed their hand. They would never go after your family, Barrett, unless they viewed you as a threat to their operation. That tells me we are close to the counterfeiters."

"Doesn't mean the currency's being manufactured locally. If past experience holds, the counterfeit's being made overseas, but the attempt on your family convinces me that Raul Carrera was connected to a Mexican cartel that is taking delivery of faked currency from someone in the Third District."

"So when are we gonna start kicking in some doors?" Bear asked grimly.

"We've already requested a warrant to search Terry's boat." Cricket offered that hope for action. "We called Homeland Security and told 'em, hey, we've got a murdered GI tied to a national threat who was employed on a shrimp boat. We're arguing we should be able to extend a search of Raul's residence to his place of employment. Kind of like searching a locker at a factory."

"Lets you search the locker, not the factory."

Cricket shrugged. "Let's just say Homeland's judges are more flexible."

Sheriff Rawlings pulled himself to his feet. "That's all well and good, but while we're waitin' on the judges, I vote we put some pressure on Raul's buddies. If Raul was muling counterfeit, those jarheads had to know."

"If they aren't in it together," Cricket agreed.

"Wish we had some reason to haul 'em in." Smoot worried his straw hat. "Might make a difference if we could split 'em up behind bars."

Barrett sat up straight in his roll-around chair.

"By God, maybe we can. Smoot, you got the tag numbers for Terry's truck?"

"I can get 'em, sure."

"And we have the tags for the motorcycle."

"What're you getting at, Bear?"

"I think you need to arrest Terry Godot and Dawana Jackson."

"For what?"

Barrett smiled grimly.

"Leaving the scene of an accident."

13

No Place Like Home

Good cops don't run around the law. Good cops know the rules and live with them. Really good cops know the rules and live *by* them, and the best cops make laws work in their favor. Barrett Raines learned early that "the law" liberates the really good investigator, even as it imposes limits on his actions. It's surprisingly hard, for instance, to make an arrest. The most basic requirement for slapping cuffs on a suspect is statutory; no one on U.S. soil can be arrested for any behavior unless that activity is criminalized by the state. And not every crime merits handcuffs. There are felonies and there are misdemeanors.

You can commit most varieties of misdemeanor without fear of arrest. Take speeding, for instance. If you're speeding at eighty miles an hour on an open road, any patrolman in pursuit has full authority to pull you over and issue a citation. That's all good. But no cop can sit on his ass as you race by, wait a week, and then arrest you at work for that violation.

Barrett Raines had full authority to issue a citation to Terry Godot and Dawana Jackson the evening he witnessed that pair tearing past his family, but the law did not allow him to arrest either party after the fact. He couldn't even arrest them for reckless driving. But that didn't mean he couldn't arrest them. Because Barrett Raines, being a very good cop, knew full well that some misdemeanors do justify arrest, and among these is leaving the scene of an accident. Especially where property is damaged. Especially when the property damaged is federal.

Like, say, a mailbox.

A call to a handful of body shops in the area netted Bear his fish. Terry Godot's Ford pickup was waiting for repair at Slade's Body & Paint. Bear knew the shop well; his Malibu was there, waiting for a side mirror and a windshield. But more important, Bear knew the shop's owner. Rolly Slade was another local familiar to Bear from long rides in school buses when returning from a basketball game in Destin or High Springs. Rolly floundered for a bit after high school before opening a shop for small-motor repairs, which grew over the years to include automobiles.

Unlike his memories of Terry Godot, the trove of memories Bear hoarded with regard to Rolly Slade were warm ones. Rolly had been a decent guard on Deacon High's basketball team. He was also a crooner never to be discovered on *American Idol*. Rolly seemed to know the lyrics to every song ever written, which had been a huge boon on those long rides back home from victory or defeat in Greenville or Madison or Cross City. Bear could remember nursing an ice pack and a Coke as Rolly sugared the miles with some

165

top-forty tune. The cheerleaders loved those performances, naturally, and Slade shared the wealth, recruiting his team-mates' cracked and adolescent voices in a karaoke spanning the dial from the Beatles to Bon Jovi.

Rolly built his shop from the detritus of construction sites. Virtually everything used to build the facility, including the commode and plumbing for the rest room, was hauled off some distant construction site. The salvaged materials dictated a simple architecture; the shop was not much more than a cube of cinder blocks topped with corrugated tin. But there were a pair of mechanics inside who were always busy, and migrants from Mexico provided cheap, talented, and undocumented labor for the body shop.

In warm weather, you entered the shop's office through a metal door. Inside, a gale of frigid air churned from a window unit propped directly above a plywood counter. During the winter, a single radiant heater buzzed out front, half a dozen coils glowing red. The decor, or what passed for decor, never changed. A virtual mural of calendars festooned the walls, bikini babes with breasts big as melons draped over lowriders and motorcycles. Advertisements for welders or screwdrivers were similarly endowed, some airbrushed brunette sticking a crescent wrench down her tight, tight shorts.

Barrett opened the shop door for Sheriff Rawlings, and, what do you know, there was Terry Godot, haggling with Rolly over his estimate for labor and parts.

Slade was still skinny as a stick of celery, a shock of white now at his temples. Terry leaning on the counter in Levi's and a civilian T-shirt.

"Sarge, you cain't just paint the passenger side; it won't look right."

"Fix the passenger side; that's all I'm payin' for."

"Or mebbe just leave her as is." Sheriff Rawlings offered that course of action standing at Godot's shoulder.

"The fuck have you got to say about my truck?" Godot challenged, his jaw bulging with a fresh pod of Red Man.

Smoot was now resting his hand on the butt of his revolver.

"Your vehicle was witnessed leaving the scene of an accident, Terry."

"What got-damn accident?"

Smoot nodded in the general direction of the shop out back. "The one that's got you scraped to the primer. That'd be on the passenger side."

"I don know what yer talking about, Sheriff. Buddy fucked up that truck trying to back through some palmetto."

Smoot shook his head. "We got a man says different."

"And who would that be?"

"Would be I," Barrett replied with deliberate formality. "Terry, you passed my family car the night of Laura Anne's fund-raiser, speeding way over the limit on the blacktop heading north toward Fenholloway. Dawana Jackson was trailing on her Harley Sportster. Lost her top along the way. Maybe that distraction's what sent you into those mailboxes."

"So I'll pay for 'em. No big deal."

"It's big enough to get you arrested." Smoot slipped a set of handcuffs from behind his back.

"Arrest!" Terry began pushing away from the counter. "You're shitting me. For a fuckin' mailbox?!"

"For leaving the scene of an accident with damage to property. Now, Terry, yer entitled to representation by an attorney, and don't say anything you don't want to, 'cause anything you say can and most likely will be used to your disadvantage in a court of law. Did I get that about right, Bear?"

"Close enough."

For a minute, Godot looked set to fight. Barrett saw the rage in his eyes, his fists clenched, a pair of cords stretching tight on either side of that sunburned neck, and for a moment it appeared Bear would be obliged to humiliate his old classmate for the second time in thirty years.

But Sarge knew he should stay off the radar.

"You son of a bitch!" he said, backing and spitting a juicy wad of Red Man in Raines's direction.

"No need to be personal," the sheriff warned genially. "Just turn around an' put yer hands on the counter."

Another long moment passed before Terry complied.

"That's good. Now spread those legs for me."

Smoot directed Terry's boots with a tap of his brogans, handing the manacles to Bear Raines.

"Son of a bitch!" Sarge spit again.

Bear moved in from behind to secure the bracelets.

"You might have heard a couple of Mexicans tried to snatch my boy?"

"The fuck has that got to do with me?"

"Why, there's absolutely no connection, 'Sarge.' None at all. Like the sheriff said, you're under arrest for leaving the scene of an accident. Got nothing to do with kidnapping. Or counterfeit, either—you see that piece in the *Herald* about counterfeited currency? Interesting reading.

"Course, as a hypothetical, if you were in bed with a counterfeiter, *he* wouldn't know we're jailing you for busting mailboxes. Would he, Sarge? Matter of fact, in that instance, he'll most likely figure we're arresting you on suspicions related to his own business. Might even think you're ratting him out. People cut deals all the time, especially if they think they need protection."

"I want protection, I'll buy a fuckin' Trojan."

Bear smiled. " 'Folks I have in mind won't leave you with

anything requiring a condom, Terry. They see a liability, they just eliminate it. Like your radioman, say. Like Raul Carrera."

"Fucking nigger son of a bitch!"

"I notice that's not a denial"—Bear wrenched Godot's wrist up toward his shoulder blade—"but keep up the lip and it might be construed as resisting arrest."

Buddy Hewitt actively resisted his incarceration. A pair of deputies arrived at the Outfit's Fenholloway trailer, to find Buddy at work outside on the dartboard. It took a half hour to get Buddy separated from his tomahawk, which added a charge of assaulting an officer to another for resisting arrest.

"I figure by the time those two can post bail, we'll have a warrant for Terry's boat," Smoot predicted. "Now what about Dawana Jackson?"

Dawana Jackson had been hanging behind the Little League stands when Los Zetas came for Barrett's son. She knew it was Ricky's men who'd made the attempt. Had to be. Not that she'd known ahead of time. No way. It wasn't till Dawana saw the tinted windows of their Suburban that she realized what was going down.

Then came the gunfire.

"Holy fucking shit!"

She ran from the ballpark on thick, muscled legs, away from the bleachers and past the charred remains of the old school, to reach the part of Mayo locals still called "Colored Town." That's where she'd parked Buddy's truck, out of easy sight. She stayed off Main Street, sticking to the wrong side of the tracks all the way to Shirley's Café. She wanted to let Buddy know what had gone down at the ballpark, but Buddy never picked up his phone. Drunk son of a bitch. Better call Sarge.

"What is it?"

"The Zetas went after Bear's little boy."

"The fuck they have."

"I saw it! It was at the ballpark; I was there!"

"The hell. Did they get him?"

"I don't know. I heard shots and people started runnin'. I started runnin'. But I saw it comin'. I *know* I did!"

"Calm down."

"Calm my ass, Gunny, first Raul and now this?"

"Ricky's not after you, awright? He's not. Long as we do our job, we're fine."

"I don't feel so damn fine."

"Where are you now?"

"Passing Shirley's."

"Get back to the trailer and sit tight. There's nothing connecting us to this other shit. Nothing connecting us to the Mexican, for that matter. But from now on, we're keeping communications secure, you hear me? Nothing operational over the phone."

"Nothing by phone, roger."

"Just get your ass to the trailer. And drive the limit, hear? Don' give some pissant cop an excuse to pull you over."

Dawana felt better with that firm direction. Deferring to authority was her default position. She drove Bud's truck back to the trailer, and for the rest of that day and a good chunk of the next, she managed to tolerate Buddy's porn tapes and toilet training. A bitter cold front blew in overnight, putting a morning rind of frost on the roof of the trailer. The pump out front froze and icicles hung like chandeliers off the trailer's ragged roofline. The wind outside was cold and damp and kept Dawana and Buddy inside the trailer. Dawana began to get the sheebies, that feeling like the one she'd had in the war when things got too close.

One minute she was listening to the wind in her Florida trailer and the next it was like she was back in-country, strapped into that goddamn Humvee one time, tied up inside a rolling tin can. Then came the IED. Not the full charge—the lead vehicle bought that honor, some raghead's cell phone triggering an artillery shell straight through the oil pan. The bright flash, the concussion, the sudden clap of thunder that burst your ears and froze your brain. It was like you were in a diver's bell, everything in slow motion and echoing. But she could still see well enough to realize her own vehicle was off the road.

Off in the ditch and burning.

A scramble then to survive, that instinct checked by the solider's ethos. Dawana remembered yelling Buddy's name, even though she hadn't been able to hear it. Remembered dragging him from the driver's seat, kicking the door open, only to find herself trapped in her own seat belt. It wouldn't let go. It wouldn't release. A panic then, her buddy in her arms, the smell of gasoline and fire, every swinging dick running hell-bent for cover. Except for one man.

Dawana would never forget her gunnery sergeant sprinting from up the side of that fractured road, firing his M16 in short bursts to cover his sprint for her Hummer.

"SARGE!" she screamed from inside her bell, yanking desperately at her belt, but her gunny already had his knife ready.

"CUT THE STRAPS!" She heard his command and complied, and survived.

That's why she bought the Harley. 'Cause there's no such thing as a motorcycle with seat belts. And most of the time, it was all right. Most of the time, she didn't think about Humvees or legless men or broken eardrums. But every now and then, something would trigger that awful claustrophobia.

Like, for example, being trapped inside a trailer.

"I gotta get outta here," she announced abruptly.

"I can make a fire on the patio," Buddy offered over his beer.

"No, I mean *out.*"

"Gunny said stay put," Buddy slurred.

"I'm just goin' to the Piggly Wiggly," she told him. "Get us some chili. Maybe a movie."

"Videos? Good, you can exchange these."

"Not that trash, Buddy. Wages of that sin is death."

"Don't give me that Jesus shit."

"Jesus is the Way, the Truth, and the Life."

"What Raul used to say. The fuck good did it do him?"

Dawana grabbed her fatigue jacket. "Thing I don't get is why they dit'n kill Raul when they had him on their boat."

"Maybe he spilled to the cops afterwards," Buddy retorted with malice. "He had a guilty conscience—maybe he opened his goddamn mouth someplace he shouldn't. Somethin'."

"Gimme your keys."

"No way. Sarge said stay. He finds out I gave you my truck?"

"Fine, then, I'll take Raul's car."

Buddy shrugged. "He won't need it."

Dawana wished she'd kept Raul off her motorcycle.

"I hadn't of loaned him the bike, he might be alive," Jackson said, punishing herself.

On the other hand, if the Mexicans wanted you dead, you were dead. There was no doubt what Ricardo was capable of. All Dawana had to do was recall the woman hanging above his bamboo floor. Jesus Lord.

But going after Bear's little boy? An innocent child!

Dawana clutched her Bible to her breasts. Suffer the children, the Good Book says. Suffer them! Better that a lodestone be cast around thine neck than to fuck with these, my little ones.

Corporal Jackson prayed there would be no lodestone hung about her own neck. It was she, after all, who texted *el jefe* with regular reports of Agent Raines's habits, his routes to work, the location of his home, and, of course, his weekly and unseasonal commitment to Little League. Sarge had given Dawana that task, and she obeyed, thinking the Mexicans might go after Bear Raines. That was acceptable, in the larger war, she had told herself. Collateral damage.

She didn't know they were going after kids.

In hindsight, she should have known. What better ways to castrate Bear Raines than to take away his son under the lights and in full view of family and friends?

Dawana put Mel Gibson's *The Passion of the Christ* into a basket with a can of chili and was headed to the checkout counter when she heard Reverend Theopolis in muted conversation with another black man. Something about Laura Anne taking little Ben home.

Took him home? So the boy was alive, praise the Lord.

"And how's Laura Anne? I heard she done boarded up her house."

"You cain't blame her," Preacher declared. "All that woman's been through."

Dawana left the store, trying to parse her own culpability for the attempt on Barrett's son. She decided it was like the war; the mission was more important than any single person, wasn't it? Even a child. Corporal Jackson told herself for the umpteenth time that she was a soldier in God's army, however impenetrable His purpose.

The kidnappers' intent was easier to divine; Ricky and his cartel knew that a snatch of Bear Raines's son would intimidate cops throughout the region. The attempt on Bear's son, even though it had failed, stripped away any illusion of invulnerability. And when you threaten a cop's family, you erode his sense of confidence; you put him on edge, make him more prone to overreach or err.

It was God's plan in God's hands; this was Corporal Jackson's manufactured epiphany. Every contingency was ordained, every action justified. All she had to do was sit tight and complete the mission. There was only one more patrol to make. One more rendezvous at sea.

Then it would be finished.

Dawana comforted herself with that solipsism as she fired up Raul's Camaro. She was halfway back to the trailer when her cell phone buzzed noisily. Dawana snapped the mobile open and found a text message waiting.

SARGE & BUD ARRESTED

"Fucking shit!"

But arrested for what? What was the charge?

Dawana heard a ringing in her head, like when you take a shot to the jaw, and the car caught the shoulder of the road and turned sideways.

Dawana stayed off the brakes and yanked the wheel to countersteer. By the time the car quit spinning, she was four feet from the ditch and heaving air like a halfback.

Arrested? Buddy! Sarge! What should she do?

Dawana felt her bowels churning. Clearly, she couldn't go back to the trailer. How about the boat? No, not there. They'd be looking there.

Her hands shook like leaves. She stabbed the pad on her phone.

WHR DO I GO

The reply appeared on the screen.

UR MTHRS

Her mama's place, that was good. That was safe!

WILCO

"Will comply" was Corporal Jackson's preferred response to any situation. Her default position. She liked hierarchy, the security to be had in a chain of command.

Dawana stayed in first gear as she eased Raul's muscle car back onto the road. She made sure she had traction before gearing up. She was alert now, exhilarated. She lowered the window and sucked in the cold, damp, briny air as though it were an aphrodisiac. But she was driving carefully, deliberately. Scanning the road for cops. It was just another recon. Another stroll down the road.

No biggie.

All she had to do was get to her mama's house and everything would be copacetic. Nobody went out to Devil's Slew unless they had to. And anyway—

There's no place like home.

14

Trojan Horse

A federal judge approved the warrant allowing agents from the Secret Service and FDLE to inspect Terry Godot's shrimp boat, but in the state of Florida, that authority did not trump the prerogatives of the county sheriff. It did not matter that the FDLE and the Treasury Department and Homeland Security had prevailed upon a federal judge to obtain the warrant allowing a search of *The Crusader*—Sheriff Rawlings was the highest authority inside his own county and was prickly with anyone stamping on that ground, so Barrett Raines made damn sure that Smoot Rawlins was first to step aboard Terry Godot's seventy-foot shrimper.

The Crusader was still moored beside the dry dock at Harvey Sykes's Marina, and with Terry cooling his heels in jail, investigators had the vessel to themselves. Barrett recruited Harvey Sykes's son to assist in the search of Terry's trawler. Roten had refurbished Terry's boat the previous summer, and performed most of the heavy maintenance.

Good chance he'd see something a gaggle of landlubbing cops would miss.

The tide was cooperating this morning, bringing the gunwale of the trawler almost dead even with the dry dock. Barrett could have made the small leap from dock to deck, but instead he followed Roten and Sheriff Rawlings across the unnecessary gangplank. In addition to the sheriff and Roten Sykes and the by-now-familiar technicians from FDLE's Mobile Crime Lab, there were three CSIs on loan from the feds and two Secret Service agents specializing in the detection of counterfeit currency who would be combing *The Crusader* with UV lights and iodine pens.

Bear mostly tried to stay out of the way as the specialists descended on the vessel. It was obvious right away that the deck had been recently swabbed.

"Lots of bleach," Julie Fannon pointed out. "And if you look, it pretty much follows a corridor, like you were covering up something dragged off of the boat."

"Or onto it," Bear amended and Julie nodded assent.

"We'll test for bloodstains, but I doubt we'll find anything. 'Specially out in the elements like this."

"I'm taking Roten and Sheriff Rawlings to the bridge unless somebody objects," Barrett declared, and with nods all around steered carefully around the work of forensic specialists on his way forward.

Bear entered with Roten and Smoot, to find a wheelhouse that was not nearly as pristine as the deck of the boat. Unwashed coffee cups lay all around, along with bottles of Gatorade, Honey Bun wrappers, and other litter.

"Some mess."

In contrast, the electronics looked in fairly good shape. A Lowrance sonar, commercial-grade Furuno radar, and Garmin chart plotter and autopilot offered high-tech backup to the old-fashioned chart spread beneath a sheet of Plexiglas on the same table now littered with cellophane wrappers and Styrofoam cups. A handheld radio backed up the standard VHF receiver, and Bear recognized an Edson satellite phone.

"He's got a ditch kit stashed forward that's got another radio and an EPIRB," Roten volunteered.

It was standard to have that sort of gear, but Bear reminded himself that a survival kit could also hide counterfeited currency.

The Crusader rolled with the passage of some other shrimper through the channel and Roten suppressed a chuckle as Sheriff Rawlings grabbed a captain's chair.

"No sea legs," Smoot said gruffly.

"No need to 'pologize," Roten said solicitously. "I can build a boat and take 'er apart, but you put me own the water, I'll puke like a damn tourist. Now, whatchu gennelmen want me lookin' for?"

Bear nodded to the banks of gear. "Can you show me where this boat's been over the last two weeks?"

"Might be on the GPS. Course, you can delete the track."

"I'm hoping Terry's not that ambitious."

"Uh-huh." Roten surveyed the instruments. "Well, we just put a new generator in this ole girl, but I got juice from the dry dock runnin' now, soooo . . ."

Roten reached over to a bank of switches.

A whine of fan, a sprinkling of lights.

"So now I got my lights and electronics," Roten said, and powered up the GPS chart plotter.

"Can I have that chair, Sheriff?"

"Sure, Roten."

It didn't take fifteen minutes to strike gold.

"Here she is."

Roten was pleased with himself, you could tell. All these hotshot cops depending on the local Cracker.

"These readings indicate course heading and speed over ground, but this right here's what you want. We call 'em 'tracks.' You can see this boat's only been out six times in the last two weeks. One of those was at night. Go back some more . . . Now, this is interesting. . . ."

"What is it, Roten?" Smoot leaned over the boy's shoulder.

"Well, there's nothing particularly unusual about fishing at night. Terry's been night-trawling maybe three times in the last couple months. But take this trip here. See this track? That's familiar. That's out toward Dead Man's Bay, an' lots of boats set nets in that direction. But see here? These coordinates? That's out in deep water."

"Can you show us on the chart?" Barrett asked.

"Sure."

Roten rolled with the boat on his way to the chart table.

"This chart runs from Cape San Blas to Tampa. Terry puts out from right about here."

"Any chance we can see his night trips?"

"Nuthin to it. Hand me that greaser over there."

Sheriff Rawlings handed Roten a grease pencil stowed with Windex and chewing tobacco. Bear read the coordinates from the GPS; Roten plotted them on the Plexiglas.

Within minutes, a pattern was evident.

"On the day trips, you can tell Terry's shrimping," Roten explained. "Or at least goin' through the motions. This here is fishing ground. Anybody shrimping sets nets somewhere around these coordinates. But on these night trips, Sarge took a sharp detour out to the Gulf."

"How far out?" Smoot asked.

"Last one's twenty miles out from where he started. And making around seven knots, too, which is close to hauling ass for this boat."

"Any idea what'd take Terry on that kinda detour?" Smoot asked.

"Nossir."

Roten shook his head.

"But it ain't shrimping."

Sheriff Rawlings met Bear's eye.

"Anything else you can tell us?"

"Time stamp can," Roten replied. "See this first trip? Now, looks like he drifted some with the wind, but basically he goes straight out, spends twenty minutes on-station, and then comes straight back. Same thing for the second track.

"But the third trip, something must have happened. They get to their terminal coordinate little after five-thirty in the morning; 0533 hours, to be precise. But look here: They don't head back to port 'til after seven! See here? First coordinate heading toward land is tagged at 0740 hours."

"There a date to go with the time, Roten?"

"Yup. For this trip here, that'd be . . . first of November."

"November first, you're sure?"

Roten swiveled back to the computer.

"Yep. One November."

Barrett felt hair rising electric on his arms.

"That's what—a Monday? Agent Mantle was kidnapped the last Saturday in October."

Sheriff Rawlings looked up from the chart. "Goddamn, Barrett, you don't think—"

"I think this whole time we've assumed Agent Mantle was put in a plane and flown to some location on land. What if she was on a boat?"

Barrett reached for his mobile phone.

"Roten, you just helped us big-time. The Marine Patrol needs to see this chart, and the Coast Guard. Do I have your permission, Sheriff?"

"You do."

Barrett was stabbing his speed dial when a ponytailed technician stuck her head into the wheelhouse.

"Sheriff Rawlings?"

"Whatchu got, darlin'?"

She entered the boat's cockpit, raising a rusted coffee can in latexed hands as though it were an offering.

"I think the feds are gonna want to see this."

Smoot frowned. "The hell is anybody gonna want with a can of Folgers?"

"It's not the can, Sheriff—" She tilted the rusted cylinder for their inspection. "It's what's inside."

Bear leaned over the can and saw what looked like a wad of white paper. Just a wad of paper.

"I found it in the head," Julie supplied, and then for Sheriff Rawlings's benefit, she added, "In the bathroom. It was just sittin' in plain view with some soap and bleach."

Smoot peered into the can.

"Why is anybody going to give a shit about toilet paper?"

"Because it's not toilet paper."

Bear heard the thrill in her voice.

"It's not ordinary paper at all."

15

Extra Soft

There are several ways to identify counterfeit currency. A security thread on the left side of a genuine bill will have microprinted identifiers of its denomination. The presidential portrait on newer currency is haloed in a series of fine random lines and shadowed by a watermarked portrait that should be visible from both sides of the bill. The notifier of denomination on the bottom right-hand corner of genuine money is double-inked to change color as the money moves in varying planes, and every major denomination when exposed to ultraviolet light will glow with distinctive colors.

Any one of these protections taken singly is hard to beat, and taken together the refinements make U.S. currency the hardest to counterfeit of any in the world, and yet with art, ingenuity, and digital printers regularly crooks can create near-perfect facsimiles of almost every usable denomination.

Fibers can be robbed; lower denominations can be bleached

and faked as higher-valued bills; watermarks and polarized ink can be manufactured. All of that stuff can be faked. But not the paper. The paper for U.S. currency is control-sourced from rag, not cellulose, and is uniquely processed under tremendous pressure—thousands of pounds of pressure. The material and process used to create that particular paper is what gives the feel of real cash. It's what makes real money fold and feel differently in your hand than crap. You can print funny money with the best technology and artist available, but without the right paper, it won't fool a blind man.

What Julie Fannon found on Terry Godot's trawler were a few wrappings of rag paper processed under very high pressure, paper that was manufactured somewhere outside the United States. Following her initial discovery, Ms. Fannon explained to astounded Treasury agents that she believed the paper found on Sarge's shrimp boat was ripped off a larger sheet for the exemplary purpose of wiping somebody's ass. Fannon's theory was confirmed when an inspection of the boat's plumbing revealed scraps of shit-stained paper that matched the wad found in the coffee can.

"We don't have a case yet," Barrett warned, and Cricket Bonet concurred.

Even in combination with the reconstructed course Terry's boat had taken, the high-value asswipe wasn't enough to conclusively prove that Terry and his crew were counterfeiters, kidnappers, or killers. But it sure as hell made them suspects for an array of felonies that far outshined busting mailboxes. And because Terry and Bud were incarcerated, it gave Barrett Raines a unique opportunity to divide and conquer.

There was no question who was the weakest link in that chain.

Barrett interviewed Bud Hewitt in the Dixie County jail. It

was apparent that Buddy was not handling his confinement well. The symptoms of PTSD were obvious. Barrett wondered briefly whether he should order a suicide watch.

"Buddy, have a seat," Barrett directed the younger man and with no preamble, he outlined the evidence found on Terry Godot's boat.

Buddy shifting his weight in the metal chair. Running his hand over his scalp repeatedly.

"Jesus shit," he said. "Fucking shit all."

"Easy, Buddy, nobody's charged you with anything." Bear slid a cold cup of coffee across the table. "Not yet anyway."

"You think I'm owna rat out my outfit, you can kiss my ass."

"Why, no, I don't expect that, Bud. Last thing on my mind. But I would expect you to help me find out who killed Raul Carrera. He was part of your team, wasn't he? Heard ya'll were hot shit in Nangarhar."

Buddy was suddenly looking at his hands.

"What do you know about Nangarhar?"

Bear spread his hands on the table.

"Not much. Elite outfit. Special Ops. Seemed like they didn't keep you in-country very long, though. Any reason for that?"

"Fucking politics. Same reason they backed off bin Laden in Tora Bora."

Bear decided to let that pass.

"Well, it wasn't a raghead killed Raul Carrera, I can tell you that. My guess is it was Los Zetas, or someone similar."

Buddy shifted his weight.

"I don't know anything about that."

"Well, that's too bad, Buddy, because I can tell there's a good chance that whoever killed Raul also killed Brenda

Mantle. Probably the same son of a bitch went after my boy, too. So whoever could help us with that connection, why, he could do himself a lot of good.

"Now, you don't have to say a word against Terry. Those ties are strong; I understand that. But why should you protect some Mexican son of bitch who's killed your buddy? You think that's gonna buy you goodwill? 'Cause I don't see the Zetas sending you bail money, Buddy. I don't know what you can expect once Smoot cuts you loose, but based on Raul's autopsy, it ain't gonna be quick and easy."

Buddy's hands continued to run over his scalp. Over and over.

"It was for a righteous cause," he said finally. "It wasn't just the money. We're doing something good. Something needs doing."

"I hear you." Barrett nodded. "Figured there had to be a reason."

"Fuckin' A. You think we were gonna keep it all for ourself? It was for the Crusade. For the fight."

"We talking your money, Buddy?"

"All our money. Like a pool. It was Dawana's idea."

"Dawana's?" Bear tried to suppress his surprise at that tangent.

"She said it was awright to steal the Devil's money, long as we tithed to the Lord. You know, like in the Bible. Ten percent. So like if I send ten dollars of every hundred to the war, it's righteous"

"To which war?"

"The war against fuckin' Islam, Bear. The war in fuckin' Iraq an' Afghanistan. Fuckin' Yemen. Africa. Won't be long before it comes to the homeland."

"Gotcha. And to whom do you send your tithe?"

"Sarge is in charge of that. It goes for medicine and stuff. Ammunition. See, it goes to help people and it keeps the homeland safe, too, which is cool."

"Cool with—"

"With Jesus. With God, the Maker. Whatever."

"But you keep nine dollars out of ten."

"Hey, man, Yahweh never said you had to starve!"

"No, I am sure He didn't," Barrett replied gravely. "Now, maybe you can help me understand how this connects to the counterfeiting business."

"What do I get in return?"

"Protection."

But now Buddy was shaking his head.

"Nah. I bring you the bacon, you're gonna have to do better than that."

Barrett raised the bear's hump of his shoulders. "All I can do right now, Buddy."

"Well then, you come back when you can do more."

Every interrogator has to know when to walk away, and in this case it wasn't a hard call. Bear had gotten much further with Buddy the first time around than he'd expected. Time now to let Corporal Hewitt stew. Let Bud think about what waited on the other side of the wall when he became a free and open target. In the meantime, the kid's shallow justification confirmed that Buddy and his outfit were pawns in the hands of foreign counterfeiters who had killed Brenda Mantle and possibly also Raul Carrera.

Bear should not have been surprised to hear specifics of Dawana's involvement. Dawana was not part of Terry's team of killers; her membership must have been qualified. Why did the men bring her into their circle? It certainly wasn't for religious justification. Sex, maybe. It seemed likely, at least, that Raul and Dawana had shared more than a love of motorbikes.

The 10 percent tithe was nice, a cheap price to salve a counterfeit conscience. Rob from the rich, give to the poor. Old as Robin Hood. And Bear wasn't the least surprised to hear Bud maintain a concern for Afghans as justification for his criminal activity. Criminals were infinitely ingenious in the justification of their crimes.

But Barrett was surprised at Buddy's reticence to discuss his personal experience in combat. Not that veterans typically or easily discussed their wartime experiences. Bear knew better than most that men who actually killed or endured killing were wary of divulging any detail linked to their own conduct, especially those actions bound to offend the unstained sensibilities of friends and family. But Buddy was a braggart. There was no clutch between his brain and his mouth. Barrett expected Buddy to brag about his exploits in Nangarhar, which made his reticence all the more interesting.

Bear wanted to know what had happened in Afghanistan to bond Buddy Hewitt so tightly with his band of brothers. He also wanted to know how Dawana gained the trust of those immodest warriors. And how did Quentin Hart fit into the picture? It was very hard to believe that Quentin would arrange a cop-assisted suicide from guilt over counterfeiting. That crime wasn't big enough. It wasn't bad enough. And anyway, as Bud had insisted, making money for God's use was a sin easily forgiven.

Those questions would have to wait. At present, it was enough to know that Terry Godot was using a remnant of his Special Ops team to man his personal boat for the purpose of making and moving fake money in collusion with a Mexican cartel. Maybe the GIs were only being paid to move the paper needed to print counterfeit bills. Maybe they were moving both paper and cash. Those details would emerge in time.

It was clear that Los Zetas beheaded Agent Mantle to

protect their counterfeit operation. Presumably, Raul was killed for similar reasons. And Bear had to assume that the same organization was behind the attempt to kidnap his son. You didn't need to go roaming in Afghanistan to find bad guys, Bear reminded himself.

And speaking of roaming—Dawana Jackson was still at large. You'd think a black woman in a GI jacket would stick out like a sore thumb in the Third District, but thus far Corporal Jackson had eluded local authorities. "We've got eyes everyplace," Barnett had been told. "Nobody's seen her."

Sheriff Rawlings drove out to Fannie Jackson's place with a warrant for her daughter's arrest. The eldery Mrs. Jackson told Smoot that she had not seen her daughter recently. Smoot went over the house with one of his deputies. They found some old clothes and toiletries, nothing definitive. A fisherman at Harvey's Marina said he'd seen a black girl driving Raul Carrera's pimped-out Camaro, but there was no sign of that vehicle at Fanny's.

Smoot Rawlings believed that Jackson was no longer in the district. "She's off the reservation."

Bear made a note to visit Dawana's mother himself. He knew from church gossip that Fannie was not happy her only child left her mama for the Marine Corps, and she was even less pleased to have Dawana come home and use the house like a motel. Even so, Bear would not be surprised to find that Mrs. Jackson lied to any white man at her door. Barrett expected Fannie to engage him differently than she had Sheriff Rawlings. Aside from sharing a racial identity, Barrett and Fannie held tragedy in common: Barrett's father died in violent circumstances in the same week that Fannie Jackson's old man got his balls cut off by some redheaded whore in Lake City. Barrett's mother and Dawana's found commiseration in their shared loss. Barrett could remember being comforted by Mrs. Jackson in gentler years. He would not be a stranger at her door.

Did he have time to see Fannie on the way home?

Agent Raines checked his watch: 4:00 P.M. Dawana's mother lived in a homestead right on the edge of Devil's Slew, but from the Dixie County jail, it wasn't much out of the way. Bear figured he could stop by Fannie's house and be on the water in his kayak before supper. Either that or he could walk straight over to Terry Godot's jail cell and begin that interrogation.

He decided Terry could wait. It wouldn't hurt to let Sarge stew overnight, wondering whether Bud Hewitt had blabbed anything to Bear that would implicate his gunnery sergeant in crimes linked to the murders of Brenda Mantle and Raul Carrera. He'd be wondering if Buddy had let himself get tricked into ratting out his old gunny.

Barrett would sleep well knowing that Buddy had.

16

Miss Fannie

It was the first time since he'd shot Quentin Hart that Bear
Raines had been anywhere near Devil's Slew, and the closer
he got, the worse he felt.

It was a clean shoot, Bear kept telling himself. Quentin
came charging out with his weapon on full automatic and
Barrett returned deadly fire and that was that. End of story.

Except the story wouldn't end. Bear continued to replay
the shooting in his head like a video on automatic rewind.
For many cops, perhaps most, this would be taken as a normal reaction, the brain's way of recuperating from a terrible
trauma. But it wasn't normal for Bear Raines.

Barrett had thrown down on suspects many times, had
killed more than his share of bad guys. Had killed his own
brother, for God's sake! Always in the line of duty. But
something about Quentin Hart was unresolved, unfin-
ished. Something about that killing stuck in his craw.

Agent Raines spotted the raised hump that snaked through

the slough's interior on its way to Quentin Hart's pull-along, but he would not be taking that primitive road. Fannie Jackson's house bordered the bogs and brooks on the other side of Devil's Slew. There was a farm-to-market road turning sharply off the blacktop a couple of miles ahead; it connected to a sandy lane leading to Fannie Jackson's homestead. Locals usually located the turnoff to Fannie's place by a microwave tower that rose some three hundred feet above farmland overgrown with huckleberry and grapevines on a sharply banked curve of the farm-to-market road. Barrett could remember seeing that tower assembled when he was only five or six years old. Was odd to see grown men in yellow hats climbing up and up to assemble an alien technology rising like some spaceship above fields of sugarcane and tobacco.

Barrett spotted the old tower now, alternating sections of red and white supports rigged at intervals with antennae that had long outlived their purpose. How much money had been wasted to build a tower used solely, now, to mark the turnoff to a single shack next to a slough of devils?

You had to slow way down on the steep bank of the blacktop to make the turn onto Fannie's seldom-traveled lane. A decrepit fence line bracketed both sides of ruts that ran crooked as a blacksnake to Fannie's front porch. Bear remembered the mimosa and magnolia trees that marked the end of the lane and his destination. He spotted the house, a true cracker shack raised up on a pier of stumps, the roof's original cedar shingles long replaced with tin. A shotgun hall down the middle shunted summer breezes to rooms on either side. A single chimney marked the kitchen.

The front porch was raised a good four feet above the muddy ground, and there was Fannie in a rocking chair fashioned of hickory boughs and covered with deer hide. She looked like a bag of sticks. Some print of flowers or fleur-de-lis stamped into the fabric of a cheap cotton dress. She was going bald, her hair sprouting in patches like weeds in a badly kept yard. Dawana's mama launched a chaw of tobacco into a yard scraped bare as a skull as Barrett pulled his cruiser beneath a bloomless arbor of redbud trees.

He grabbed the top of the door to haul himself out of the cruiser.

"Hello, Miss Fannie," he called, brushing his hand past his hip to make sure his firearm was where it was supposed to be.

"I doan need nuthin," came the high-pitched voice from the porch. "Whatever you sellin', take it someplace else."

"Miss Fannie, it's Bear."

"Who?"

"Bear Raines, Miss Fannie. You knew my mama."

He saw her jaws working.

"Why sho' I knew you mama, Bear. Whatchu come out here fo'?"

Bear strolled up to the sagging steps of her porch.

"Miss Fannie, I am trying to help your daughter."

"My dawta?"

"Dawana, Miss Fannie. She's in some trouble."

"She always in trouble." The old woman spit. "Trouble her middle name."

"Yes, ma'am, but if you can help me locate her, I believe I can help."

"Hep Dawana?"

"Yes, ma'am."

"You mean arrest her, is what you mean. Shaff done been out heah."

"There is a warrant for Dawana's arrest, yes, ma'am. But she's also in danger. There've been some killings."

"Don' I know." She spit off the porch again. "Killin' here.

Killin' there. I don' know why the Good Lord don' juz come down and make an end of days."

"Maybe 'cause we're doing a pretty good job of it ourselves?" Bear offered, and she cackled.

"I always like you, Bear. You funny."

"Yes, ma'am. But I am serious about Dawana."

She shook her head.

"Cain't hep you."

"Can't or won't, Miss Fannie?"

"She ain't nowhere to be seed, is all I got to say. You kin look in my house, you ownt to, but she ain't here."

"I hear you." Barrett scanned the grounds. As Smoot had reported, there was no vehicle of any kind in sight. Nothing outside the house but a pasture gone to seed and what was left of the old sugarcane mill.

"You remember us making syrup, Miss Fannie? In the old days?"

"Old days," she repeated slyly. "You ain't old. You don' know what old is."

Barrett flirted back. "You're not doing too bad yourself."

She smoothed her printed skirt over her knees.

"You won't some corn bread and tea?"

"Oh, Miss Fannie, nobody makes corn bread like you. But, no, I spect Laura Anne's got something on the oven."

"You better eat it, then. You don' let a woman go to awl that work and not eat."

"No, ma'am. Will you tell Dawana I came by?"

"I see her, I will. But like I say . . ."

She wasn't paying attention to him anymore; he could tell. She was somewhere back in her own memories. Some distant call of days. Barrett was already turned away himself and headed back to the cruiser when she stopped him.

"I 'member the day yo' daddy was kilt."

193

Bear Raines pulled up short. There was the slightest pause before he turned to face the old woman.

"Yes, ma'am?"

She was smiling. A wicked, wicked smile.

"Yo' mama, she knew how to keep her mouth shut, too. Diddun she?"

It would take a sharp eye to see the slender change of cadence in Barrett's stride as he made his way without reply to his unmarked sedan. He'd been wrong about Fannie Jackson. She wasn't going to give him a goddamned thing. Nothing he could afford anyway.

Bear drove to his wife's restaurant with a different set of memories to ponder. It will be good to get out on the water tonight, Barrett told himself. A good way to sweat off that cold, unnatural chill.

In fact, it was essential.

17

Play Swing

Dawana Jackson waited until the taillights of Raines's unmarked Ford were out of sight before allowing herself to
breathe. For two days, she'd been hiding with the hens inside the sugarcane mill behind her mama's house, distant
from Fannie's sullen wrath and the indifferent passion of
deputies on the border of Devil's Slew.

And now Bear Raines was after her black ass.

Dawana knew she could not count on her mother's loyalty, but thank God she wouldn't have to depend on it much
longer. She had a protector, a guardian angel. It was he who'd
alerted Dawana of Buddy's arrest. It had been his idea to pay
cash for her mother's silence and it was he who'd reminded
Dawana to hide Raul's spider-hubbed Camaro in the tangled
underbrush of Devil's Slew. All she has to do now was wait.
Just a little while longer and he would come for her and
they'd be together. Finally. Just the two of them. Just like
he'd always said.

The sun was well set. The tree line looked like the teeth of a saw on a matte of blood. Dwana felt the tickle of her cell phone. Another text:

BUG OUT 2100

She tapped out a terse reply.

ROGER

Dawana pocketed her throwaway phone and checked her watch. Two hours to kill. God, she was tired. So tired. Dawana pulled up the hood of her fatigue jacket. The chickens were already bedded for the night, warm as toast in their roost of milk crates. Dawana wished she could do that, just fold her wings and sleep. She could use some shut-eye.

Well, why not? She'd followed every texted instruction to the letter. Everything was ready, all essentials neatly arranged in her GI backpack: a change of shorts and shirt and cammyies, her Bible, a toothbrush, the .45 automatic, loaded, with magazines to spare.

The Lord helps those who help themselves.

A few other items were kept closer to hand. Corporal Jackson fished a Ziploc bag and Zen papers from a pocket of her service-issued trousers. Took just a moment to roll a pin on the kettle's iron lip. She cupped a Bic to light the joint and took a deep, deep hit.

She'd been introduced to weed in Nangarhar and had told herself on that first occasion that it was really just a kind of cigarette, and anyway, the Bible never said a thing about smoking pot, or any other leaf, for that matter. Not anywhere. That was Dawana's rationalization for her new habit, and it was a blessing now, enduring the fear and anxiety of a felon's flight to find respite in a sin barely venial.

She exhaled a warm vapor into the frigid air and imagined her soul rising in winding tendrils to commune with the spirits of slaves released from the slurry of Devil's Slew. Either that or devils and demons. An unholy congregation.

"Don' matter." She closed her eyes. "We awl God's chillun."

She tried to conjure her daddy's face and couldn't. She remembered that he'd loved making syrup. Those leaf-burning days, juice foaming in a boiling kettle. Scooping the rising foam for candy. The smell of syrup and smoke. Sunlight bent into rainbows through whiskey bottles and mason jars. He'd liked to watch her chase the boys, she remembered. And she could remember his broad hand in the small of her back at the play swing he rigged on the long axle that drove their grinder. Sailing high into the air. Squealing laughter.

Those were memories worth keeping.

She wouldn't miss the chickens, though. She wouldn't miss getting up before dawn morning after morning to gather that meager protein. And as for cutting okra? Stringing tobacco? Fuck that shit.

Dawana indulged another toke. She would never again gather eggs for breakfast. She would never sleep in come-stained sheets or chase snakes from a filthy privet. And she wouldn't be humping the boonies, either. No IEDs or ragheads or heathens. *No mas.* She had fought the good fight. A mansion was waiting, and before the night was out, she'd be delivered to her reward on the wings of a dove. Or maybe the tires of a fast car. Too bad she couldn't keep Raul's Camaro.

Whatever.

She regarded her roach's glowing ember. No need to be edgy, really. No vehicle could approach her mama's house without being seen, and even at night the sweep of headlights would give away any approach. The only way to get to the house unseen was to trek in from the back side of the property, and that meant crossing Devil's Slew. That was the path her private angel would tread, her counselor, her shield. But only He knows the moment of His coming, she reminded herself, thinking of that line in Scripture. Like the Bridegroom. Like Jesus.

She stubbed out what was left of her joint, spread her arms on the kettle like a schoolgirl at her desk, and cradled her head.

When she wakes her bladder feels fit to burst.

Lord, what time is it? she wondered. Dawana yanks back the cuff of her GI jacket to check her watch. Ten minutes after nine. He's late! He's never been late!

She snatches out her throwaway phone and stabs in a message:

WHN WLL U B HR?

The answer comes with three quick strobes from a flashlight triggered across the pasture from the barbed-wire fence that marked the edge of Devil's Slew. The Bridegroom come for his bride—

"—Like a thief in the night!"

Days of fear and hope found release with her bladder. No matter! There was no time for shame now. And no need, either! Dawana pocketed her phone and hefted her bulky pack to her shoulders. The torch winked twice more, like a lighthouse on a distant beach. The light of life beaming from a demon's den.

She sprints across the pasture, those thick, hard legs churning, churning. The girl who always outran the boys at cane grinding, racing now for freedom, for salvation. She vaults the fence line like a startled doe and a rusty barb snags her thigh, but she does not slow down. She doesn't even care. Let it bleed! These are her wounds, her holy wounds. The stigmata of martyrs.

"Praise Jesus!" she cries full of faith.

And leaps into her Savior's embrace.

18

Gathering Eggs

Dawana's mother woke the next morning to a sky gravid and gray, peeved that her daughter had neglected her chores. There were still chickens to feed and dishes to wash. When Dawana came begging for a place to stay, her mother warned her, "This ain't no motel."

"DAWANA?" she called out, to no reply.

Where in the world?

Fannie pulled one old stick of a leg and then the other from beneath the ratty blanket, slipped on an unwashed robe and slippers, and shuffled down the freezing hallway to Dawana's room.

"Dawana?"

She wasn't there. Fannie frowned at the empty soda cans and underwear littering the floor. Surely that girl didn't spend the whole night with the chickens? But there was no point worrying. Dawana never told her mama where she was going. Always running off on that damn motorbike, though

Fannie could not recall hearing the noisome contraption fire up in some days.

Well, maybe one of those boys came out to get her. Or maybe Dawana just walked out to the hard road to hitch a ride. Either way, she wasn't here to help with chores.

First thing was to eat. Fannie went out to gather eggs, pausing to pee in the porcelain pan that was her latrine. She washed her hands at the pump out back, the long iron handle so cold, it burned. Her fingers went numb in a gush of water. She cupped her hands and waddled, cursing, across the yard toward the sugarcane mill. Once past her grassless yard, the pasture's Bahia rose knee-high and just this side of frosting. Put chilblains on an old woman's shins.

"To hell with you, Dawana!"

What daughter worth a tinker's damn would let her eighty-year old mama freeze of a winter morning for a handful of eggs?

"Ungrateful hussy!"

The rooster's crow pulled her feeble eyes forward to the sugarcane mill. Fannie was surprised to hear that raucous salutation and even more surprised to see the little fart puffing up outside the mill's shelter. Normally at the first hint of frost, Fannie's rooster retreated inside the mill to squat alongside the hens. The only time he acted like a proper cock was when Fanny arrived to scoop cornmeal from the Igloo cooler onto the yard outside. He'd leave the warm to feed, the little shit.

He was cock of the walk when it came to feeding.

But something today had roused her rooster away from his warm-feathered hens, some violation of territory or a threat too serious to ignore. Probably a possum, Fannie thought to herself. Fox, maybe? Too late in the year for snakes.

She slapped the grass at her knees, looking for a stick, and startled the rooster to flight. Just a flash of feathers black and red rising seven or eight feet to perch on the very end of the cane grinder's long axle. But the rooster wasn't the only thing on that long pole. Fannie squinted her feeble eyes.

Was it a burlap sack? A feed sack?

For a moment, Fannie was reminded of the swing her husband used to rig for the children when the grinding was done. Those little legs and feet rising and falling.

"Dawana? Dawana, girl?" she implored.

Wringing her brittle hands.

"Baby, it's too cold to swing."

Barrett Raines had just seen his boys onto their YellowBird school bus when he got a call from Sheriff Rawlings, who told him that Dawana Jackson had hanged herself.

"God o'mighty, are you sure?" Barrett asked.

"Only sure thing is death and Democrats, Bear. Why don't you come out and see for yourself?"

By the time Agent Raines reached Fannie Jackson's homestead, Smoot Rawlings had already contacted the medical examiner in Jacksonville. Florida law mandates that any policeman or other lawman finding any homicide has jurisdiction over the crime scene and its associated physical evidence, but the medical examiner is given authority over the body of the deceased, along with any physical evidence in direct contact with the body.

The only things in direct contact with Dawana Jackson were her camouflaged trousers and T-shirt and the rope around her neck. Her hair was crowned with a rind of frost, a white tiara on coal black hair. Her breasts sagged toward her belly inside the olive green shirt. Her GI-issue boots were laced paratrooper-style. Piss had frozen in the crotch of her trousers.

Smoot tugged on the zipper of his leather jacket.

"Looks like she used those milk crates to throw the rope over the grinder's axle." Smoot pointed to a pair of plastic crates overturned beneath the swaying body. "We found Raul Carrera's Camaro. It's hid behind some mimosas back of the mill here."

"Christ, I was just out here. Just yesterday."

"So Fannie lied to you, too. I'm thinkin' of charging that woman."

"Where is she now?"

"Settin' in my cruiser. Like a grieving mama."

Bear decided to let that go, for the moment.

"We got a time of death?"

"After nine-thirty-three, for sure."

"For sure?"

"We found a cell phone." Smoot indicated that Bear should follow him. "One of them like drug dealers use? You use 'em, you throw 'em away. Well, Dawana left one in the sugarcane mill. It's got a suicide note. Time on the phone was nine-thirty-three P.M."

"She called herself?"

Smoot shook his head. "Left herself a text message. An' not just about the suicide, either. You got to read this, Bear. Bennet, can you get Agent Raines a pair of gloves?"

Bear thanked Smoot's deputy as he snapped on a pair of latex gloves. The phone was propped on the iron lip of the mill's kettle.

"Just pop 'er open, ah hah," Rawlings coached. "Now, see that little mailbox?"

"I got it, Sheriff."

Barrett activated the appropriate icon and opened "Messages." There was only one text to look at:

JESUS FGV ME 4 MY SINS   FGV BUD & SARGE 2
PLS KP RAUL SAF N UR ARMS   I THOT I WS
DNG UR WORK   IFB ABOUT ALL THE KILL-
ING   U CANT GET GOOD FM THE DEVIL   WAS
RICARDO WHO KILLED THAT WOMAN   HE KLLD
RAUL 2   IAS SORRY I JUDASED RAUL TO THE
MEXICANS   I NVR TOLD SARGE OR BUD   I
MADE MY DEAL W SATAN   MY BAD   BUT NOW I
CANT SLEEP   I CANT EAT   I CANT LIVE W IT.
FORGIVE ME

"I could use a transcript of this text." Barrett was digging in his Eddie Bauer parka to retrieve his spiral pad.

"Surely." Rawlings supplied a pen from the band of his straw hat. "You get done, you might want to see this dope we found. Right over here."

Rawlings indicated a Ziploc bag on the dirt beside the kettle's kiln, along with a lighter and Zen papers.

"She had a wallet in her trousers. Driver's license, VA ID, some cash. A prescription for Zoloft."

"Zoloft is an antianxiety med."

"Can be a deadly cocktail. She was smoking, is my guess. Lighter and papers in her field jacket."

"Field jacket?"

"It was freezing damn cold last night, Barrett."

"And yet she took off her coat to hang herself?"

"People strip naked sometimes. An' anyway, she was prolly stoned. Maybe fucked-up on antidepressants. We won't know till the ME does an autopsy."

"That's true."

Barrett finished his transcription and returned to the throwaway phone.

"She sent the text to her own number, but did she dial out anyplace else?"

"Three places. Twice to the trailer in Fenholloway. That was around seven last night. And then the third call was nine-twenty-eight P.M. She called nine one one; looks like maybe she was lookin' for some help, but when the dispatch answered, she just hung up."

"Damn shame," the deputy contributed.

"And damned inconvenient," Bear countered. "Without Dawana's voice, we can't say for sure who called nine one one. You mind if I take a look at the victim, Sheriff?"

"Course not," Smoot groused. "But it's pretty straightforward, Bear."

Barrett had to admit the scene was a match for any of a dozen suicides he'd investigated. Even the victim's profile fit. You had a discharged GI who was under obvious stress taking antidepressants on top of illegal drugs. She was scared to death of Los Zetas, and for good reason. Add to that a sense of guilt for ratting out Raul Carrera and you had a suicide in the making.

The note was hard to authenticate without handwriting, but the diction and grammar certainly fit. And the allusion to Judas Iscariot was important; Dawana certainly knew that Judas was the disciple who betrayed Jesus to His enemies. And she would know that Judas hanged himself for that treachery.

"I wonder how Dawana contacted the Zetas?" Bear wondered aloud. "She couldn't betray Raul Carrera without some way to contact those bastards."

"Prob'ly used another one of them throwaway phones," Smoot replied.

"To call what number? It's not like they're listed."

"They met Los Zetas at sea. Coordinates more than likely came over a phone or computer. Dawana could of used that route to send back a message of her own. Or maybe she just dropped a note inside a bale of counterfeit. She might of even told 'Ricardo' personally; she said she made a deal with Satan."

"She did, yeah."

Barrett snapped up the collar of his Windbreaker and circled Dawana's hanging corpse as it turned in the breeze. He saw the young woman's tongue lolling purple and obscene, as though she'd spit it from her mouth. He smelled urine. That was consistent with a hanging, the systems letting go.

"Doesn't look like her neck's broken," Barrett observed.

"No." Smoot shook his head sadly. "Choked to death is what we figure. Like most of 'em."

Bear affirmed this with a grunt. That fit, too. Most suicides using a noose died of strangulation.

"Any defensive wounds?"

"Not that we can tell," Smoot replied.

"Looks like she cut her thigh," Barrett remarked.

"Yep. We don't think that had anything to do with the suicide, though."

Barrett scanned the lay of the land around the sugarcane mill. There was a barbed-wire fence between the mill and the house that ran completely around the pasture. Dawana could have cut herself anywhere along that rusty line.

"Or she could have just cut herself inside the chicken house," Smoot said, as if reading his thoughts. "There's all kinda nails and tin cans in there. All sorts of crap with an edge."

"You called the Mobile out, Smoot?"

"Yep. Be another hour at least."

Bear backed away. "Like you said, Sheriff, we can't call it

a suicide till we get the medical examiner's report. But Terry and Bud don't need to know that."

"What you got in mind, Bear?"

"I'm thinking we show Sarge and Buddy the text message left on the phone, but we don't say anything about how Dawana died. Let Sarge and Buddy believe the Zetas murdered her just like they did Raul. Buddy's already asking for protection. Let's see if we can't use what we've got to up the ante."

19

Switch and Bait

One of the greatest tools in the interrogator's immodest kit is deception. A question about a suspect's girlfriend going off on the sly is really about establishing motive. A question about the way the local Korean dry cleaner fucked up the suspect's tuxedo is really about placing the suspect one block and five minutes away from his partner's murder.

And in the business of deception, half-truths beat lies any day for planting seeds of mistrust between dual suspects. Except, to Bear's mild surprise, it was not Buddy Hewitt who first confessed to smuggling counterfeit; it was Terry Godot.

Barrett's interrogation of Terry had been delayed by the discovery of Dawana Jackson's body; Agent Raines left Sheriff Rawlings at that scene to return to the Dixie County jail for his first interview with Sarge.

"Terry, I got something to read you," Bear began. "It's a text message sent last night. We found it on a mobile phone out at Fannie Jackson's place."

Barrett spread his spiral pad on the table separating him from Dawana's gunnery sergeant. "'Jesus, forgive me for my sins . . .'" he began, and by the time he was finished, Sarge was swearing vengeance and sweating bullets.

"Fuckin' Dawana? Ratted out my radioman? Got-damn religious freak! I never trusted that nigger bitch!"

"You sure it's Dawana wrote this?" Barrett closed his pad.

"Well, who the hell else could it be? Couldn't have been me or Buddy. We're in jail!"

"Good point."

"How did you turn her?"

"'Turn'?"

"Dawana. You got the bitch to roll. How? Finger-fuck her? One nigger to the other?"

Barrett kept his gaze level.

"How do I know you didn't kill Raul Carrera, Terry?"

"WHAT? The fuck are you talkin'?"

"You had motive, means, and opportunity. Especially motive. Raul put your entire team at risk. He literally gambled with your lives. Tell me you wouldn't kill a man in the field for that. 'Field expedient'?"

"SHE RATTED HIM OUT! NOT ME!"

"What the note says, but that doesn't mean you didn't kill him. If 'Ricardo' told you to."

"Hold the fucking train! I did NOT kill Raul Carrera."

"Well, that's good to know. And as it happens, I didn't turn Dawana Jackson."

You change direction when questioning suspects. You lay a bread trail you have no intention of following. And then you double back.

"What do you mean, you didn't turn her? What—she just walked in with a confession? Just walked in off the street?"

"She's not walking anywhere, Terry. She's dead. Stone-fucking-cold dead. Just like Raul."

Bear leaned into Godot's face.

"I see a pattern here, Sarge. Mexicans want counterfeit. Gringos create a problem. Mexicans take care of problem."

"They killed Dawana?"

"Well, you didn't. Buddy sure as hell didn't. Is there anybody else running paper in the county?"

"How'd she die?"

"Let's just say it was ugly and it puts you on the short list."

Sarge stirred in his metal chair.

"They won't kill me. Not yet anyway."

Not yet? Bear leaned back.

"Tell me about the paper."

"What about it?"

"Cut the crap. The counterfeiter's got to have rag paper. My guess is you got it from the Mexicans."

"Just the once. Onetime deal. A shitload of it, too."

"Enough to wipe your ass with, apparently. Where'd you drop it?"

"Devil's Slew. Not far from the turpentine mill."

"And you have no idea who picked it up."

"Don't know. Don't wanta know."

"When's your next pickup?"

"Of counterfeit? Didn't say there was one."

"Come on, Terry, the only reason you're alive is because the Zetas aren't going to take you out, or Buddy, until they've got everything they paid for. But what about afterward, Sarge? You go out on the open sea without backup, without protection? What's to keep Ricardo from wasting your ass as soon as you make delivery?"

Godot shifted his eyes to the middle of the table.

"You want to give me something I can use here, Bear?"

"I don't want to give you shit, Terry. I'm not even sure the feds would give you a deal just to bust a counterfeiter. But they'd protect anyone can help them nail the son of a bitch who killed their Treasury agent. That's the 'woman' in the text, isn't it, Terry? That was Brenda Mantle. So why don't you start by telling me where and how you happened to be in the company of Agent Mantle and this Ricardo?"

"I want a lawyer first."

Barrett sat back in his chair.

"You sure you have that kind of time?"

No reply.

"When's your next rendezvous with the Mexicans, Terry?"

"Why should I tell you?"

"Lawyer can't help you. I can. You agree to help me set up a sting to catch this Ricardo motherfucker and intercept the next shipment of counterfeited currency and I'll fully endorse a witness protection plan that will keep your ass out of jail.

"But this is a first-come, first-served arrangement, Terry. And I should warn you that Buddy Hewitt's already asking for protection."

"That weak-ass son of a bitch."

"Him or you, makes no difference to me. Now, when's the next shipment scheduled?"

"This coming week. Wednesday."

Barrett pushed the yellow pad in front of the gunnery sergeant.

"Then we don't have time to waste."

The statement that Bear Raines pulled from Terry Godot provided about equal parts of benefit and frustration. The bennies included verification that Sarge and his outfit had delivered three large shipments of facsimile cash to Los Zetas. Sarge also offered the timely details of a final shipment scheduled to deliver over two million dollars of faked currency.

"Where do you pick up the counterfeit?"

"So far, it's been Devil's Slew."

So far, so good. But also Terry maintained vociferously that he had no clue who manufactured the counterfeit or even if the faked cash was printed in the Third District.

"Personally, I think it's made someplace else," Terry told Pam Goerne during a follow-up interrogation. "I figure we're just a cutoff. There's prolly a couple places it goes through before it gets to us."

"But you are always the last in line?"

"We pick up after dark. We deliver the same night."

"And when do you expect to be contacted next?"

"Next Wednesday, if the pattern holds."

Goerne voiced her frustration privately to agents gathered at the District Office in Jasper. "That doesn't give us much time to plan an interdiction."

"Won't take any time to cordon off Devil's Slew," Smoot Rawlings countered. "If that's where the counterfeiter's droppin' off, we can just camp out and wait for him."

Cricket Bonet shook his Viking's mane to reject that idea.

"We spook the drop, we don't get the bags, and just as important, we don't get the throwaway phone. Without the phone, we can't confirm pickup and we can't receive the co-ordinates for Ricardo's boat."

Barrett agreed with his partner. "Ricardo's our target. We nail this son of a bitch, we'll bag a killer and a drug lord along with our counterfeiter. That's a lot of birds to kill with one stone. But we've only got one throw."

The decision was made to let the counterfeiter plant his bags without interference. But would the counterfeiter keep to his normal schedule if he knew his mules were either dead or behind bars?

"We have to release Terry right away," Barrett insisted. "But when we do, we'd better convince the counterfeiter that he and Buddy weren't jailed for any crime remotely related to counterfeiting. Otherwise, he won't set foot inside Devil's Slew."

The local paper once again proved valuable. Barrett filled Terry Godot in on the details.

"Mike Traiwick's giving you cover. He's running a story in the *Deacon Beach Herald* saying you're out on bail and that you deny a charge of leaving the scene of an accident. He's also saying that the reason Buddy's not released is that he's facing additional charges of assault and resisting arrest.

"We're letting you out, Terry, but you're going to be on a leash. By day, I want you highly visible and working on your boat. At night, you'll be in a safe house with federal agents. By the way, where's your phone?"

"In the Dixie County evidence room." Godot snorted. "Smoot took it along with my wallet and watch the day you boys cuffed me in Rolly's shop."

Bear was reasonably confident that Terry's cover would hold and he had no qualms about a nighttime recon into Devil's Slew, but he got the shakes thinking about chasing Los Zetas on deep water. Bear had chased bad guys on the water before, of course. On one of those occasions, he'd run into a hurricane and had to be rescued by a crazy woman. In another case, he'd taken fire from automatic weapons and hand grenades. None of those coastal forays came close to matching the complexity and danger of an assault on a drug cartel with military hardware on the Gulf of Mexico, but that wasn't the cause for the churn in Bear's gut. He wasn't afraid of boats or bullets.

But Barrett Raines could not swim.

Many black people of Bear's age growing up in the socially segregated counties along Florida's northwestern coast never learned to swim. There were no swim classes, for blacks or whites, in Barrett's palmetto neighborhood. No pools or YMCA. Black people were discouraged or forbidden from bathing in the artesian springs habituated by local crackers seeking relief from the heat, and even white folks didn't learn to swim in the springs. Bear's pale-skinned classmates bragged they dived for dimes at the bottom of the boil in Blue Springs, but they couldn't crawl a hundred yards over calm water.

Barrett forced himself over the years to confront, if not overcome, a fear of water. He learned to boat with relative confidence from Deacon Beach to the better-known ports of call along the local coastline. He learned to take modest forays in a kayak. But the fear of deep water was never expunged: the fear of drowning, a pillow closing about your mouth, your nose, toes thrashing frantically to touch bottom.

He felt a sense of shamed relief when Captain Henry Altmiller said flat out that any plan to capture Los Zetas at sea was just too risky, but unfortunately for Bear, Pamela Goerne had the Treasury Department and the Department of Homeland Security in her corner.

"Just give me Agents Raines and Bonet," Pamela urged Captain Altmiller. "We'll make it work."

The plan that emerged was to use Terry Godot's trawler as a Trojan horse. Hidden with the counterfeit on the shrimp boat would be green units of the U.S. Coast Guard. Once Los Zetas accepted the contraband, the Guard's PSUs would storm the Mexican vessel to subdue and capture Ricardo and his crew, with support from separate teams of commandos manning assault boats and helicopters.

Responsibility for commanding the operation was unified under the Coast Guard. Federal law prohibited the navy or other armed services to open fire on a civilian vessel; the Coast Guard was not bound by that statute. Once Ricardo's yacht was sighted, all authority would rest with Comdr. Malcolm Stennis, a quiet, windburned native of New Hampshire. It was his job to get the Trojan horse inside the gates.

"There will be no time for rehearsal," Commander Stennis warned the bureaucrats and military personnel who were briefed on the operation. "Once we get the okay to go after this vessel, there will be no time to recant or rethink. So don't ask me to put my men in harm's way without giving me the authority I need to do the job."

By Monday, the commander had his orders, the Coast Guard was ready to move, and Terry Godot was waiting anxiously with his handlers for the text message that would launch Operation Mantle. Which gave Bear from Monday until Wednesday to tackle the other crises clamoring for his attention.

Crime did not pause in the Third District, not even for counterfeiters. In a single week, the sheriff in Madison County reported a homicide in connection with a meth lab run out of the parking lot of the junior college. In Hamilton County, a man and wife posing as tourists in a recreational vehicle were caught cooking. There was a case involving electoral fraud in Lafayette County that Bear would have to address soon, and somebody near Perry was dumping kerosene into the Fenholloway River.

On top of that came the medical examiner's autopsy report on Dawana Jackson.

Barrett caught Cricket on the fly with the report. "Did you see this?"

"No. Bottom it out for me."

"Suspicious. There were drugs in her system; we expected that. She'd been smoking and was on Zoloft. But there were also residuals of Rohypnol."

"Ah, the date-rape drug. Was she raped?"

"No sign of sexual contact of any kind, no."

Cricket frowned. "She could have easily taken the Rophy herself, Barrett. It's a benzodiazepine. Works for anxiety, panic attacks. Might be the drug of choice for someone considering suicide."

"It might. But it might also be the perfect tool for a killer wanting to incapacitate somebody long enough to put a noose around her neck."

"I hear you, partner, but we already have about eight full plates. Gonna have to wait for this one."

"I'll wait." Barrett slipped the file beneath his arm. "But I won't forget."

Cricket Bonet and Bear Raines reached Steinhatchee in time to see a sinking sun refracted through crystals of cirrostratus clouds in fantastic ribbons of gold and copper and ruby red. The safe house's stuccoed walls were bathed pink in the falling dusk, an ordinary cube of lumber and plaster no different from other weekend retreats along the coast. Certainly the fence did not convey special status; any number of condos lay hidden behind iron gates and security systems, the snouts of their cameras like the beaks of birds.

The architecture was banal, but the setting was spectacular. You could sit on the balcony and imagine you were living in the time of the Seminoles. There was no sign of modern life beyond the condo itself. A channel of salt water ran like a vein of silver through a sea of grass that stretched interminably toward the horizon.

"On a good day, you can maybe tell where the grass ends and the Gulf begins," Bear remarks to his Viking-size partner.

A pair of pelicans working the water jogged memories.

"I used to take a cane pole and a can of worms all along these channels," Bear tells Cricket.

He remembered looking for supper as snakes and otters fed along the boundary of brine and freshwater. A red-tailed hawk circling overhead. Squirrels scratching bark from yellow-heart pines and cypress trees. Then walking home at sunset to the sough of a sea breeze. The hoot of owls and the grunt of alligators. By the time Bear got home from one of those modest expeditions, the sky was so thick with stars that he couldn't make out the constellations. And there were no condominiums.

"Somebody's pussy palace." Cricket snorts aloud.

Bear keyed the ciphered lock, allowing entry through the gate, and a windowless door up ahead rolled up, revealing a Chevy Suburban crowding a garage that was Sheetrocked but unpainted. Bear squeezed his unmarked vehicle along-side the Suburban and got out to follow Cricket up a steep set of grated steps to a heavy metal door and intercom.

Cricket punched the intercom and was answered. Moments later, the door opened framing an armed FBI agent dressed for a winter's trek in cargo pants and hiking boots. A shoulder holster underneath a parka bore the instantly recognizable stitched letters *FBI*.

"Credentials, please, gentlemen. Thank you. I am Special Agent Kidd."

Kidd was an athlete; you could tell. Square and lean and taller than Barrett. They followed Agent Kidd into a kitchen that looked out to a lanai and balcony. Fans were suspended from a vaulted ceiling. The inside of the condo looked like it had been fitted out with second-tier Ikea. Except for a few scattered tables and chairs, it was practically unfurnished. Bear saw a second agent monitoring a bank of radios and CRTs.

"Gentlemen, meet Agent Sandford."

"Call me Sandy."

Sandy settled soft as a doughnut at a picnic table set along a salmon wall. Bear recognized a satellite radio and saw a cable snaking from a laptop to a dish on the balcony. Sanford shoved away a cellophaned sandwich and a bottle of Gatorade. Terry Godot was placing queens and jacks in neat columns on a coffee table.

"How you doin', Terry?" Bear asked.

"Itchin' to get out of this fuckin' cage," Terry complained.

"Shouldn't be long now." Barrett unzipped his FDLE Windbreaker.

Terry turned then to his handlers. "The phone charged?"

"The phone's fine, Terry," Agent Sandford replied with affected nonchalance.

Barrett saw the phone plugged to its charger, within easy reach.

"You sure it's tonight, Terry?" Cricket asked.

"It's Wednesday, ain't it? Little after nine, usually."

He doesn't look good, Bear notes. He's sweated through his olive greens. A sheen of perspiration brightens his face, his lips. Smoot Rawlings sees it, too. So do the feds.

"I could use a beer."

"It's just another, patrol, Terry." Barrett scanned a map pinned up like a poster on the wall. "Just an out and back, that's all it is."

"Out and back, yeah." Godot ground a napkin into his forehead. "Just a walk in the fuckin' park."

About that time, the phone danced on its plate.

"Your call, Sarge," Agent Kidd told him.

Godot jumped for the phone, snapped it open.

"Sumbitch," he said, and displayed the text.

There they were, latitude and longitude in degrees, minutes, and seconds.

Agent Sanford grabbed a laptop. "If you'll give me the coordinates . . ."

Within minutes, the fed had an infrared shot zooming in from a satellite. The topography showed up in patterns of gray and green on the fed's small screen. Barrett waited for the cursor to settle before checking the computer's posted coordinates against the map positioned alongside.

"It's Devil's Slew. For sure."

Barrett notices Terry testing the laces on his boots.

"Damn near the same location as last time. Closer to the rail bed, maybe."

"Wait a minute, wait a minute." Bear squinted at the grainy image materializing on the laptop. "Sandy, what's that there? That structure?"

"See if I can improve the resolution," the agent replied.

For a second, it looked as though he'd lost the picture altogether. But then the screen blinked and the cursor centered like a gun sight over an image crisp and clear and green.

"I'll be got-damn," Sarge said.

It was Quentin Hart's goosenecked trailer.

20

The Trap

Bear Raines guided Agent Kidd straight to Quentin Hart's abandoned fifth-wheeler. Cricket brought up the rear in Bear's unmarked Ford. Rolling through the gloom on the ghostly ruts of the railway bed, Bear recalled childhood stories of the devils in Devil's Slew. The KKK and the bogeyman. Before the Civil War, bounty hunters invaded the slough in search of runaway slaves. Barrett used to regale in harrowing tales of pursuit and escape, snakebit slaves running to hide from plantation agents and Seminole Indians. Fannie Jackson claimed a bloodline descent from some survivor of those encounters. It was as likely a genealogy as any.

"They's lots of bones in this wilderness," Terry Godot remarked, and Cricket tipped his chin.

"Just make sure ours aren't among 'em."

Agent Kidd and Cricket Bonet took a flanking position on either side of Quentin's fifth-wheeler, bracketing the trailer with their headlights. There was no sign of activity. The crime-scene tape drooped like a beauty queen's banner over the tit of a broken door.

"Cover me."

Barrett Raines ran at a crouch between twin cones of light to reach the trailer. He brushed aside the yellow tape feebly guarding the door, the 9 mm small as a bar of soap in hands the size of basins.

"BARRETT RAINES, FDLE. IS ANYONE THERE?"

No answer. Not a sound.

"Am I covered?"

"We have you," Kidd replied from his flank.

Bear popped his head through the door, then withdrew it. No response.

He listened closely. No sound. No shift of weight inside. No telltale movement. The trailer was dead.

"I'm going in."

Barrett followed the gun sight of his Glock into the trailer and immediately spotted two large duffel bags on the kitchen sink.

"I SEE BAGS."

"I'm right behind you, Agent Raines."

Special Agent Kidd vaulted into the trailer and Bear stepped aside to make room in the tiny kitchen. There was a window above the sink—an open window.

At first, he didn't see anything, only an intimation of movement, a shift of shadow or wind. But then a jolt of adrenaline hammerd Bear's heart as he realized—there was somebody outside, looking straight into the trailer. Somebody looking at him.

"FREEZE!"

Bear walled off Kidd to clear a shot.

"CRICKET—BOGEY OUT BACK."

"ROGER."

Bear heard the thud of boots on soft earth. Saw the flashlight bobbing in Cricket's hand as he pounded past the trailer.

"Who the fuck is it?" Kidd rasped.

"Couldn't tell."

"Go get him. I've got our witness."

Bear Raines bolted out of the trailer and around the side of the pull-along in time to see Cricket plow into the underbrush at the edge of the clearing. Cricket wasn't hard to follow, the flashlight in his fist swinging with the barrel of his handgun.

"HALT!" came the formal command. "FDLE—HALT!"

Bear heard the tear of pursuit through the tangle of vine and palmetto. He saw the swing of the light in Cricket's hand in rhythm with the stride of his legs. Back and forth, back and forth.

"FDLE—"

But then the light dipped precipitously and the rhythm broke and Barrett heard something else.

A bellow of pain.

"CRICKET? CRICKET!"

Barrett charged toward the unmoving light and then he saw it: the long anchored chain, the iron jaws.

"FUCKING HELL!"

Cricket Bonet pounded the ground with his fist, his leg snapped in two in the teeth of a massive trap.

"MAN DOWN!" Bear yelled back to Agent Kidd. "BUT BE CAREFUL! THERE'RE TRAPS!"

Bear cleared a path to his partner. It was worse than he'd imagined.

"I . . . I think I broke my leg," said Cricket, trying to joke.

Barrett was reminded of the first serious injury he ever saw. It was on a basketball court, some young kid heading east when his knee was heading west. On another occasion,

Bear was slurping beer at a college game in Texas when he saw the Longhorn's leadoff hitter snag his foot on the bag white sliding into second base, and on any number of Sundays he had groaned on the couch with buddies, watching the instant replay of some quarterback hit dirty below a knee. Never failed to turn your stomach, that odd and unnatural angle between a dislocated limb and torso, but if you soaked one of those fleeting moments in blood and twisted the limb a couple of more times, you'd still have only a shallow approximation of Cricket Bonet's shattered leg.

The trap had caught Bonet fairly high, about halfway up the calf. The lower portion of his leg stuck out at ninety degree angle, snapped off like a stick of asparagus by massive saw-toothed jaws. Blood, bone, and meat laid open.

"Kind of rig is this?" Cricket fights to stay conscious.

"It's a bear trap," Raines told him. "Just stay still. We'll take care of it."

Agent Kidd jogging up, now, with a medic's kit.

"I've got morphine."

"Good. Where's Godot?"

"Handcuffed to the cruiser, no worries. Now, Agent Bonet, if you'll show me some skin . . ."

Kidd bends the needle afterward, slides it back into the kit.

"I've never seen an injury quite like this."

"We can't risk opening the trap." Barrett had reached that verdict quickly. "We open an artery, he could bleed out. We're gonna hafta haul him out trap and all."

Kidd snapped his kit shut. "I'll call Commander Stennis."

"NO, YOU WON'T," Cricket Bonet snarled from the ground. "No, you will not! You finish this damn job. You can take me to the medics. Bear's plenty able to escort the witness

223

and those fucking bags to that fucking boat. Don't use me for an excuse, Agent Kidd. Don't you goddamn even think about doing that."

"Okay." The fed seemed both embarrassed and encouraged to receive that permission. "But let's check the bags first. Make sure everything's there. If we've got our contraband currency and a cell phone, we're still good to go."

"Outstanding," Cricket declared, and passed out.

Barrett and Agent Kidd hauled Bonet back to the Suburban in a two-man carry, the shattered leg dangling in its bloody chain and trap.

"The fuck?" Terry Godot scanned the clearing nervously. "The fuck is this?"

"Get the bags from the trailer. Go!" Bear gasped.

Kidd reclined the Suburban's passenger seat as far back as it would go. It took a couple of heaves to get Cricket inside.

"Elevate that leg best you can," Bear suggested as Terry returned with the twin bags. "What about it, Terry? We good to go?"

"We got the counterfeit, got the phone—" Sarge displays a wrap of tinfoil.

"And what about my cut?"

Barrett Raines delivered Terry Godot to the Coast Guard's authority around 10:15, escorting Sarge in handcuffs to his own bridge. *The Crusader* was still moored at Harvey's Marina, and that was intentional. A casual passerby would see nothing unusual about the activity. Stennis had his team out of sight, including a sniper, who was invisible against the nets. The two PSUs chosen to pose as Terry's crew meet Bear and Agent Sandford on the dock and received the twin bags of counterfeit. Bear Raines uncuffs Terry Godot on the pier below his own bridge.

Commander Stennis leans over the side of the shrimper, crisp and sharp in workaday khakis. Barrett recognizes a chief petty officer's rating on the sleeve of a Coast Guardsman at the commander's side. A lieutenant with two silver bars confers with a warrant officer alongside.

"Permission to board, sir," Bear offers the usual courtesy.

"Granted. And you as well, Godot."

"Gunnery Sergeant Godot, if you please, sir. Agent Raines, after you secure Mr. Godot I'd like you to meet me at the bridge."

Bear boards the shrimper and stows Terry out of the way before climbing to the wheelhouse. The bridge is alive with activity.

Stennis shakes his head.

"No, you've squandered that privilege."

A constant stream of communication buzzed over the radios and computer screens. Lots of personnel and hardware to coordinate. The Coast Guard cutter that was Operation Mantle's mother ship orbited as if in a training exercise ten klicks south of Pensacola. Twin MH-68As from the Helicopter Intercept Tactical Squadron in Jacksonville were already forward-deployed to Cedar Keys.

Bear was grateful for air support. Each HITS team included a pair of gunners with M240 machine guns and a marksman with a .50-caliber sniping rifle. Coast Guard snipers routinely disabled Cigarette boats making seventy miles an hour over rough water with a single slug to their motors, that feat accomplished while hanging in a strap from a low-flying Stingray. Barrett was glad to have a marksmen like those looking down on the decks of the *Mi Casa*.

"Agent Raines."

"Yes, Commander."

"Find a vest for yourself and our witness, please. In case we go swimming."

For the next two hours, Stennis pantomimed the patterns of a boat dropping nets for shrimp. Bear felt the spike from his earlier rush petering off when sometime near one in the morning the cell phone warbled and shook.

The lieutenant grabbed the phone.

"We have coordinates," he sang out, then handed over the phone with its text message to Commander Stennis.

"Ready to receive, Nav?"

"Yes, sir."

"Read and confirm. Latitude twenty-eight degrees, twenty minutes north."

The WO repeated the coordinates as he tapped them into the autoplotter.

"Longitude is eighty-four degrees, fifty minutes west. Confirmed? Roger. Petty Officer Grimes, please notify command and pass the word to our teams. ETA to intercept, Lieutenant?"

"Oh three-thirty hours, Commander."

"Thank you." Stennis turned then to Bear Raines. "Remind Mr. Godot that we will not board the Mexican vessel until the counterfeit is delivered and accepted."

"Excuse me, sir," Godot said, "but what if they tell me to come aboard myself?"

"Then you will."

"I don't know, Commander. Last time out, it was a pretty rough reception."

"You knew the risks going in, Mr. Godot."

Ricky Ricardo was watching *24* on TiVo and could not believe how the series had changed. "Where are the hombres?" he raged aloud. Where were the drills and prods and truncheons?

It was in the midst of that critique that a crewman arrived to tell his *jefe* that *The Crusader* was in sight.

"*Sí, sí.* Meet me at the boarding net," Ricardo growled from his widescreen.

"What you want to do when we get our product, boss?"

"Kill them. And scuttle the boat. I don't want anything left but an oil slick."

Ricky toyed with the diamond in his ear. He was willing to pay for additional consignments, at nearly any price, but the delivery had to be secure, and Ricky's supplier had told him the Marines were compromised. The Artist agreed that to ensure their mutual safety, the delivery boys had to be neutered.

A handful of gringos on a shrimp boat? *No problema.*

Ricky returned to the TV fix, shaking his head in disgust.

Even Jack Bauer was going soft.

Stennis had Terry's boat running dark on its approach to Ricardo's yacht. Terry stood as directed with the Coast Guarders posing as his crew when his boat pulled alongside the *Mi Casa*. Terry hoped that Ricky's men would simply toss a line, as usual, to haul the bags aboard. He didn't want another dose of the Zetas' hospitality.

"What if they tell us to come on board?" he asked the female commando at his side.

"You go. Don't worry, we'll be with you."

"That's a got-damn comfort."

Bear Raines looked on from the concealed vantage of the bridge. Stennis had already cut loose the assault boats from their towline. Those STABs were already low in the water on the other side of the *Mi Casa*. The choppers were hiding minutes away on the pad of an offshore rig. With luck, they wouldn't be needed.

"Looks like we have our horse to the Trojan's gate," Stennis observed coolly. "Just Greeks bearing gifts."

But the gifts had yet to be accepted.

Terry Godot notices that Ricky has killed the lights on his pleasure boat. On previous trips, the Mexican had had his show-off toy lit up like a Christmas tree stem to stern, but not this evening. Tonight, she was running dark.

"I don' like this shit," Terry groused, and then a search light speared him from the Mexican's deck.

"*BUENAS NOCHES, SEÑOR*," a voice boomed through a bullhorn.

"That's him. That's Ricardo," Terry muttered, and the female commando at his side relayed that intelligence to the bridge.

"We have this on video, Lieutenant?" Stennis asked from the bridge.

"Five-by, sir."

From his concealed vantage point, Barrett sees Ricardo lean far over the boarding net that sways down the hull of his ship. The drug lord smiling down on Terry Godot and his faux crew. The long hair falling to his shoulders. An ascot and cravat setting off his tux. The earring sparkling like the morning star.

"Dressed like a vampire," Bear muttered to himself.

"What is the matter, Gunnery Sergeant Godot? Cat got your tongue?"

"BAD MEMORIES, SEÑOR." Terry tried to put some balls in his reply. "BUT IT DIDN'T KEEP ME FROM DE-LIVERING YOUR COUNTERFEIT. IT'S ALL HERE."

"You are sure you did not take a little bite? Maybe some cards? Blackjack maybe? Or poker?"

"Naw, that was Raul, señor. Not me."

"Very well, then."

"You throw me a line, I can get these bags right up to you, señor."

Terry makes that offer as though it were a prayer.

But the gangster shrugged off that idea.

"I think I send someone over," Ricardo declined. "My people. No offense."

"None taken, but that's a whole lot of trouble," Terry shouted back. "If you could just throw a line . . ."

"I want to verify before I take delivery," Ricky declared grandly.

Barrett Raines sees the problem from the bridge.

"If Ricardo doesn't take those bags onto his ship, he can claim he didn't receive counterfeit," Bear tells the captain.

"Understood," Stennis acknowledged, and triggered the intrasquad radio. "Command to teams. Hold all action. Repeat, hold all action until my command. Confirm, please."

Whispered confirmation came in from all over the ship—from the assault crews amidships, from the snipers in the nets, from the engineers and boatmen ready to take over the *Mi Casa*'s engine room.

Stennis killed his ISR. "We have to play it out," he said.

By now, a pod of Zetas was snaking down the boarding net toward Terry's trawler. There were probably half a dozen men. They weren't bothering to hide the fact that they were armed. They dropped onto the shrimp boat's deck leisurely, like spiders.

Terry kicked the bags over. "See for yourself."

The nearest Mexican stood aside and another man carried a flashlight, a UV light, and a microscope over to the bags.

He opened both bags, dug out wads of bills, and laid them on the deck. Each man on the American side held his breath until that inspection was complete.

The inspector tossed the bags of fake bills into the duffel bags and looked up to Ricardo.

"*BUENO,*" he called out, and gave a thumbs-up.

"Bring it up."

Each of the two Zetas grabbed a bag. The remaining gunmen covered their climb back onto Ricardo's yacht, weapons trained casually on Terry and his crew. The bags were delivered into Ricardo's outstretched hands. Ricky pulled out a handful of counterfeit bells, kissed them. It was all recorded on video from the deck of Terry's trawler. And then Terry Godot did something he didn't need to do.

"BEST DAMN COUNTERFEIT YOU EVER BOUGHT, SEÑOR. AM I RIGHT?" he said.

"AND IT WON'T BE MY LAST," Ricardo promised. "BUT NOT FROM YOU, GRINGO."

Bear didn't see the shooter. No one did. The camcorder recorded the sharp report of a rifle. Terry Godot jerked back as if yanked on a ski lift. When he hit the deck, there was a red corsage blooming on his chest.

"RETURN FIRE," Commander Stennis ordered. "BOARD-ING TEAMS ARE GO. SNIPERS ARE GO. AIR SUPPORT TARGET AT WILL."

Within seconds, a small war was raging in the Gulf of Mexico. Ricky had his own teams laced on the deck of his yacht, well protected in the superstructure and with the advantage of height.

"HIT THE DECK," Stennis yelled, and yanked Bear Raines off his feet as machine-gun fire ripped through the bridge.

There's a saying that the best-made plans are thrown away once the shooting starts, but that's only half true. The

Coast Guard commandos kept to their plan. Stennis and his men had been in this situation before; they were ready with lines of fire and tactics designed to break out of this sort of ambush. That didn't mean things couldn't go wrong.

Barrett scrambled from the bridge, pulling his own sidearm on reflex. He saw Terry dead on the deck. He saw the muzzle flashes from the deck of the yacht, heard men cursing in Spanish.

But then Bear saw an assault boat bearing down fast on the stern of the Mexican-flagged boat. A commando steadied what looked like a fat tube on his shoulder. Barrett saw a bright white streak, a missile's flight. Seconds later, a TOW missile slammed into Ricky's yacht.

They're going for the rudder, Bear realized. They're going for the skeg or the rudderpost.

The first assault boat peeled off and a second boat made its run from the other side. The assault had the immediate effect of dividing Ricardo's fire, some of his men hosing the deck of Terry's trawler with automatic weapons as others diverted, sending rounds after the assault boats.

The Coast Guard's commandos never flinched. Those on Terry's shrimper battered the superstructure and deck of Ricky's vessel with short, controlled bursts of fires. The green's sniper picked off Zetas one by one. And then Barrett heard an explosion at the waterline—a satchel charge set amidships.

And then came the Stingrays.

Bear heard the familiar *thwop-thwop-thwop* of rotors and saw the steady flash of automatic weapons. The choppers strafed the deck of Ricky's ship with 40 mm slugs. You could see the chew of metal along the deck. Railings were cut in half like strings of spaghetti, as were the men. The hail of death from the sky broke the yacht's defense. There was confusion everywhere now. The boat was rudderless and taking on water. Ricky's men were taking fire from above and below and there was nowhere to hide.

The momentum swung, and in that instant the Guard's commandos snatched the advantage in the fight, one squad of greens hitting the nets as other PSUs provided laid down covering fire. In less than a minute, the first wave of shock troops fanned onto Ricky's deck almost unopposed. Then the crews from the assault boats pulled alongside for a second and has a third wave of assault. Once aboard, the fight turned urban. Coast Guard commandos fought Ricky's men from bulkhead to bulkhead, bow to stern, shooting, moving, and communicating.

It took all night, but by the break of dawn, the Coast Guard owned the listing vessel. It didn't come without cost. Three commandos had lost their lives in the firefight. Eight were wounded. Over twenty Zetas were wounded and nearly that many killed. Add to those casualties the former gunnery sergeant, Terry Godot. Medics tended the injured of both sides on the yacht's open deck until rescue choppers could effect evacuation. The dead would be put in body bags and loaded on Terry's trawler.

But Ricky Ricardo was nowhere to be found.

"He's either on his ship or he's gone overboard," Commander Stennis told his units. "Keep looking."

The sun had been up for an hour or more before Barrett Raines climbed the swaying grid of rope that led up to the deck of Ricky's yacht. The carnage triggered memories of his own months in combat. So long ago, so far away. Bear saw the splatter of blood on bulkheads, that timeless graffiti. He smelled cordite. It was all familiar.

"I believe these are yours, sir." A Coast Guardsman held out the twin bags of counterfeit. Barrett took the bags. He'd fill out paperwork to ensure a chain of custody. As for other evidence aboard the yacht, that would have to wait. Members of the Treasury Department and the FBI would pore over Ricky's vessel once it was towed to port. Bear was sure of that. The FDLE might even be invited to participate.

"A floating city of evidence" was how Bear described the ship to his Coast Guard escort.

Once the counterfeit was secured, there was not a lot to do but wait. It was odd to be so footloose in the midst of so much activity. Medics ran back and forth with IVs and compresses. Commandos combed the yacht. It didn't take long for Barrett to feel like he was just in the way.

"Commander, if it's okay with you, I'll just post back to the shrimp boat and start the report my boss is gonna want to see."

"Certainly, Agent Raines," Stennis approved graciously. "Tell Petty Officer Grimes he is now in command of the trawler. I will remain on the *Mi Casa* for the tow to port."

A pair of commandos assisted Barrett as he climbed down the rope ladder to what used to be Terry's shrimp boat.

"Thanks," Bear gasped as a PSU pulled him to the trawler's deck. "Shit, I think I'm gonna be sick."

"Happens to the best, sir. Feel free."

His guts spilled like a fish over the side. It took a minute or two after that for the dizziness to pass.

"You all right, sir?"

"Not exactly a sea lion," Bear confessed.

"Helps to find the horizon, sir," the young seaman offered. "And I believe there's some Gatorade in the deck box."

"Gatorade sounds good, thanks," Barrett said, and wove sternward.

The shrimp boat's deck box was longer than a freezer and deeper, set right behind the wheelhouse. No working fisherman could afford to have loose lines or fenders or other gear

233

unsecured, so the deck box was situated for safety as well as convenience. Bear wouldn't have been surprised if Terry'd cooled his beer back there.

He climbed over a pile of net to the whitewashed box. A padlock's U-bar was looped through a brass hasp to secure the lid, but the box was unlocked. Barrett slipped off the padlock and raised the lid. A cooler sat atop a foul-smelling tangle of lines and Styrofoam fenders.

"Messy," Bear said, but it felt good to plunge his arm into the cooler. He pulled out a Gatorade, snapped the Igloo shut, dropped the deck box's lid, and threaded the padlock's U-bar back through the hasp. He was heading sternward with his ice-cold drink when he heard a scratch of movement behind, some gull or perhaps a pelican. But when he glanced back, there was nothing there. Nothing but the white deck box.

A white box.

But Bear missed something when first opening the box, because now he saw that there were smudges along the top of its freshly painted lid. Dark brown streaks ran right along the top. Most folks wouldn't think twice about a white box getting soiled on a shrimp boat. Could be grease off somebody's hands. Could be the slime off some net or line tossed on the deck box. Could be paint, even. But Barrett has seen these streaks before—many times, in fact. The texture and color were familiar and he knew it was not grease staining the deck box. It was not the mark of some carelessly tossed line.

And it was not paint.

A fresh wave of nausea came at the very instant he couldn't afford it. Bear fumbled the Glock from its holster, making damn sure the safety was disengaged. He leaned over and carefully slipped the padlock free. Then he staggered back to take cover behind a pile of netting, his gun extending in a cup and saucer grip.

"I'm covered here, Ricardo. You got one chance to get out of that box alive, and you best take it, or I'm going to stitch your ass end to end."

No reply. No movement.

Barrett sights along his barrel and fires. The wood splinters.

"Next one's for you, Ricky."

The lid opens, exposing a soaking-wet hand attached to a soaking-wet tuxedo.

"Throw out your weapon."

"I am unarmed," comes the voice from inside.

"Throw it out or I'm killing you, Ricardo."

The movement was a little slower this time, but the second hand emerges with an Uzi.

"Drop it."

The weapon clatters to the deck.

"And I'm guessing you carry a handgun."

This time, it took a little longer, but a Beretta rattled on the deck near the machine gun.

"All right, now get out. Hands on head."

His head came up first, the dark hair framing an acne-scarred face, the rock bright in his ear. Ricky was wounded; Bear saw the crease of a slug across his shoulder.

"You must be . . . the Negro."

"And you must be the son of bitch tried to take my son."

The yacht's spanking-clean gymnasium became the drug lord's calaboose. Bear cuffed Ricardo to the steel rack on which Brenda Mantle had been tortured. Barrett noted the video cam on its tripod nearby, the stack of DVDs. Evidence of other crimes, no doubt.

"You're going to jail, Ricky," Barrett informed his prisoner. "If you rat out your enemies, which I expect you to do, and if you finger the source of your fake currency, you might, just might, avoid the death penalty for murdering a federal agent. Maybe. In which case, you'll spend the rest of your life begging guards for smokes in Colorado.

"On the other hand, if you decide to play macho man, my boy will be playing center field on his Little League team just about the time they strap you to a gurney."

"I never rat my people!" Ricky spit from his chair. "As for the counterfeiter, the artist? All I do is wire the money. He delivers. I pay. There is no face, no name."

Ricardo lifted his shoulders, dropped them.

"He is not my people. If I could help myself by giving that one up, of course I would do it. Why not?"

Ricky eyed Barrett.

"If I had an e-mail address? Maybe a phone number? I give you that, can you get me off for the woman?"

"Let's not forget Raul Carerra. Or maybe Dawana Jackson?"

"She sister to Michael Jackson?"

"Yeah, keep that up, Ricky. That'll help."

The drug lord grabbed his shoulder and groaned.

"I need another shot."

"You cain't always get what you want, Ricardo. But comes to needles, you'll get what you deserve."

21

Unfinished Business

The Mi Casa was towed safely to Pensacola and impounded. Investigators would be gleaning evidence from that vessel for weeks and weeks, but Barrett Raines and the FDLE were not invited to contribute. That was okay by Bear. It wasn't like he didn't have a ton of work piled up. Not to mention personal obligations.

Bear could not avoid Dawana Jackson's funeral. Corporal Jackson was buried in the cemetery behind Barrett's home church in a donated plot beneath a grove of water oaks. Not a stick of grass on that sandy yard, which would make Dawana feel right at home. Preacher Theo brought Fannie's daughter back to her community, never once alluding to suicide.

"She wanted to be a hero, a warrior," the preacher told his congregation. "However misguided, she wanted to serve God. Our Dawana was not perfect. 'For all have sinned and come short of the Glory of God.' We're all sinners, Lord knows. But in Him, we are sinners with hope."

Chaplain Frank Swain attended Dawana's funeral, but not in a formal role. Barrett saw the priest make a special effort to console Fannie Jackson.

"She was one of my best," the chaplain told Dawana's mother.

There was a potluck dinner afterward—chicken and rice and banana pudding, sweet tea by the gallon. And singing. Lots of singing.

Terry Godot, on the other hand, was buried unsung, unclaimed, and without honors in a county grave.

"He betrayed his men," Chaplain Swain told Bear sadly at their Little League field. "It's a shame, it really is. A damned shame."

The only veteran of Terry's outfit left alive was Buddy Hewitt, and Buddy would not be leaving jail. He was facing multiple federal charges related to transport of counterfeit and seemed resigned to doing time. That case alone buried Barrett in paperwork.

Bear completed his last interview with Corporal Hewitt a few days after Dawana's funeral.

"You're a pain in the ass, Buddy, you know that?"

"Sorry for the bother."

"One thing I still am not clear about is Quentin Hart."

"Quentin? He was just a mule. Just like the rest of us."

"And that ate at him so bad, he'd kill himself?"

"Not for that, no. It wasn't the counterfeiting."

"What was it, then?"

Buddy leaned back from the metal table separating them, and for the first time Bear thought he saw some sign of genuine remorse.

"Bad as you think we are, Bear, we done things worse."

That was all he would say. Barrett couldn't get any more out of him.

Cricket Bonet wrote off Bud's cryptic remark as a tease, a ploy for sympathy.

"Hewitt's going to use PTSD as a justification for every crime he ever committed. It was the war, he'll say, and tell us we should all feel sorry for him."

"Not gonna fly," Bear countered that prediction at his partner's bedside in an orthopedic ward in Gainesville.

Cricket had been rushed to surgery directly from Devil's Slew, but was back in the hospital so the pins drilled into the bone of his fibula could be adjusted. The pins were inserted from outside the shattered limb. Looked like his leg was stuck in a bird cage.

"Jesus, what a mess." Bear offered that crude sympathy to his partner.

"Be better when I can get back to work. Speaking of—did you see those records I sent you?"

"Records?"

"Military records. For Dawana Jackson."

"They're probably under a pile on my desk."

Cricket nodded. "I took a look."

"Yeah? See anything interesting?"

"There was a letter of reprimand."

"For Dawana?"

"Yes indeed. Poor judgment. Conduct unbecoming. Specifically, she attempted to intimidate a local woman, an interpreter in Nangarhar, who'd accused some GI of rape. Must have pissed Dawana off big-time. She cornered the local woman at chow hall and called her out."

"Any idea who, exactly, she was defending?"

Cricket shook his head.

"The accused wasn't named, for obvious reasons. But there was an officer mentioned in conjunction with the case, a JAG."

"Dawana's lawyer?"

"No, the interpreter's. Some air force major. Track him down, maybe you could get something useful."

Barrett got the major's name off a letter appended to Dawana's Article 15. That letter specified the name of the Afghani interpreter assaulted by Dawana in the chow hall as an indigenous person whose legal claim was still under review. The person accused of raping Gulpari Bhotri was not provided. In fact, the name of the accused was protected officially, which convinced Barrett that the person had to be someone Dawana had known personally. More than that, someone she felt honor-bound to protect.

First candidate on Bear's list was Quentin Hart. Had Quentin raped a married woman in Afghanistan? Was that the sin that led him to an early grave?

Barrett fired off an e-mail to his air force liaison, seeking contact information for Maj. Steve Saitta, but he was told the major was discharged from active duty. Figuring that Saitta was probably returned to private practice, Bear hit the professional rosters available over the Internet and came up with four possible matches. After that it was a matter of leaving phone calls on message machines or with indifferent secretaries.

He was surprised how quickly Steve Saitta called him back.

"I'm returning a call from Agent Barrett Raines? Regarding a letter of reprimand for a former service member?"

"This is Agent Raines."

"Steve Saitta. How'd you get my name?"

"You had a letter attached to Dawana Jackson's Article Fifteen file."

"So how'd you get those records, Agent Raines?"

"Dawana Jackson is dead. We haven't ruled out homicide. She was also connected with criminal activity resulting in federal charges. The Office of Homeland Security authorized release of her records to the FDLE."

"I see. Well, assuming that is the case, I'm not sure how I can help you. Jackson wasn't my client."

"Understood. But then, Corporal Jackson was reprimanded by article for verbally threatening a local translator named in your letter. A woman who came to you with an accusation she'd been raped?"

"Gulpari Bhotri, yes."

"Can you tell me what came of that accusation?"

"Nothing."

Bear paused over the phone.

"Excuse me, Steve, but something must have happened; otherwise, Dawana Jackson wouldn't have accosted Miss Bhotri in a base cafeteria."

"Mrs. Bhotri—she was married. And by 'nothing,' I mean that no legal action was taken against any service member connected with the alleged rape of Gulpari Bhotri. There was no administrative action taken, no articles or court-martial. Not even a preliminary hearing."

"Why not?"

"Because Gulpari Bhotri and her family were killed by a Marine Corps Special Ops squad within days of her complaint."

Bear felt the hair rise on his arms.

"Any chance there was a gunnery sergeant named Terry Godot involved with that operation?"

"Not at liberty to say."

"Or a Randall Hewitt? Or a Raul Carrera? How 'bout Corp. Quentin Hart?"

A silence fell on the other end of the line, and for a second, Bear thought the attorney had hung up on him.

"Here's what I can do," Saitta said finally. "Mrs. Bhotri

has a relative living in Florida. Her brother. You can contact Dr. Jangi Nuhrani through the Department of Engineering at the University of Florida. I have his number. But a word of caution: This is an incendiary topic. He will not be happy to get your call."

Barrett took the number and thanked the attorney, but as he hung up, he couldn't help wondering if he was chasing geese. Certainly there was nothing an Afghani engineer could tell him that would help him find the still-unidentified source of counterfeit in northern Florida or improve his understanding of Raul Carrera's murder or Dawana Jackson's hanging. Certainly, Dawana's letter of reprimand did nothing to disprove the received judgment that Los Zetas was responsible for Raul's death.

But a war crime might explain Quentin Hart's drive to suicide. It would certainly explain why military commanders pulled the plug on Gunnery Sergeant Godot's Special Ops unit. The report of action clearly established that Sarge and his squad were solely responsible for the attack on the translator's home. The report also buttressed Barrett's conviction that the translator's accusation of rape threatened somebody in Terry's unit. Dawana Jackson's cafeteria tirade made that connection probable, and Buddy Hewitt's veiled reference to overseas sins could certainly include a rape and a cover-up. Those sins might lead a young man with a troubled conscience to suicide.

But how could a rape overseas run Raul Carrera off the road or put a noose around Dwana Jackson's neck? Those questions crawled like lice in Bear's scalp.

He started by contacting Gulpari Bhotri's brother. Bear found a good head shot of Dr. Jangi Khan Nuhrani on a University of Florida Web site dedicated to petroleum engineers. The professor was very clear he was not happy to be called at work by anyone from any law-enforcement agency, and he was openly hostile to a request for a meeting until Bear told him that the female marine who verbally assaulted his sister in Afghanistan had been found hanged behind her home.

"Ah," came the immediate response. "Then perhaps there is some justice."

Barrett decided he'd better interview the professor on his own time, which meant a Saturday drive to Gainesville. He wanted to take the Malibu, but Rolly Slade told him the car would not be finished until midafternoon.

"The side mirror we got in was for an Impala. Sorry, Bear. Tell you what, though, I'll put in your satellite radio for free. How's that?"

"I'll see you this afternoon," Bear assented and then called Mike Traiwick to request a ride for the twins to their Saturday practice.

"No problem," Mike assured him. "It's right on my way."

Those chores accomplished, Barrett swung by the restaurant for a cup of java to go, kissed Laura Anne good-bye, and hit the road, his XM receiver plugged into the cigarette lighter and the eighties channel.

It took about an hour and a half to reach Gainesville. Nuhrani had directed Bear to meet him at some joint called the Reggae Shack, which turned out to be a funky venue for Jamaican cuisine set across University Avenue from an office-supply business. Bear arrived way early. He liked Gainesville. It was nice to see pine and oak and Spanish moss lining a city boulevard.

Could be crowded, though, especially during football season. The Florida Gators were playing Tennessee in 'the Swamp' and every parking spot for miles was taken. Barrett passed lots filled end to end with expensive RVs, Newells and Marathons and Prevost motor homes fitted with push-outs and satellite dishes. Fans feasted beneath rollout awnings on beer and barbecue.

You'd never guess one out of every eight Americans was on food stamps. One child out of every four.

Barrett found a place to park his car in a lot behind the café. He stepped out of the way at the street-side door in deference to a bevy of giddy coeds in tight sweaters and tighter jeans before entering. Dr. Hurani was already waiting in a wraparound booth.

First impressions: a well-groomed beard, slight build, a full head of raven hair, and deeply set eyes. The professor was dressed like an Ivy Leaguer in ribbed slacks and a sports coat. But he wore sandals with his wool socks. And no tie. He was Pashtun, Bear guessed. Most Afghans didn't have surnames; Nuhrani might refer to a tribe.

"Am I late, Doctor?"

It was more polite to address Afghans by title than by name; he remembered that much.

"No, I prefer the advantage," the professor replied. He did not stand from his booth or extend his hand.

"I'm sorry to drag up bad memories." Bear seated himself without asking permission. "And I am sorry to intrude on your privacy, Professor, but as I imagine you know, it's next to impossible to get information from the military chain of command about operations overseas. Especially where the deaths of civilians are involved."

"These were not normal deaths, Agent Raines. This was butchery, a massacre."

Barrett was taken aback. He thought he was prepared for some expression of vitriol from the reclusive professor, but the abrupt claim of a massacre, delivered flat and without emotion, was not expected.

Nuhrani eyed him carefully. "How much do you know about my sister, Mr. Raines?"

"Nothing," Bear replied. "Next to nothing. I know she worked for U.S. forces in northeastern Afghanistan. She was described as a translator."

"An interpreter, yes. She worked hard at it."

"And she was married?" Barrett asked.

"To my wife's brother," Nuhrani confirmed. "He was working in Pakistan at the time, which is the only reason he is now alive. Alive, I might say, and killing Americans."

"He have some special reason to kill Americans?"

"Would he need one?"

Nuhrani nodded to the street outside.

"Imagine there is some barricade out on this street. This lovely Florida avenue. But there is a checkpoint manned by, say, Chinese military. Your wife is on the way to pick up your kids. She sees a roadblock, thinks it's an accident, pulls around the sawhorse, and is machine-gunned to death. How would you feel about that?"

"I'd hate it, of course."

"Well, that is daily life in Afghanistan," Nuhrani told him. "That and death from jetting aircraft, death from Predator drones."

"Death from the Taliban, too. In fairness."

"In fairness, yes." The professor nodded. "But there was nothing fair about my sister's death. She had nothing to do with the Taliban. Hers was not 'collateral damage.' It was murder."

"Tell me about it."

The Afghani man took in a deep breath, exhaled.

"It is hard to make this effort. We have spoken to authorities before, my family and I. Many times. We have engaged attorneys. We have written congressmen, senators. No one listened."

"I'm listening."

Nuhrani sized him up a moment more.

"Is that a pen in the pocket of your blazer?"

"It is."

"Then use it. Because as my students will attest, I hate repeating myself."

The story came out in one short narrative.

"I am Muslim, as you may have guessed, but my sister was Christian. Catholic, actually. The discredited Gospel of Thomas has Saint Thomas preaching in Bactria, in what is now northern Afghanistan. I was raised in the faith myself until submitting to Allah."

He smiled.

"A powerful experience. I recommend it. At any rate, when the Americans came, my sister, then living in abject circumstances, saw a way to support herself and her family by serving U.S. forces in the capacity of interpreter.

"Gulpari courted death every day she went to work, but she accepted that risk. She had no illusions about the Taliban. Unfortunately, with Americans, she proved to be naïve.

"You already know that a specially trained cadre of marines was sent to Nangarhar. My sister was embedded with that unit. She wrote me letters about the excellent Gunnery Sergeant Godot, and the pitiful efforts to impress from Corporal Hewitt. She went to combat with these men. She even went to Mass with them.

"But someone in their company put something in Gulpari's food or drink, because though she was raped—repeatedly, according to an examining physician—my sister had no memory of the event. It was as though twelve hours of her life had been erased.

"Imagine being put in that position in Afghanistan! Her family disowned her. Her husband, I am sure, would have killed her had he learned of it. She wrote to me and told me she had an idea who had drugged and assaulted her and that a DNA test was possible."

"She give you a name?"

"No." He shook his head. "She wanted to get the DNA test first. Gulpari was not one to falsely accuse. Can you imagine anyone more noble?"

"No, I can't."

Nuhrani took a moment to compose himself.

"I told her to have the doctors check for drugs. I don't remember which."

"Rohypnol, maybe?" Bear suggested. "Addicts call it the 'Forget Pill,' the 'Mind Eater.'"

"I am unfamiliar. But in any case, she was not tested until four or five days after her assault, and by then, whatever was present had passed from her system."

Barrett shook his head. This was a difficult crime to investigate even in enlightened jurisdictions with forensic support. But in Nangarhar?

"So nobody believed your sister," Bear said, filling in the blanks. "They figured she would have sex if it meant keeping her job."

"Or worse," her brother added. "But there was one gentleman, an air force lawyer—"

"Major Saitta." Bear jotted a note. "That's how I got your name."

"Saitta, yes. Very professional. He was skeptical of Gulpari's claim initially, but he became convinced that my sister was raped by someone close to her when, within days of filing an initial report of sexual assault, Gulpari was killed with her mother and sister by marines in an action officially described as a raid on a Taliban safe house."

Barrett looked out the window to the avenue beyond, a winter's light softened by pine needles and moss. Barrett pictured a Chinese soldier lipping a cigarette on the street outside the café window. The red star.

The banana clip of an AK-47.

"Was there ever any specific tie between the action that killed your sister and Sergeant Godot?"

"Was his unit. The summary of action claimed the Taliban were using my sister's home to cache weapons. There were guns found in the house after the assault. Naturally. Someone in the chain of command obviously was not fooled, because the whole battalion was sent home early. A cover-up, from my point of view, and probably not the only one."

Bear folded the worn covers of his spiral pad.

"For what it's worth, Doctor, I believe you. I don't know if there's a damn thing I can do about it. I won't promise you that. But I'll try. I will try."

It was then that Gulpari Bhotri's brother extended his hand.

"Then we part as friends."

The drive back to Deacon Beach gave Bear Raines a chance to digest the import of Dr. Nuhrani's testament. Bear started by granting the premise that Terry Godot's unit murdered Nuhrani's sister to prevent Gulpari from pressing charges of rape. Next question: Which member of their outfit were the Crusaders protecting? It could have been any of the twenty or so noncoms assigned to the company, obviously, but Dawana's angry defense predisposed Bear to believe that someone in her inner circle had to be the accused party.

There were many cases of GIs using drugs in connection with sexual assault. Certainly the marines in Godot's inner cadre could have obtained Rohypnol or something similar. GIs got pills from home or from Internet sources. Military personnel working in pharmacies too often stole controlled meds for sale on the black market. It would not be hard to get a "Forget Pill" if you had cash to pay. So who among Dawana's favorites was the most likely candidate to have doped and raped a local translator?

Could Buddy Hewitt have done it? Barrett remembered Nuhrani's comment about Buddy's efforts at flirtation. Buddy was not the sort of person who'd endure snubs lightly. Clearly, Hewitt had a short fuse, and of all the mules on Terry's crew, Bud was conspicuous for striking out with the girls. He was pissed off and repressed and he abused drugs. On the other hand, an equally compelling case could be made that Quentin Hart had committed the rape and that his buddies, protecting him, slaughtered Gulpari Bhotri with her mother and sister. That would explain Quentin's guilt and his suicide-by-cop.

And then there was Sarge. Barrett had no basis to rule out Terry Godot as a candidate capable of rape. At a minimum, it had to have been Gunnery Sergeant Godot who organized the translator's slaughter and who planted evidence to implicate Gulpari as a Taliban sympathizer. If Sarge did not commit the rape, he certainly orchestrated the execution and cover-up. And, finally, it was entirely possible, maybe probable, that Dr. Nuhrani's sister was gang-raped by the entire squad. That was a scenario so common in war as to have become, from a certain perspective, jejune.

Did Quentin Hart hold back? Barrett wondered. Is that why he was not fully trusted by his comrades?

But how could Bear prove any of it? Three of the Crusaders were already beyond justice, including the gunny himself. Buddy Hewitt was the Outfit's sole survivor and Bud was not about to implicate himself. Bear could see nothing on the road ahead but a NO OUTLET sign.

He made it back to Deacon Beach by early afternoon. The boys were still at practice, which gave him time to check on the repair of his Malibu. The little bell above the door of Rolly Slade's tin-can shop tinkled as Barrett entered.

"Bear, how are you?"

"Itching to drive my muscle car."

"She's ready. Come on back and let me show you what I did with your sattelite radio."

Rolly opened a service door for his customer and followed Barrett into the body shop. A pair of fans churned, even in winter. A high roof, no ceiling. Trusses all the way across and benches of tools and tires. Bear spotted his Super Sport right away. Maroon and spotless, the SS logo prominent in polished chrome.

"You washed her."

"Detailed, actually."

"You didn't have to do that, Rolly."

"I kept the damn thing long enough to own it, Bear. Felt like I owed you something."

" 'Preciate that. How 'bout the radio?"

Rolly opened the door for Barrett.

"Why don't you pop that console? That's your new receiver, see how I got it installed? This way, when you're not driving, you can take it out. I usually put mine in the trunk."

"That's slick, Rolly."

Barrett closed the console and ducked his head as he pulled out of his car. That's when he spotted a pickup across the shop. A pickup minus a bumper.

"Whose truck is that?"

Rolly followed Bear's line of sight. "The Chevy? That's Frank's truck. Frank Swain."

"Where's the bumper?"

"Out back in the pile. He wants a new one."

"A new bumper?"

"He hit a deer. Came in wanting a new bumper and grille. I told him I could fix up the bumper just fine. Beat it out. Paint it. I could even chrome it, but Father Frank said, no, he wanted a new one, something tougher, so I ordered a brush guard. Four hundred damn dollars. Should be in this week. You need a truck?"

"Thought about it. Between baseball and Boy Scouts, and then there's the kayak."

"Well, this one's for sale, and check this out—Father Frank's donating every dime to the Veterans' Center."

"That's generous," Barrett replied. "But I'd be happy with the original bumper. Knock four hundred off the price?"

He saw the younger man hesitate.

"Rolly, you said you could fix the old bumper."

"Except Frank told me to get rid of the original."

"Father Frank told you?"

"He said it really bothered him, hitting the deer, which I fully understand. And then he told me to make sure the bumper was never used for anything other than scrap metal. Gave me fifty dollars."

"Nothing wrong with that."

"No. Except I didn't do it."

"Why not?"

251

" 'Cause it's foolish, is why. A waste. Bear, I can clean that bumper up and chrome it and put it on somebody else's truck for a hell of lot less than I would spend on a new one."

Bear strolled over to Swain's pickup. A Chevrolet Silverado. Late model. Single cab.

"Hit a deer," he repeated. "Look that way to you?"

"It was all nicked up."

"Any blood?"

"He'd run it through a car wash."

Car wash? For a deer?

Bear knelt down to look beneath the truck.

"Don't remember when this happened, do you? Just approximately?"

"Couple of weekends back. I can check the computer."

Couple of weekends?

Barrett checked his mental calendar. Then he stood slowly. Dusted off the knee of his slacks.

"Rolly, I'd appreciate you pinning down the date Frank brought in this vehicle."

"Sure."

"But first I need to see that bumper."

Bear Raines used plastic to pay for the Mailbu's repair and headed straight for the practice field. The Little League field looked great, freshly mowed and marked off in anticipation of the final game of the season. It was great to see Mike Traiwick coaching the boys in the subtleties of a double play. Ben was taking his turn on second base. And Brady Hart was back on the field with his team.

"Thank you, Lord," Bear prayed aloud, and settled into his usual spot on the bleachers.

It was perfect weather for any sport—bright and crisp,

hardly any wind. Bear stretched out in the sun and waited for Father Frank Swain to mosey over.

"Barrett. How goes it?"

"Well, Father. You?"

The priest nods toward the field.

"I see Brady's back in his cleats."

Barrett smiles.

"Noticed that myself. Damn good thing."

"Too much sadness lately," the former chaplain said, settling beside Barrett. "Maybe things are about to improve."

"They might, they just might." Barrett bobbed his head. "And speaking of improvements, how's it look for our Veterans' Center?"

"Mike Traiwick says we have almost two hundred thousand banked and commitments for at least fifty more."

"I heard you were making a contribution."

"How's that?"

"Your truck."

"Oh, well, I hardly deserve credit. I don't need the thing, and we need every nickel we can find for this center."

"I'm thinking of buying it," Barrett declared.

"Are you?" Frank kept his gaze on the field.

"What with baseball and Boy Scouts." Barrett rolled his shoulders.

"You've got plenty to haul." The priest chuckled.

"Gotta shave some off the price, though."

"I'm sure Rolly will work with you."

"He's already trimmed off four hundred dollars."

"That's a pretty decent discount."

"Not a discount, really. I just told him I didn't need the new bumper."

"You planning on buying a truck without a bumper?"

"No, no. I just told Rolly to put the old one back on."

Frank Swain kept his eyes on the field of play.

"I told Rolly to get rid of the original."

"And he was going to." Bear nodded. "Matter of fact, Rolly'd already thrown your old bumper on the scrap pile, but we figured if repairing the original means I can afford to buy the truck, then the Veterans' Center gets over four thousand dollars cash. I'll pay you back the fifty you gave Rolly. Pay you in cash if you like. Seems like a fair proposition. What do you think, Father?"

The priest adjusted the visor of his hat. "Caveat emptor, Barrett."

"It's just a truck bumper," Bear assured him. "Doesn't matter to me if it's scratched up."

Father Frank Swain knew he had to get his bumper back. He made small talk with Barrett Raines for a few minutes more, but then left practice early in the parish's battered Corolla. Frank hated to admit it, but he knew he was slothful in many ways, and this time it had come back to bite him.

A truck bumper! He should have taken it off himself. Frank always said he wasn't handy with his hands, but that was a lie. He just hated getting his hands soiled. You paid people to do that sort of work. Clear a sewage line. Shovel snow off a sidewalk. Pull a bumper off your truck.

Of course, he might be overreacting. He'd cleaned the Chevy's damaged grille and guard before taking it to Rolly's shop. Well, he ran it through a car wash. That should have been enough, but with all the new science available, you couldn't be sure. It took only one speck of paint to put a man under suspicion, and Father Frank could not afford any prolonged examination. That's why he'd told Rolly to destroy the bumper.

Crush it. Bury it. That's what Slade was supposed to do. That's what he'd paid him to do!

And now for a savings of four hundred measly pieces of silver, the simpleton had put him at risk of being discovered! He could not allow it. Especially with Buddy Hewitt still alive. The onetime chaplain struggled to remain calm, at peace. The good news was that Rolly's shop was closed from Saturday night through Monday morning, and the chain-link fence out back would not be a problem, not even for a man who hated dirty hands. He'd break into the yard, take the bumper, and destroy it himself. That's what he'd do. Time enough, then, to deal with Corporal Hewitt. Prisoners were always happy to see their chaplain. He would come, Frank told himself, like a thief in the night.

He always had.

22

Stakeout

Barrett Raines established a stakeout inside the junk-filled yard fenced off behind Rolly Slade's shop. It was Bear's decision to establish surveillance from inside the chain-link fence. Frank Swain wasn't going to risk a break-in if he saw any hint of surveillance outside the perimeter of Rolly's shop, and it would be extremely tough to plant deputies and vehicles unseen around Rolly's exposed location, so a stakeout was established right in the middle of Slade's spare parts.

They'd already gone through three shifts, Bear keeping vigil with Smoot and his deputies on rotating shifts from Saturday night onward. So far, no one had breeched the yard, much less taken the damaged truck bumper. If by Monday morning the bait remained untaken, Bear was beat and he knew it, and it was now close to three o'clock, Monday morning.

"First time I ever set up a stakeout in a car that couldn't chase," Smoot remarked.

The sheriff had the passenger seat next to Bear in the fiberglass shell of what used to be a '63 Avanti. The hood was raised for easy cover to display a cavity where the 327 V-8 ought to have been.

"Goddamn crime, car like this settin' out to rot."

"Totally," Bear said, appropriating his kids' patois.

"You think he'll come?"

"If he's guilty, he'll have to."

The Avanti sat on rusting wheels with a sheltered view of Rolly's pile of parts, everything from transmissions to tire irons. Before leaving for the ballpark, Bear helped Rolly locate Frank's damaged bumper. He'd dragged the battered guard out from beneath a pile of scrap iron and made sure to place it in easy view in the middle of the yard.

The Studebaker provided a good view of the yard's interior and also of the gate allowing access. Nothing but a padlock on a thin chain secured that portal. The light wasn't great. A pitiful bulb at the gate wasn't much help, and scuds of clouds passed at intervals to crowd out a fickle sliver of moon.

And Smoot missed his radio.

"My cruiser, I can get Rush Limbaugh round-the-clock," the sheriff said.

Barrett ignored the bait.

"We got a bogey."

Sheriff Rawlings craned for a look over his shoulder.

"I don't see— Hold up. Yessir. Somebody's busy."

The moon pulsed briefly, outlining a silhouette at the gate.

"Hooded up. Like a sweatshirt," Smoot whispered.

Or a cowl, Bear thought.

"Bolt cutter," Rawlings rasped. "He's cuttin' the chain."

"That's what we want." Bear nodded.

The gate opened and the intruder stepped in, hesitated.

"Come on," Bear urged. "Come on in."

"He's spooked," Smoot whispered. "He's backing off."

But, no, a flashlight dropped a pool of light at the trespasser's feet.

"Here he comes."

Wouldn't you know that after planting the truck's bumper in plain sight, the intruder would work the whole damn periphery before reaching the center of the yard?

"Here he comes, here he comes." The sheriff's hand wrapped about the stock of a shotgun.

"We don't nail him till he's out the gate," Barrett warned. "We don't want any doubt."

The intruder finally reached the pile of scrap in the center of Rolly's yard. He saw the Chevy's bumper right away, dropped a bag to the ground.

"He's riggin' a sling," Smoot mouthed. "So he won't have to drag it."

"That's good," Bear acknowledged. "That's premeditation."

It takes only moments to tie off the rope on the bent and damaged bumper. The man slips that rude sling over his shoulders and hoists the metal guard.

And then he stops.

"He hears us!"

"He's paranoid," Bear disagrees. "Just let him get back to the gate."

The thief scanned the yard carefully. Finally satisfied, he turned back for the gate, the heavy bumper banging off his shins. It seemed to Barrett that it took a half hour for the hooded thief to cover the thirty yards back to Rolly's gate. It took about two seconds for Agent Raines and Sheriff Rawlings to pile out of their classic car.

"HALT." Smoot aimed a flashlight down the barrel of his shotgun to frame the thief at the gate and Barrett leveled his fast-repeating handgun.

"BARRETT RAINES, FDLE. Just hold what you got, Father Frank. I'd hate to nail a man carrying his own cross."

By the time Sheriff Rawlings had Frank Swain printed and booked, the sun was well risen and Frank Swain had a lawyer.

"First time I ever arrested a priest." Smoot shook his head. "And for murder! Hard to believe."

"That's what he's counting on," Barrett replied. "He still thinks a jury will let him off. And they might for a single murder supported only by circumstantial evidence. But I don't think a jury will let him get away with two in a row."

"Two murders—are you talking about Dawana Jackson? 'Cause you're gonna need a hell of a lot more than a truck bumper to make that charge stick."

"You're right, Smoot. No doubt. Which is why I'm making one more trip back to Devil's Slew."

23

Back to the Scene

It didn't take long for Devil's Slew to swallow up Fannie Jackson's sharecropper's shack. The fence was already down. The yard, always raked and spotless before Fannie moved away, was sprouting a beard of Bahia and johnsongrass and the beam of the porch sagged over a pier given way to rot. Bear Raines could have driven his Crown Vic right up to the front steps if he'd wanted to.

Nothing inside but a porcelain pan and muslin curtains. No photos, no furniture. The house listed like a boat taking on water, the sun pouring through unscreened windows to catch motes of dust in whimsied transport. A slough of wind playing the solitary chimney like a flutophone. Somebody said Fannie put everything she owned in the back of the preacher's truck and still had room left over. She was at Dowling Park now, a ward living on Social Security.

Nothing is emptier than an empty house.

The cane mill out back fared better in comparison, as it

had been broken for years. The hens were gone, but that ornery little bantam rooster remained, the cock of a walk now abandoned. Barrett did not intend to research the house, or the mill, but there were a couple of things that had brought him back to the scene of the crime. The first was the suicide note. Was too easy to plant a text message, and even though her prints were on the phone, Barrett had never been sure that Dawana composed the self-incriminating note so conveniently available to investigators.

The next thing that bothered Agent Raines was that the FDLE never found Dawana's fatigue jacket. It was the only coat Dawana owned, and Bear could not imagine her lasting through a freezing evening without it, but the jacket was never found. And lastly, there was the wound on Jackson's thigh. Bear was reasonably sure that Dawana got cut going over the barbed-wire fence that ran the perimeter of the pasture behind her home. Sheriff Rawlings was sure this was the case, but there was no blood found on the fence between the sugarcane mill and the house.

That didn't mean anything, really. Only in TV shows was evidence perfectly preserved. There was dew all over the crime scene when investigators arrived that morning. It might even have showered sometime the night before. That would have been more than enough to wash a speck of blood or a thread of fabric off a fence line.

On the other hand, what if they'd been looking at the wrong part of the fence?

When the FDLE's techs joined deputies at Fannie's homestead, they approached the house from the only road available, the same road Barrett used to return to the scene on this morning. In the initial search, everything from the road to the mill out back was gridded off. Working toward the center of the scene, Julie Fannon scrubbed the house and mill thoroughly, including the surrounding yard and grounds. But no one extended a search beyond the pasture and into Devil's Slew. Why would they? Dawana was hanging in plain sight of the house and there was only one road coming in.

But Barrett Raines was thinking a killer might not have come by the road. If he was determined. Or if he was desperate.

Bear walked straight through the shack's dog-run hall and out the back steps of Fannie's house, taking a line past the sugarcane mill, past Dawana's gallows, and over the pasture of Bahia grass to the fence line beyond.

By the time he reached the far side of the pasture, Raines was shivering with cold and his trousers were soaking wet. The fence line was as broken-down as the rest of Fannie's property, the posts hanging in barbed wire like rotten teeth in rusty braces.

Barrett walked the line back and forth for twenty yards or so. He did not expect to find anything on the wire, and he wasn't disappointed. But beyond the fence was Devil's Slew. Beyond the verge of knee-high grass were rattlesnakes and wild boar and gators and traps with teeth large enough to snap off a man's leg like a stick of celery. Barrett took out a pair of wire cutters from his pocket and cut the fence. When he stepped through, his shoes sank to his ankles.

Barrett tested the ground carefully. Be a bitch to come out here and die in quicksand. He cast about for a walking stick and settled on a length of deadwood pine. With that timber, Bear prodded about and quickly found a rim of terra firma leading around the bog that bordered Fannie's fence. Within a few yards, he recognized a trail. It was a pig trail; Bear knew the signs from childhood. Wild pigs knew what ground was safe and what wasn't. This particular patch ran past a riot of mimosa trees for a good hundred yards, snaking deeper into the slough, past hardwood trees and pines and blackberry vines nude of fruit, to reach an open glade bordered by sentries of gray-green palmetto. That was where Barrett found what he hoped to find. It had been buried hastily behind the palmettos in a shallow hole, but the hogs had dug it up.

Drawn without doubt, by the smell.

Frank Swain would eventually be charged with a felony burglary and two counts of first-degree murder. In addition to other evidence, a grand jury would receive unclassified documents identifying Lieutenant Colonel Swain as the accused rapist of Gulpari Bhotri. Buddy Hewitt would confirm in his testimony that Dawana Jackson had insisted Gulpari Bhotri was working for the Taliban in Nangarhar.

"We didn't find out that the translator had accused Father Frank of rape till afterward," Buddy told investigators. "It really bothered Quentin. Bothered Raul some, too, but it shouldn't have. We didn't do anything different with her than we did any of the others."

That remark made Buddy eligible for charges under the War Crimes Act, in addition to the federal charges already pending. Swain's case, however, was much trickier to prosecute as a crime of war. Without a victim to bear witness about the rape and with Dawana Jackson dead, Father Frank was beyond the reach of military justice.

However, the truck bumper hanged Chaplain Swain for a crime closer to home. Barrett Raines personally drove Frank's damaged bumper to the FDLE's forensic lab in Tallahassee, where an examination revealed that metal and paint from the Harley Raul Carrera had been riding were imbedded at high impact into the leading guard on Frank Swain's Chevrolet truck.

"You killed Raul Carrera," Barrett accused the priest. "My guess is Raul had second thoughts about covering your ass in Afghanistan. So did Quentin Hart, but Raul was going to talk to somebody in the chain of command. Maybe even to me."

"I don't know what you're talking about. I did not rape anyone and I cannot be held responsible for what Sergeant Godot and his men imagined they were doing on my behalf."

"You can be held responsible for running Carrera's bike off the road. And for murdering Dawana Jackson."

"Dawana? Outrageous. You have no proof of that."

"Oh, but we do. Recognize this?"

It was a fatigue jacket, Dawana Jackson's jacket, the rank still proud in chevrons on the sleeve.

Barrett throws the coat open and turns it over to display the stain on the back.

"DNA matches your semen. You doped Dawana first, and then as you choked her to death, you gratified yourself. Which is why you had to get rid of the jacket, wasn't it, Frank? You took off her jacket and buried it and then you had some really dirty work. Hauling a dead corpse all the way back to the cane mill? Nasty. And then more work to stage the suicide.

"It was easier to leave the text message on the phone. That's white-collar crime, isn't it? Especially in your case. And of course you planted the other calls on the phone, including the nine one one. That was a nice touch."

"You can't prove any of that."

"You want to explain to a jury how your semen got on the back of the victim's jacket, which was buried a hundred yards into Devil's Slew?" Barrett smiled.

"I had sex with her. Kinky sex. Doesn't mean I killed her.

We had congress. She felt guilty. I felt guilty! She committed suicide afterward."

Barrett shook his head. "Bullshit. You had Dawana tell Terry Godot that their interpreter was working for the Taliban. The unit had just been hit with an IED; they'd lost men. You knew they'd be looking for payback.

"I'm guessing Dawana didn't care whether Mrs. Bhotri was assisting the Taliban or not; she had no problem killing infidels. Besides, it was all to protect you, wasn't it? And that was Dawana's job. To defend you with her own life!

"Maybe even Terry and Buddy didn't care whether you lied to get Bhotri killed. But Raul did. And Quentin did. They kept a lid on while the unit was overseas, but then the outfit comes home and gets sucked into muling counterfeit, and suddenly you're faced with the possibility that any one of those dumb shits, if caught, can rat you out. No telling what a man will say to save his ass from prison, and these jarheads didn't have to prove anything to be a threat; they just had to point investigators in the right direction.

"Because you've played these games before, haven't you, Frank? You're a serial rapist. And a killer. That's why you moved from parish to parish. That's probably why you jumped at the chance to go overseas. See, I checked with police in the jurisdiction of your former congregations. Three unsolved homicides involving strangulation, and an unusually high incidence of date rape. Usually your victims didn't recall a thing, but Gulpari Bhotri was the exception, wasn't she? She knew who put the dope in her Communion wine. She knew who was to blame."

"That's blasphemy!"

"So is confessing criminals to cover up your own crimes. Prosecutors in other jurisdictions will find more of your victims, Frank, but it won't matter, because in a few months the state of Florida is going to put a needle in your veins for the premeditated murder of Raul Carrera and Dawana Jackson. The judge will beg God to have mercy on your sorry-ass soul—

"Who are you going to beg?"

24

The Artist

In the following weeks, Ricky Ricardo, aka Juan Molinas Ricardo, was indicted for the murder of Treasury Agent Brenda Mantle and for purchasing counterfeited U.S. currency. The onetime kingpin claimed he did not know the artist of the clinquant, and Bear was predisposed to believe him. Ricky was not the sort of fellow to take a hit for a stranger, and since the facsimiled denominations were being circulated in Mexico, "the artist," as he had come to be known, was insulated to some extent from discovery. In fact, not a single faked bill of any denomination had turned up in northern Florida for over two months. The case of the missing artist was, in investigator parlance, going "long-distance."

Smoot Rawlings held the opinion that the counterfeiter never had resided anywhere local. "He prob'ly is familiar with the area, but my opinion he just used the Slew for a drop-off," the sheriff declared. "We haven't caught the sumbitch, 'cause he ain't here to catch."

Barrett was unconvinced.

"We have meth labs all over the flatwoods that operate for months at a time. If you can cook meth in a house trailer, you can print currency."

"Print it on what?" Smoot challenged. "You realize we haven't seen a single bill in two months? And no paper, neither, which tells me it's all used up."

"That, or maybe if he figures we're too close, he's just gotten rid of it."

"Doubt he'd burn it. Too damn hard to get a source for that kind of paper. Not to mention expensive. Sell it for asswipe, maybe?"

"I doubt that." Bear chuckled. "There are smarter ways to hide rag than that."

You didn't need a fixed structure to hide paper. Could be in a trailer or an RV. Barrett knew the flatwoods were littered with abandoned campers and trailers and the like, and so he organized a systematic search of that wilderness, trying to identify anything with wheels that might be used to hide the artist's hard-to-get canvas. Bear even enlisted the Civil Air Patrol for long flights over the featureless lowlands and pine forests of Taylor, Dixie, and Lafayette counties to look for abandoned campers and trailers, with the result that in six weeks the Third District and local sheriffs busted six labs cooking methamphetamine.

But no high-rag paper. And no counterfeiters.

The artist was at large and given the coverage of newspaper and television coverage, Bear began to suspect that he, or she, had closed up shop and moved on.

Bear needed to move on, too. He had fences to mend with Laura Anne, and the boys needed their daddy home at night. The Little League finished its first fall season and the twins seemed eager to continue a tradition of year-round play.

That was a remarkable achievement, considering the allure of football, but now it was time to steer Ben and Tyndall to focus on exams and research papers, those essential duties competing with the seasonal replay of Virgin birth, wise shepherds, and stars over Bethlehem.

And Laura Anne could use some help, Bear knew. She was throwing a huge party at the restaurant in honor of donors to the Veterans' Center. Mike Traiwick asked Bear's wife if she could top her initial fund-raiser; Laura Anne told Mike to put together a list of guests.

The four thousand dollars gotten from the sale of Frank Swain's Chevrolet truck was contributed anonymously.

The party was scheduled to take place a week before Christmas. Laura Anne decked out her cypress-beamed halls with boughs of local holly, wreaths of wild pyracantha showing off their firey orange berries against fronds of palmetto, and vanilla-scented potpourris of deer tongue. Pinecones making a manger in beds of Spanish moss.

Guests seated themselves in booths or tables beneath the restaurant's cypress beams and paddle fans to feast on country ham or sea bass with sides of cheese grits and hush puppies and a bouillabaisse you could smell all the way to Cross City. It was a perfect way to begin the season of giving, which Bear had every reason to hope would continue when he and Laura Anne got home later that night.

"You are one good-looking woman."

"You soft-shoeing me, Bear?"

"Yes, I am."

"Well, keep it up. Maybe you'll get lucky."

Barrett reached up to the mistletoe.

"Not now, Barrett. Later."

But she pecked him on the cheek, which for a man decompressing from months of bloodshed felt like the balm of

Gilead. Mike Traiwick was grinning at him from across the booth, pale and bald and still skinny. Eyes set close as a grouper's.

"Watchu lookin' at?" Bear felt his face splitting wide.

"A happy man."

"You got that right. Come over here. Tell me whassup with the center."

Mike collected his iced tea and slipped into the booth opposite Raines.

"We probably have a good quarter million in the bank, which isn't enough to build anything, but, Bear, I believe Dowling Park is willing to let us have the old chapel if we'll create a fund that will pay for counselors and administration."

"So you're thinking of putting the money into people instead of buildings? Seems smart to me."

"Without the park's support, it wouldn't work. Another alternative would be to use the annex of the Catholic church in Mayo, but some folks feel queasy about that."

Bear nodded. "Understandably. How's the paper, by the way? Still afloat?"

Mike shook his head. "Not for long. Circulation's holding, but I can't raise subscriptions, and advertising's way down."

"Sorry, Mike. How much longer, you think?"

Traiwick shrugged. "I figure I can make it through the holidays, but after that I'm closing her up for good. I hate losing the paper, Bear. I really do."

"Not your fault. You've done this town a ton of good."

"Thank you, sir. And how 'bout you, Barrett? How're you holding up?"

"Good, at least for tonight—I don't have to be a cop."

"I hear that." Mike raised his glass. "I, on the other hand, still have work to do."

"Go ahead, go on," Bear said, waving him off. "I'll be fine."

Barrett settled back with a Bud Light and watched the several threads of local society weaving through his wife's restaurant: locals in their holiday rags, black people and white people mingling, kids in Dockers mixing with older folks in their Sunday best. Bear was glad to see Brady Hart with his wife. Felt good to see Brady engaged again with his neighbors; Bear had hopes to get his old friend back on familiar ground.

Maybe. You couldn't rush those things.

There was a wind ensemble from Florida State set up by the baby grand, the coeds in starched white blouses and black skirts, the boys in tuxes, their classic instruments rendering noels familiar to everyone gathered. Of course Laura Anne would take her place at the baby grand at some point in the evening. She was wearing a white evening gown for the event, low over the shoulders and lots of bare skin visible down the back. Barrett smiled to himself. He was a lucky man.

He picked up a napkin to wrap around his sweating glass of brew and shoved out of the booth for a stroll on the pier. The stars were bright above the Christmas bunting. Boats winked lights port and starboard in the channel. You could see the flicker of somebody's TV below a boom folded with new sail. Some weekend mariner. It was cold, but Barrett didn't mind. He finished the beer and strolled over to the blue bin designated for recycling.

There was a paper hung up on the rim.

It was Mike's paper, the *Deacon Beach Herald*. CELEBRATION FOR VETS' CENTER ran the banner, with a thermometer crudely sketched below to indicate the progress of contributions. Was a crying shame to lose the town's only newspaper, Bear mused. He dropped his bottle and napkin into the recycling bin and salvaged the *Herald*. If this were Saturday's edition, the fortunes of any high school halfback would trump donations to the Veterans' Center. Smart of Mike to push that story a day early.

He opened the local rag and scanned the columns. FUTURE FARMERS OF AMERICA PLACE SECOND ran one header dedicated to a local competition. AMY LAWSON WINS SCHOLARSHIP. You could bet Amy's parents would be proud to see their daughter's picture in the paper. Somewhere in the back fold was a header to remind Barrett of his impact on the community: LOCAL PRIEST ON TRIAL IN FEDERAL COURT.

Ancient history, Bear told himself. He was about to discard the paper, when something stopped him. He was never able to explain later what made him hang on to the newspaper, what kept him from tossing the *Herald* into the bin.

What made him feel the rag in his hands.

He kept the paper, quit the pier, and returned to his booth in the restaurant. He ate a good meal. He bantered with neighbors and friends. The evening ended splendidly with Laura Anne leading her college-aged orchestra in a slow recall of "Silent Night." Bear helped bus the tables and clean up.

"Thank you, sweetheart," Laura Anne said.

"You're welcome."

He played the evening out as he had hoped. This was no time to be a cop, and except for that one lapse out on the pier, Bear was able to keep that commitment.

Laura Anne kept hers, too, and before morning Barrett Raines was once again a lucky man.

He got up early and shooed Thelma out of the kitchen. "You just sit right here." Barrett guided his aunt over to the rocking chair by the TV. "I'll make breakfast this morning."

By the time Laura Anne and the twins were out of bed and in their robes, there were pancakes waiting and linked sausage of pork and venison, courtesy of Harvey Sykes. Bear poured orange juice for the boys and made coffee for Laura Anne. He gave Aunt Thelma a bottled water and a glass of prune juice.

"Why you bein' so nice, Bear?"

"Making up for lost time, Aunt Thelma."

It wasn't hard around midmorning to make an excuse for going out.

"I haven't got you boys a present yet," Bear told his twin sons, which was true. "I'll be back by early afternoon."

With that promise and a kiss for his wife, Bear Raines climbed into his much-repaired Malibu Super Sport and drove less than half a mile to make the only visit of the morning.

It was a Saturday, and Bear knew that Mike Traiwick would be busy pasting in scores from local gridirons all over the district. Barrett parked his car in front of the *Deacon Beach Herald*'s brick facade, stepped over the cracked sidewalk, and opened the aging double doors.

Mike had his back to the street, consumed with a vector graphics editor to lay out pages for the coming edition. Barrett saw stacks of unsold papers crated along the wall—stacks and stacks of paper.

"'Lo, Mike," Bear greeted him from the counter.

"Jesus!" Traiwick jumped in his seat and then turned around. "Barrett! Sorry. I'm on a deadline."

"You're going to want to hear this, though. Big story. Breaking story."

"Can't use her today, Bear. I'm full up."

"I even have the headline. What you call it—the banner?"

"The banner, sure. Well, let's hear it."

"It goes something like, 'Local Paper Hides Counterfeiter.'"

The forced smile on Mike's face faded and the grouper eyes narrowed.

"Never known you to be cute, Bear."

"Only with friends. People I know well. Or at least thought I knew well."

"You asking me to print a riddle, Barrett?"

"Riddle's solved. Should have cracked it sooner. What better place to print counterfeit, after all, than a local newspaper? You've got the equipment, the space. And the privacy, that's the most amazing thing. Put your business right out in the open and no one's going to look. Especially when you charge for advertising."

Mike Traiwick remained seated in his roll-around chair. "You have a search warrant?"

"Why would I? You've moved your gear out by now, or at least most of it."

Barrett nodded at the unsold newspapers stacked along the wall.

"But those papers are in plain sight, and I'm pretty sure when a judge hears what they're printed on, we're going to be having an extended conversation."

"You're still talking riddles, Bear."

"You printed two editions of last week's paper, Mike. The papers you sold, you laid out on regular paper, but this stack over here—it's different."

Mike shrugged. "It's just newspaper."

Barrett wagged a finger. "Not just any paper. See, it takes a special kind of paper to print counterfeit, and Terry said he'd hauled in a shitload, which got me to thinking, If there was extra rag lying around, where would a counterfeiter hide it? He wouldn't get rid of it. I was sure of that. Shit is too goddamn hard to find. Too expensive.

"He might stow the paper in a camper in the flatwoods, or in a U-Lock-It off Highway Twenty-seven, but that would risk calling attention to himself. Or he could do 'The Purloined Letter.' You familiar with that story, Mike? The one by Mr. Poe?"

"I'm just a reporter."

"Allow me to broaden your education. Story starts out with some jerk who's stolen a lady's letter. The inimitable Detective Dupin contrives a visit to search the minister's house and sees what everyone else has missed, that the letter's in a torn envelope hanging in plain view from a card rack or some such.

"That's you, Mike. You used your newspaper to hide your facsimile in plain sight. You're the counterfeiter. You're the artist. You're the man who dropped off the duffel bags in Devil's Slew. And you are the son of a bitch who enlisted Terry Godot and his Crusaders to do your dirty work."

"You expect me to just 'fess up, Bear? Just write the story myself, is that it?"

"I'm giving you the story, the headline of the day. You can print it or not, but when I come back, it's going to get worse, because it isn't just a prosecution for counterfeiting you're facing, Mike.

"People have suffered because of you. A Treasury agent was tortured to her death. My partner damn near lost his leg chasing your ass. It's because of you that my son was damn near kidnapped, and if you think you're immune from those charges, you are one dumb fucking journalist."

Mike's mouth opens like a goldfish, closes.

Opens again.

"You know most of the money donated to the Veterans' Center . . . came from me."

"It's poison."

"That's harsh."

"Not as harsh as a gurney."

"I can't take that, Barrett. I hate needles."

275

The artist swiveled in his chair to the rolltop desk and opened a drawer. When he swiveled back, he had a revolver in his hand.

"Put it down, Mike."

Bear crouches with his Glock behind the counter.

"Don't make me goddamn do this."

"Tell the boys we had a good season," Traiwick said, and put the revolver in his mouth.

Ten feet and a waist-high counter separated the counterfeiter from Bear Raines. You'd think anybody could have gotten off a shot inside that distance, especially with the gun already past his teeth. But Barrett cleared the counter before Traiwick could pull the hammer to single action. Here was a man heavy as a barrel of wet cow shit vaulting the counter like some high school hurder. One bounce to reach the rollaround. Raines slapped the revolver aside as the hammer fell and a shot exploded harmlessly into a buffer of costly rag.

"You're not getting off that easy, Coach."

The Bear snatched Mike Traiwick off his seat like a bale of hay, jerked him high overhead, and with a bellowed rage slammed his narrow face straight into the hardwood floor.

Epilogue

Pauline Traiwick returned to her familiar haunt for the sole purpose of completing the final edition of the *Deacon Beach Herald*. There were some nice pictures of the dinner party at Laura Anne's restaurant, a terrific picture of Bear with Laura Anne, some shots of kids, one of Brady Hart dancing with his wife. There was no photo of Mike Traiwick. Pauline composed no paean to her only nephew, nor an elegy. There was just a short, curt paragraph pasted in an inside fold.

A grand jury has indicted Mike Traiwick for counterfeiting U.S. currency and conspiring to kidnap a federal agent. Sheriff Smoot Rawlings, while acknowledging Mr. Traiwick's contributions to local charity, reminds all citizens that no one is above the law. We hope that is true.

There was some hope that Pauline might be able to resurrect the paper in a cheaper, smaller format. No guarantee.

Barrett turned over the thousands of pages of disguised rag paper to agents of the Treasury Department. Pam Goerne informed the FDLE that in typical denominations Mike Traiwick could have printed millions more in faked currency.

"Good work." The well-suited fed shot Agent Raines that e-mail, with the promise of a letter to follow.

Meantime, the twins passed their exams. Laura Anne raffled off a piano for the new Veterans' Center. The Florida Gators lost to Alabama in the last game of the season, the Crimson Tide running as usual.

And as winter warmed to spring, Barrett Raines could be seen dragging a used kayak from the bed of an old Chevy pickup.

Somebody said it'd look a lot better with a bumper.